JACK BE QUICK

STRIKE FORCE (BOOK TWO)

FIONA QUINN

JACK BE QUICK

Strike Force

BOOK TWO

FIONA QUINN

THE WORLD OF INIQUUS

Ubicumque, Quoties. Quidquid

Iniquus - /i'ni/kwus/ our strength is unequalled, our tactics unfair – we stretch the law to its breaking point. We do whatever is necessary to bring the enemy down.

THE LYNX SERIES

Weakest Lynx

Missing Lynx

Chain Lynx

Cuff Lynx

Gulf Lynx

Hyper Lynx

MARRIAGE LYNX

STRIKE FORCE

In Too DEEP

JACK Be Quick

InstiGATOR

Uncommon Enemies

Wasp

Relic

Deadlock

Thorn

FBI Joint Task Force

Open Secret

Cold Red

Even Odds

Kate Hamilton Mysteries

Mine

Yours

Ours

Cerberus Tactical K9 Team Alpha

Survival Instinct

Protective Instinct

Defender's Instinct

Delta Force Echo

Danger Signs

Danger Zone

Danger Close

This list was created in 2021. For an up-to-date list, please visit FionaQuinnBooks.com

If you prefer to read the Iniquus World in chronological order you will find a full list at the end of this book.

This book is dedicated to Devin

And to all of those who have had loved ones in harm's way for our greater good.
I recognize and honor you for your sacrifices. Thank you.

1

Suz

11:15 p.m. Sunday, February 13th
Suburban Hospital, Bethesda Maryland

Suz perched on the edge of her vinyl-cushioned hospital chair to study Jack's face. He was pale beneath his tan. His bruised and unshaven skin lay slack over the chiseled angles of his jaw and cheekbones. His mouth hung slightly to the left, following the tilt of his head as his lips slid open and hung loose.

Balanced on one hip, a good two feet from his face, Suz could smell smoke clinging to the black ebony of his hair. She brushed her hand down Jack's bare arm, stopping to dance her thumb lightly over the IV and tape.

"Here you are again," she whispered. "Here *we* are again." She lifted her gaze and let her focus take in his little corner of the post-op. They were the only ones there. It must have been a slow night for the emergency surgeons. They were probably in a back room somewhere, sipping coffee and playing Angry Birds, waiting for the next car accident, or gang beatings, or special forces operator who felt compelled to jump off a building. . .

Her eyes scanned over the room with its beeping machines and bright lights. It hadn't been bad this time. Well, not life-threatening. Something to do with the meniscus in Jack's knee. When the surgeon tried to explain about the cartilage tearing from a massive impact and twist, he pointed to the images on his tablet. Suz's stomach jumped at the sight. With a sour face, she shook her head, pushing the photos away. She didn't need to know the details. She didn't want to know them. Deep down, in a place that she hadn't yet acknowledged, Suz understood that these kinds of details weren't going to be her burden to carry anymore.

The two points that got through her resistance were that Jack was going to be okay, and there was a three to four-month recovery time.

She laced her fingers into Jack's and, while she squeezed to hold him tightly, his fingers hung unaware. Three to four months. Jack would turn that into a week, maybe two. He couldn't sit still. He certainly couldn't lie still in a hospital.

Suz's mind drifted back to just a short time ago when he was fighting for his life after being shot in the thigh and through his chest, collapsing a lung. A covert mission that had gone very badly, jeopardizing his whole team. No one had come out of that one unscathed except for Blaze, their communications officer. She remembered how she had waited for the surgeon's report, waited for the "I'm sorry. We did everything we could. . ." She had pulled herself into the fetal position on the hard, plastic, waiting room chair. Her head rested in Jack's teammate's lap as she sobbed, and Blaze offered up what comfort an alpha male could offer up — which meant he pet her like she was a puppy and dropped a brotherly kiss onto her hair every once in a while. Jack and his friends were much more comfortable fast-roping into the fray than dealing with emotions.

"How in the world did we end up together, Jack?" It was the ubiquitous question that she had been asking herself since they started dating almost four years ago.

Jack mumbled something as if in response. Suz had been in this position too many times, watching him come out of his medicated stupor, to pay much attention. His work as an Iniquus security operator assigned to Strike Force put him in constant danger. And he loved it. Loved the adrenaline rush.

Suz preferred yoga and meditative quietude. Adrenaline was something she tried to avoid. She looked down at her hand so small against his bear paw. She was five-foot-two, and he was six-foot-five from his bare feet to the top of his tight military haircut. She weighed in at a hundred and ten pounds, and he doubled her without an ounce of fat, just pure heart and muscle. A mountain of muscles. Unconquerable. Unless, of course, it's your job to jump off three-story buildings as they exploded somewhere in the far reaches of the world. He'd have to be more robot than human to be able to do that and not end up here in the surgical wing.

Suz knew little other than what he had texted her from the ambulance. Apparently, as he flew off the top of some building — somewhere that required a plane to evacuate him and eighteen hours of airtime — he landed on the roof of a car which collapsed, absorbing the impact of the fall, and he walked away – hobbled away.

His last text said: I'm home for a once over at Suburban Hospital.

That text struck her as the nail in their coffin. She couldn't. She couldn't keep doing this. For someone who sought to be peaceful and centered, Jack brought life-or-death energy to their relationship on a daily basis.

He loved it.

She hated it.

"Jack be nimble," Jack mumbled. ". . .quick."

Suz leaned in, her ear hovering just above his mouth, trying to catch his words. "What? What are you saying, Jack?"

"Jack jump over. . . candlestick." Suz made that up. She thought it might be what he said – but nursery rhymes? Could be. People said awfully weird things while sedated.

"Thank you, Lynx. . ."

That last one was clear, and it hurt. Lynx's name was on his lips, not hers.

Lynx was Strike Force's newest teammate, Lexi Sobado. She was fun, kind, unduly attractive, as smart as they come, and Trouble with a capital T. Lynx had a way of magnetizing the bad guys to her, and then the Strike Force team of good guys would have to save her life, time and again.

Lynx was supposed to work in the office doing their intelligence and wasn't supposed to be a field operator like the others.

Yes, for sure, where Lynx went, trouble followed.

Suz scowled. That was really unfair of her to think. And not any more true for Lynx than the other team members. Jack had been in danger since before Suz, and he started dating back when he was still a SEAL in California. His life had been on the line long before Lynx had shown up. *This is a stupid thought process.* Suz twisted her copper-colored curls into a make-do braid. She was just looking for a bad guy – someone to blame for Jack's wounds and her misery.

"Jack, jump. Jack. . . candlestick." Jack breathed out.

"What candlestick?"

"Jump."

"Jack, did you jump over a candlestick?" Was that code for something? Maybe the dynamite that blew up the building as he stood on the roof? Not that she actually knew why the building had blown up.

He lifted his free hand inches off the mattress and made a gesture that she read as jumping over.

"Why did you jump?"

"Lynx," he said.

Frustration painted over Suz. Jack never gave her a straight answer about his missions. It was as if he lived a parallel life. It was one of the things Suz hadn't been able to work through. She stared at the engagement ring glittering on her right ring finger – the "thinking spot" until she made up her mind to say yes.

Or to hand it back.

Could she marry someone and not know what happened during most of his life? Their only reality as a couple turned out to be the short, sporadic bursts of time they were together. That just didn't sit well with her.

She had heard the soldiers laughing back in California, "Are you married?" "Not overseas, I'm not." Jack wasn't like that. She trusted Jack because he deserved her trust – but that many secrets wore at a relationship. Made it threadbare and fragile. And then it ripped, leaving ragged edges that were all but impossible to mend.

In that moment, Suz needed an answer. Just one clear answer. "Lynx told you to jump. And you did. You jumped off a building. And then it exploded. Lynx was on this assignment with you? I thought she was here in D.C."

Nothing.

Suz tried again. "You jumped, and you're alive because Lynx told you to."

Nothing.

"Come on, Jack. I need to know this. How would Lynx know the building was going to explode? She was in Washington, and you were. . ." Suz had no idea where Jack had been. She frequently didn't even know he was leaving. They needed him – he ran toward the enemy. There were plenty of bad guys out there. Plenty of hostages that needed rescuing. Plenty of CIA or FBI or DHS or any other government agency who signed private contracts, preferring to use mercenaries over their own folks, especially in politically delicate areas of the world. Yes, there was plenty of extremely lucrative work for the operators at Iniquus. Suz hated that money. She'd rather Jack were poor and home.

And safe.

"Jack?" Suz shook his shoulder. "How did Lynx know you needed to jump off the building before it exploded?"

Jack pulled his hand towards his head and tapped a finger to his temple.

"She figured it out?"

"Psychic," Jack said. Maybe. Suz wasn't sure; he had barely mumbled. He had merely twitched his lips.

Suz plopped her bottom back in the chair. She felt as if she had just opened the door on a stranger using the bathroom, and she wanted to shut it as quickly as she could. If it were true, it wasn't something she was supposed to have seen. Suz shook her head and convinced herself that Jack was out of his mind on drugs, and she didn't really know what he was muttering.

"Jack, be quick! Jack jump!" His body jerked, and his hand landed on the brace that locked his leg out straight.

The hum of the ice water pump that cooled Jack's angry surgical site filled the sudden silence.

A wash of cold doused Suz's body, leaving her trembling and sweat-covered – because this time, Suz had heard the voice of someone leaping to their probable death. If Jack had missed the car roof, if it weren't engineered to absorb impact energy, he'd be dead.

She couldn't do this.

She lived in terror. All the time. Terrified.

Every single time her phone buzzed, she was sure it was *the* call. Jack was dead. Or worse, Jack was injured to the point that he wished he were dead and now would live in a broken body with no adrenaline surges to electrify and power his system.

Jack scraped his teeth over his lips, and Suz reached for the moistened washcloth that she had been using to dab his mouth. "My world is so vivid, Suz." He had tried to explain. "You can't imagine how bright the colors are, how meaningful every nanosecond is when you're in survival mode." He tried to help her see why he did what he did. Even when she felt willfully blind to the pictures he tried to paint, Jack was always patient with her. She couldn't imagine him ever raising his voice or his hand to anyone. There was nothing about Jack that was violent. She knew intellectually that he had killed people. But it didn't make sense to her. Jack was a gentle giant. A reader. A thinker. A devoted would-be fiancé, waiting patiently for her to decide to say yes.

Suz bit her bottom lip to stop its trembling. She was tired of crying. Bone tired. Wrung completely dry. She didn't understand why Jack chased those adrenaline highs. Her system didn't brighten with fear; her system crashed under heavy cotton-filled emotions, buffering her from the moment, keeping her hidden inside of her body. Her limbs became dull and heavy. Her thoughts slowed. She vibrated with anxiety and inability like she was doing now. And this was no way to live.

Suz disentangled her fingers from his – when she tucked her fingers up into the web of Jack's hand, her joints stretched too far apart as the distance splayed her palm. The difference between them was physically painful. They didn't fit comfortably together.

She lay her forehead on the cool sheet by his elbow. "I love you. Oh my god, I so desperately love you." Her words tumbled out in sobs. "I can't do this anymore. I can't, Jack. I'm so sorry."

2

LYNX

05:35 Hours, Monday, February 14th
Panther Force War Room, Iniquus Headquarter, Washington D.C.

St. Cyril and Methodius.
St. Mogila
St. Basil's
St. Clair

LYNX POSTED the list in red marker on the whiteboard at the front of the room. She turned and saw that the Panther Force team was taking in the information, silently mouthing the words, trying to make sense of what they saw. Titus Kane, the Panther Force commander, stood beside her with his arms crossed over his expansive chest. Special Agent Steve Finley, FBI Counterterrorism Division, stood to his side.

Titus angled toward him. "Mean anything to you?"

Steve shook his head slowly, scrunching his lips together. "No," he finally said. "But when Lynx put up that last saint's name, my electrical grid lit up so bright I could swear it singed my hair. Last time that happened was when my task force took down a white supremacist threat on a judge. They didn't think a black man should be putting good white men in prison. They were about to blow up the Supreme Court of Virginia."

Lynx snapped the cap onto the marker. "This is bad juju then."

"If you believe in that kind of precognizant stuff," Steve said with a self-conscious chuckle.

The note had been found in the top desk drawer in Pavle Zoric's home office. Pavle was in custody. He was being held on child trafficking, murder, and terror charges.

Lynx let her gaze dance between the names of the saints. "It feels significant, though."

Titus nodded. Whether that was in agreement or just acknowledgment of her sentence, Lynx couldn't tell. Titus had one facial expression and one expression only – "stay out of my way." So, Lynx had a hard time reading his body language. She had no idea what boiled beneath his surface. Lynx glanced over to see who had poked his head around the door.

"Special Agent Finley?" the man asked.

Only Finley and Lynx were dressed in civilian clothes. Everyone else at Iniquus wore the uniform of gray camo BDUs–battle dress uniform–with long-sleeved compression shirts, which showed off their company's dedication to being fit and ready for action.

Finley walked over and signed off on a thick file that was passed to him.

Lynx moved toward the coffee machine. They had been

working around the clock for the past couple of days. And Lynx hoped they were wrapping things up.

"What's the sitrep on Jack?" Titus asked, pouring a mug of coffee from the carafe at a side table.

Lynx smiled. Titus was the only guy she knew who would ask for a situation report on the well-being of a friend instead of just an easy, "Hey, how's Jack doing?" "His fiancée texted me last night." Lynx peeked at the clock; it was zero six hundred. She needed to find a bed and get a few hours of shut-eye.

Lynx had been loaned out to Panther Force while the Strike Force team was on its extended mission in the Middle East. It was interesting trying to fit in with this new group of operators. Lynx thought Strike Force was a far better fit for her. Titus was a little tightly wound. "Jack's out of post-op and in his private room at Suburban, resting comfortably. And by that, I mean, passed out on his IV cocktail. Suz is home getting some sleep. She has to teach this morning." Lynx's eye caught on the whiteboard where St. Basil's was written second from the end. "Surgery went fine. Jack should be back on the team soon enough."

"I heard Strike Force's downrange time got extended."

Lynx reached for a ceramic mug. Coffee was a high priority. "Yeah, complications with the mission when that building blew."

"Jack took one hell of a leap. That guy's got more lives than a cat." Titus leaned his hips back into the table and crossed his ankles. His clean-shaven head glowed dark brown. "But good that they're gone a little longer."

Lynx raised a questioning brow.

Titus lifted his mug toward the whiteboard. "That means we get to keep you on our team for a while, and maybe you can figure this puzzle out."

She raised her mug in salute. "Aw, thanks, Titus, that almost sounded like a compliment." Taking a sip of the coffee, Lynx moved toward where Steve stood by the door, fanning through the new file. "Did they bring you anything that's actionable?"

Finley lifted his gaze. "It's the forensics information from Pavle's cell phone." He slid into a seat at one of the long conference tables and started sifting through the pages from the phone logs and texts. "Looks like they were able to access his email through his phone–they have it translated already." He seemed impressed. But this was par for the course here at Iniquus. Time always seemed compressed once a contract was signed. It usually meant lives were on the line, and every second counted.

Lynx settled behind her laptop. "Hey, Gage, can you put up some notes on the whiteboard for me?"

Gage moved into place and picked up a blue marker.

"So, I'm going to do a quick Google search on St. Cyril and Methodius because – well, who's ever heard of them before?" She turned toward Steve and tilted her head.

He shrugged in response.

"Well, here, right away, I can tell you these guys are the patron saints of Slovakia. Steve, are the Zorics' Catholic? Would their terror activity be motivated by religion?"

Steve rubbed his chin. "The Zorics' don't go to any kind of house of worship. They present as atheists, both those that are here in America and those in Slovakia. Their drive is political power. Their politics are firmly attached to Russia and Russian Middle Eastern policy, especially Hezbollah, but they're also pro-Iranian."

"Hmmm. Let's see if we start getting matching pings – I'm attacking this puzzle-like it's a message to take action. I'm looking for repeated threads."

"Sounds good – I'm going to scan through this and see what leaps out at me." Steve tapped the folder.

Lynx toed her tennis shoes off. Being barefooted helped her think. She caught Gage's gaze. "These saints apparently devised the first alphabet to be used for Slavonic manuscripts. So, these guys were intellectuals." Lynx ran her finger down the page. "They arrived in Rome in 868, where they were warmly received. This was partly due to their bringing with them the relics of Saint Clement." She tilted her head back and forth. She said the details aloud just to pick out any commonalities when she moved down the Saints list on the board.

Gage dutifully noted the information.

"It says here that Cyril felt his end approaching, so he became a monk. He died fifty days later."

"Geezis." Steve's gaze fixed on the paper in his hand. He jumped up to slide the page into the projector so everyone could see the image illuminated on one of the three screens hanging in the room.

"This is a series of four separate text messages that came in yesterday. The first phrase was written in English."

Let us prey. May the saints bless our endeavors. Amen.

"The next three texts were written in Slovakian and translated in the forensics department." Steve dragged his finger down the sheet.

The time has come, my brothers and sisters.

Great changes come at the price of great sacrifices.

. . .

I BELIEVE, though, that our plan is sound, and all is being readied. Nothing should prevent our success.

"THAT'S A GREEN LIGHT," Titus said.

Everyone agreed.

"February 14th 869 CE," Lynx said.

"What's that?" Titus moved over to stand behind her, where he could see her screen.

Lynx pointed to the sections she was reading. "February 14th is the feast day of both Saints Cyril and Methodius."

Gage quirked a brow. "Today's February 14th."

"Let's not jump ahead of ourselves," Lynx said. But as soon as she saw the date, her heebie-geebies—her personal warning system—began to buzz. Either she or someone she cared about was in mortal danger. Too bad it was such an imprecise warning system. She had no idea whose life was on the line or how she could help.

Lynx ran through the possibilities. Certainly, she was safe here at Iniquus Headquarters. Jack had come through his surgery with flying colors. The rest of the Strike Force team. . . well, they were off-grid right now, playing in a Middle Eastern sandbox. Her mind flitted to her fiancé, Striker Rheas, Commander of Strike Force. It was terrifying to love someone who went downrange into the heart of the battlefield. Every day was a struggle with a low-level hum of life-or-death survival fear. Even though she had contact with the team and what "need-to-know" information about their missions, she came into contact with – that didn't help. Loving someone who lived with their foot poised over a mine and an AK pointed at their heads was a physical and mental battle all its own. Loving someone who was in constant danger . . . well there was a reason why so few Iniquus operators were married.

Lynx pulled her thoughts back to the present moment. She could do nothing to help anyone right now other than try to figure out why her warning system had gone off when she saw the date, February 14th.

Steve yanked his chair up to her left, crowding in beside her. Lynx liked space to think. Her thoughts needed light and air, and she was getting neither with these two men looming over her. She called out, "Nutsbe, can you run this list and all of the permutations through the analysis software and see if it can find something interesting – I'm particularly interested in St. Basil's since it's the only one that is possessive – I think that might be a place rather than a thing – like St Basil's Church or St. Basil's grave." Lynx hated using Nutsbe's call sign – his fellow pilots had picked that moniker for him back in his pre-Panther Force days when he flew F-16s. Nutsbe's birth name was Thaddeus Crushed.

She looked at the board. "While you do that, I'll Google St. Mogila. That's a pretty obscure name." She hammered her fingers into the keys. "Only one Saint Mogila. Saint Peter Mogila"

"What's his claim to fame?" Titus moved to a chair, and Lynx felt instantly better.

"Hmm. He's from a later period. In the 1620s, Mogila traveled to Ukraine. It says here that that's when Poland annexed Ukrainian lands. . . he founded a church. . . settled in Kyiv. This doesn't seem pertinent. Pavle worked out of America. Right, Steve? He wasn't involved in planning things in Europe?"

Steve stuck his finger on the paper where he left off reading. "That's right. There are family leaders in Slovakia, and they directed Pavle. And Pavle, in turn, instructed the family members here on the East Coast of the US. There are other family groups that have positioned in other parts of the country."

"So logically, since Pavle was in possession of this list." She gestured toward the whiteboard. "We're concerned that it has implications to terrorist activity here in the Washington D.C. area where he was operating."

"And that could mean a direct terrorist attack," Steve said. "But we have no information on his family actually engaging in anything even remotely like a terrorist attack. Their main objective was to fund organizations in the Middle East."

"But Pavle never got the message." Lynx pointed out. "It came in after he was arrested, and you had confiscated his phone, right?"

"The messages were received Sunday, February 13th at 12 hundred exactly. These are the only texts that came in after the raid."

"They originated from a burner phone?" Titus asked.

"That's what your forensics department notated," Steve said. "The call, though, originated in Bratislava, the capital of Slovakia. It took a circuitous route from country to country until it was spoofed as a Pennsylvania Pizzeria."

"We need the CIA in on this, Steve. You were working with John Black and John Green. . ."

Steve's gaze traveled to the wall clock above the whiteboard. "Green's my contact in Slovakia. Black is here in Washington. I'd like to have a little more to hand them if I can."

Titus's phone buzzed, and he moved to a more private corner of the room to answer it. Steve went back to his file. Lynx turned back to Gage, who stood patiently by the whiteboard.

"Gage, it remarks here that Kyiv was not only the political and cultural center for the area but also an educational center.

Mogila was part of a group of intellectuals there. It seems they wanted to use Latin in the universities, and there was retaliation against the teachers and educational facilities. Again, with education." She turned to look at her colleague, who was working the computer searches. "Nutsbe, I'm just checking in on your parameters. Can you run a search with education or school or university and each of the saints' names?"

Nutsbe scratched his nose. "Here's an interesting ping – the 'Slovakia and St. Clair' search turned up that Brandon St. Clair is the chair of the Senate Arms Committee."

"What's the correlate?" Lynx asked.

"The document I'm looking at is a small article that mentioned that St. Clair was not available for comment because he was in a meeting with the Slovakian ambassador." Nutsbe squinted his eyes and tapped at the keyboard. "I have another hit. This one is on the combination of St. Clair and St Basil's. St. Basil's Preparatory School. The senator gave a speech three years ago."

"Where's the school?" Lynx asked.

"Bethesda, Maryland. But here's the part you need to hear. His granddaughter was a kindergarten student there."

Lynx moved over to stand behind him. "Follow that lead – what's her name?"

"In this photo, Senator St. Clair is standing with a family of three children. The article says, 'Second-grader Rebeca Levinski and her brothers enjoyed a lovely day, listening to their grandfather speak about the importance of respecting each other for their differences.' There are three children in the photo with Brandon St. Clair." A couple of swift clicks on the keyboard and the image was projected onto a screen for everyone to see.

"Another ping," Nutsbe said, tapping more keys. "It's coming off the directive for 'schools and St. Mogila' – good catch on that one, Lynx. Looks like in March 1939, Hungary wanted to take over more territory from the newly established Carpatho Ukraine. But the autonomous section of Czechoslovakia wouldn't allow that to happen. Aryan terrorists attacked St. Mogila's School in Czechoslovakia. They went in and shot some of the children, then held the students and faculty in the cafeteria for days with their parents outside, trying to at least get food and water to them. Some days later, the school was exploded, children and all. The threat was that this kind of terror would continue if the region tried to remain autonomous. They joined Hungary throughout World War II."

Steve was standing, wiping his hands over his face, then leaned back and stared at the ceiling. "Shit. Shit. Shit."

Titus moved up in front of Steve and planted his knuckles on the table, leaning his weight onto them until they were eye to eye. "You have more on this." It wasn't a question – it was a command to fill in the blanks.

Steve took a step back and spoke to the room. "The assault on St. Moglia's didn't work by blowing up the children." Steve's skin lost its color. He had been pushing himself without breaks for over a week, trying to cross all the Ts on the Zoric takedown. He hadn't looked well even before this last bit of news. Whatever was going through his mind now seemed to lick at the last of his vital energy. "One of the Carpatho-Ukrainian leaders was a power-hungry sociopath. He didn't care for anyone or anything except his sons."

"Were his children or grandchildren in the school?" Lynx asked.

"Worse. His children were taken from the school. The school was merely a smokescreen, hiding what the terrorists were doing. They kidnapped the leader's children and held them, using their pain as leverage throughout the war. Allowing for untold atrocities to take place."

"I know it probably doesn't make a difference to this narrative – but what happened to the children? Is there any way there is a familial correlate?" Lynx asked.

"They were killed when Hitler suicided."

"So, never rescued?" Lynx asked.

"No one knew they were gone – everyone assumed they were victims in the school."

"But their father. . ."

"Was under duress and didn't let anyone know. The children were being held in Berlin–if there was an attempt to rescue them, it was off the records."

"And you know this how?" Titus asked, rocking his weight back onto his heels.

"It was one of the case studies we looked at in one of my counterterrorism classes," Steve replied.

"Okay, no waiting. Get Black and Green on the phone now," Titus said.

Lynx leaned over the computer desk. "Nutsbe, can you get a roster of the students at St. Basil's? Maybe also check the birthdates for the two boys and see what grade they might be in. Titus, we should get eyes on the Levinski home." She checked the clock, zero seven-fifteen hours. "The children should be just about ready for their ride to school. Could a few Panthers head over? If they go now, we could get the children in sight before they leave."

Titus turned and pointed at three men: Thorn, Brainiack, and Dagger. They jogged out of the room. He pointed at Nutsbe. "Text them the address."

"Roger that." He tapped his phone. Then moved back to his work at his keyboard.

"What are you thinking, Lynx?" Finley asked.

Lynx moved over to the board and took the marker from Gage. She wrote parenthetically next to each saint.

"St. Cyril and Methodius." (when)

"St. Mogila" (what)

"St. Basil's (where)

"St. Clair" (why)

"The who… that's missing. And the end game. If I see this correctly, we're looking at an attack today. But we might be lucky. Perhaps taking down Zoric on Friday night before he got the green light means that whatever this is—" she tapped the board, "has been thwarted."

Nutsbe cleared his throat. "The granddaughter is in fifth grade, Mrs. Peabody's class. The boys are twins in first grade. Hang on. . . Mrs. O'Grady's class and Miss Molloy's class."

Lynx turned from the board the pen held mid-air. "Wait. What's that last teacher's name?"

"Gillian S. Molloy."

Lynx's gaze caught on Titus. "That's Suz. That's Jack McCullen's fiancée."

3

Suz

8 a.m., Monday, February 14th
St Basil's Preparatory School, Bethesda Maryland

Suz was exhausted and distracted that morning as she got ready for school. That it was Valentine's Day had completely slipped her mind as she dressed for her mood rather than the occasion, choosing all black.

When she unlocked her classroom door, though, she was greeted with bright red and pink decorations and the new reading words carefully lettered and posted behind her desk — words that meant love to her students: hugs, family, home, safe. . . Suz picked up a sheet of stickers that lay on her desk, ready for her to use on the kids' workbook pages that day, and she tapped a few hearts onto her turtleneck sweater. It was the best she could do under the circumstances – all she had energy for.

The kids filed in, filling the classroom with excited chatter.

"Good morning, bright and shining faces. You look very happy today. You would think that it was a special day or something." Suz smiled down at her first graders. They plunked gifts and cards on her desk, then went to hang up their coats. It was a blustery winter day. The temperature hovered in the upper twenties, and there had been warnings of possible snow. The children worked to untangle themselves from their layers of outerwear. Suz waded into the crush to help with buttons and stuck zippers.

"Miss Molloy, I want to give out my cards." Michael held up a crushed paper bag. Suz was sure his mother had handed it to him in pristine order, but Michael was a rough and tumble kind of guy. Suz was a little surprised the bag had made it to school at all.

She raised her voice. "Class, after I take attendance, you can distribute your Valentine's cards to the student post boxes, okay?"

Her class was only sixteen strong today. It was a particularly bad flu season this year, and four of her students were out sick. She should have called in sick herself and had a substitute cover for her today. By the time Suz had left Jack at the hospital and climbed into her own bed, heartbroken by her decision and her loss, she couldn't sleep. All she was capable of was lying there feeling miserable. The long night left her exhausted and not completely in command of her emotions.

She watched the kids running around, making their deliveries, and a wave of melancholy washed over her. She wanted kids of her own. A bunch of them. But she also wanted them to have a father who was around for them. Yet another reason why she couldn't marry Jack. She bent over and pretended to pick something up off the floor as she surreptitiously swiped a tear from her cheek.

This is just fatigue, she tried to convince herself. "For heaven's sake, pull yourself together," she muttered as she lifted her head to find out who was tapping on her shoulder.

"I lost a tooth last night." Miranda opened her mouth wide and stuck a finger in the open gap. Her mother had pulled the wisps of Miranda's silk-fine hair into pigtails and tied them in pink ribbon to match her jumper.

"Oh, that's so fun! I can already see your adult tooth trying to pop through. Did the Tooth Fairy come?" Suz pulled her enthusiasm out of thin air. Losing a first tooth was a huge deal to these kids, and she wasn't going to mope and bring Miranda down.

"Yup!" Miranda danced off, and Jenny stepped into her place. "Miss Molloy, can we read stories this morning? I want to know what happens next to the Velveteen Rabbit."

Suz actually felt relieved. It was a good idea. She'd settle the kids on the floor with hearts and flowers coloring pages to build their finger muscles and fine motor control while she read to them this morning. This afternoon, one of the room-moms was coming in with a little party she had planned. The kids would play games and open their Valentine's cards then. Suz would make it through today and let the principal know she wasn't well. That would give him plenty of time to arrange for a substitute.

"Children," Suz said with the kind of gentle authority that made the children turn and pay attention. "Today is such an exciting and happy day. We get to show each other how much we care for each other and what good friends we can be."

Suz's gaze took in the sweet faces of her students, and she felt a sting of tears burn her eyes. She grabbed a Kleenex from her desk. "Oh my, it looks like I'm catching a cold. My face wants to drip. Four of our classmates are out sick. So today, we are going to be careful to use the hand sanitizer on my desk. We're going to make sure that if we cough or sneeze, it will be into our elbows. And we aren't going to share any food or drink. Understood?"

The children each gave their version of agreement, and Suz congratulated herself on having an all-day excuse for looking like an emotional mess. "Let's gather on the reading rug for more of Velveteen Rabbit."

There was a quick rush as her students scrambled toward the places they wanted.

"Red light," Suz called, and all the students froze in place. All noise ceased.

"I would like you to first go to the activity center, and each of you get a clipboard and some crayons. Greenlight!"

As the kids surged forward, Suz rounded her desk and pulled out a file folder of coloring sheets. And that's when she heard it.

PopPop Pop. PopPop Pop. PopPop Pop.

TRIPLE TAPS. Two shots to the chest and one to the head. The sound of death. Nothing else sounded like that. Suz had heard it time and again when she was on the firing range, waiting for Jack to finish up. Jack had even tried to teach her once. He thought she might like to learn to use a gun. He was wrong. Guns made her vomit.

PopPop Pop.

IN SUZ'S MIND, she was standing behind her desk, shocked to be hearing that sound here in her school. Her body, though, was already standing at the classroom door, moving with lightning speed. Her mouth had already called out, "Red light!" The children were frozen in space.

If the other teachers had heard and recognized the noise, they'd be turning off their lights, locking the doors, and herding their children into a corner. Jack said that was absolutely the wrong thing to do; if she did nothing else to defend her children, Suz needed to keep her students spread out. Suz flipped off the light switch and turned the lock on the door. Jack had told her that these doors were hung the wrong way, and a gunman could easily kick them open. Jack had bought and installed industrial floor bolts, and now she stepped on them to slide the metal spikes into place as she pulled out her phone.

I'm wrong. I'm hallucinating, Suz told herself. She quick-dialed the school's secretary, who sat at the front desk to sign in the tardy students. The rings ended with an out-of-service recording.

The children looked around, bewildered. A few of them must have caught hold of Suz's anxiety because she saw frightened faces and tears as she scrambled behind her desk to look out the window. There was nothing out of the ordinary. Her fingers shook as she tapped out 9-1-1. It didn't go anywhere as if she had no bars.

"Children, come quickly. We're running a very special fire drill. This time we're going out a different way." Suz said as she pushed open the window that Jack had cut loose from the layers of paint and carefully oiled for ease of use and silence. Outside on the ledge rested a box painted to match the beige façade of the building, and therefore, it had gone unnoticed by the administrators and ground's staff alike. Jack had said all she needed to do was push the box off the ledge and let it fall unencumbered, so she did. The box dropped to the ground with a resounding bang, leaving a rope ladder stretched tautly.

They're going to fire me if I do this. I must be wrong. This is so dangerous. Gunfire here? I must be wrong.

But screams and a man's shouting flooded up the corridor and gushed under their classroom door. It was the nightmare that she had been having ever since Sandy Hook. Suz was terrified that someone would come into her class and hurt one of her kids. That she'd leap in front of a bullet for them was not in doubt, but other teachers had done that, and the kids had died anyway. Their heroic actions just upping the horrific body counts.

This escape plan was Jack's gift to her – a plan, so she had some better course of action than piling the kids into a death pack. Jack had come to the school and offered to instruct everyone to come up with strategies and plans to do the training for free. But the principal thought that would make the parents feel nervous for the safety of their children. He had turned down Jack's offer. So, Jack had done this for her alone.

"Tad, come here. You're my brave leader. Down the ladder, then help the others. Michael, you're next." Michael's face was set in grim determination as he climbed out the second-story window. "Come on, guys, fast. Move. Move. Move." She watched her best athletes scramble down the ladder-like little monkeys, showing the other kids that it could be done. "Miranda, you're next. You're line leader. All the way down then to the edge of the building toward the field." Suz hefted the girl up by the waist and pushed her through the window. "Then crouch down as small as you can get next to the wall. Go. Go." Suz watched Miranda start her climb then turned to the other thirteen. "Come on. Everyone follows. Go as fast as you can. But be safe. Watch that you have a good grip. Make sure your feet are centered on the rungs."

Tata tat tat.

Gunfire strafed the hallway and seemed to be working its way toward them. Suz was picking up the children and thrusting them through the window as fast as she could.

She unplugged, then grabbed up the backpack from its place under their exit window, threw the coil of rainbow-colored rope over her shoulder, and shimmied her body through the small opening. She stood on the second rung and pulled the window back down into place. Jack said that every second that she confused the attackers meant time when they weren't watching her running the kids across the field.

As she scrambled to the ground, she counted heads. Sixteen. They were all out of the building and farther away from the crazy person wielding the weapons. Her ears, primed to take in sound and their slightest nuances, picked up on gunning engines and then the solid application of brakes in the parking lot. Surely, that was the good guys come to rescue them. Maybe she should run the students towards the parking lot instead of the woods. Suz looked up and took in all the windows that they'd have to race under, and it seemed like a dangerous gauntlet.

Jack had said that once she was deploying her escape, she needed to move forward as planned. He insisted that second-guessing would lead to indecision, and indecision could lead to deaths.

Deaths. Shit.

Suz ran forward, dropping the line beside her students, whispering, "Grab hold of the rope. Don't let go for any reason. We're all together. Everything is going to be okay." When she got up to Miranda, Suz pointed at the large oak across the field. "Miranda, do you see the pink dot on the tree?" Jack had put a long piece of pink duct tape on the trunk at a child's eye level. At this distance, it was reduced to a speck of bright color. That it was still in place was a testament to Suz that there were angels with them.

Miranda nodded.

"Sweetheart, I need you to hold the rope and run to the pink dot."

Miranda didn't need to be told twice. She seemed very glad to pelt in the opposite direction of the gunfire. Suz let Miranda set the pace. It was slow. These little six-year-old legs were only but so long and could only move but so fast.

Why did Jack want her to have the children run across such a broad expanse in the open? True, he had told her that at this angle, they were all but invisible from any of the windows at the school, but the word that looped through her brain was "unprotected." Suz tried to replace it with repetitive base notes of, "God will help us. Please. Help us." It didn't seem to dull her anxiety.

Almost immediately, Lolli fell to the ground. Lolli was their class's fairy-child. A precious little girl who was as light as a breeze, with the air of fragility like the gossamer wings of a dragonfly. Suz scooped her up and set her back on her feet, but Lolli reached down and touched the plastic supports on her ankles and started to cry. Without further thought, Suz swung the little one up on her hip like a toddler and continued her slow jog beside her students. "Good job," she whisper-cheered them on. "You're doing great. Keep going, guys. I'm so proud of you."

Slow. Their little first-grade legs made them so slow. The woods didn't seem to be getting any nearer. Suz glanced over her shoulder at the school's main building. Why would Jack have her make these babies run across a field like this? She asked herself for the hundredth time. This was crazy.

Another child, Grayson, went down, pulling the rope to a stop. Tad, her big boy, the one who always reminded her of Jack for his intelligence and kindness–her class's gentle giant—

looked around and saw the problem. He ran back to where Suz was bent over, lifting the second child.

"I've got him, Miss Molloy," Tad said as he hefted his classmate up and pulled Grayson's arm around his shoulder. The two hobbled together, and their slow caterpillar run continued. It was torturous.

Suz had no idea what was happening at the school. Time played out oddly in her brain. She felt as if things were going their normal terrestrial pace, and at the same time, things were slowed way down. It gave her plenty of time to wonder if abandoning her classroom meant she wasn't there to help with the other students. Wonder if there was a muzzle pointed their way right now. A sniper could pick off her little children, one after the other, right in front of her, as they trudged onward, growing slower as they fatigued. In one more step, the bullets could come flying. Nowhere to hide. They had little energy left to move. What would she do? Fall to the ground and crawl? But movement caught the eye. Fall to the ground and lay still? But the kids were all dressed in red and bright pinks – like the centers of sixteen bullseyes.

Suz scanned the faces of her students, who all seemed to have their expressions frozen in single-minded determination. How odd that looked for their cherubic cheeks, still plump with baby fat, to suddenly be held with concentrated ferocity. They were babies. Just babies. They hadn't had a chance at life yet. She needed to save them. Suz's heart squeezed down so hard that she almost cried out. She sucked up a lungful of air. "You're doing it," she whispered along the line. "Great job. Keep going."

Suz tossed a glance over her shoulder at the school where screaming could now be heard, seeping through the cracks in the windows, though the shooting seemed to have stopped.

The wail of sirens rose up over the hills, and Suz knew that the first responders were hurtling toward them from all directions. They seemed to be gathering and holding near the off-ramp. She wondered why they weren't coming closer to save the children.

Her class was getting closer to the tree line. Suz could see patterns in the bark. Soon they'd be safely out of view. She needed to get the kids to Jack's cache fast. They had left, as Jack had instructed, without coats. But in this cold, they were escaping from one life-or-death situation just to find themselves in another. Soon the kids would be hypothermic

Maggie broke off the line, sprinting back to the school, calling, "My sister! My sister's in there." Suz tore off after her, bouncing poor Lolli against her hip bone. Lolli hunkered down and wrapped noose-like arms around Suz's neck, cutting off her airflow. Suz reached out a rigid hand to grab at Maggie and ran harder. As Suz got closer, she clawed at the air until she caught hold of Maggie's ponytail. Suz yanked the hair backward like she was reining in a wild stallion. Maggie fell back on her bottom and opened her mouth to screech. Suz knew from past experience just how loud Maggie could be. Without forethought, Suz reached down and wrapped her arm around the girl's head and mouth and pressed Maggie into her hip. In that position, Suz rose, Lolli on her right hip, and a partially dangling Maggie on her left, sprinted back into the tree line where her students waited.

4

Suz

Somewhere around 9 a.m., Monday, February 14th
The Woods Behind St. Basil's, Bethesda, Md.

Suz took over the lead on the rope now that they were hidden by the tree line. The children were bent over, catching their breath. They were damp from the exertion, and that had Suz worried. Maggie had been paired with her best friend, and they were hugging each other and sobbing. If the children hadn't been convinced that something horrible was happening before, the sight of their teacher gagging and dragging their classmate into the woods made everyone acutely aware now. Suz set the backpack on the ground and pulled out the hats stored inside. Each child yanked a camo fleece beanie over their heads with gratitude. They were still shaking in the twenty-degree weather. Suz had to get them to Jack's hide. Fast.

She counted heads. Sixteen. Four at homesick. They were

such lucky kids to be in bed sick today. She had almost called in. Gotten a substitute. The substitute wouldn't have known Jack's plan. Her kids would still be in the school where bullets were flying. The enormity of her decision pushed a sob out of her throat, which Suz covered with a hacking cough. Her kids needed her. She had to act as if she were brave and in charge for their sakes.

A loud explosion erupted from the school, and all of them froze in place with wide eyes. Suz checked to see if she could call 9-1-1 and got nowhere. She opened the compass app on her phone to follow due south, as Jack had told her to do when they had practiced. He had also written a reminder on the duct tape tacked across the plastic bag that held the hats. That was a good thing in that her mind was short wiring, and Suz was forgetting simple things, like nouns. Also taped to the bag was a hand-held compass in case she had escaped without her phone. "One is none, and two is one." It was a phrase Jack often used to explain the redundancies that he put in place. It had something to do with Murphy's Law–she had never cared enough to really pay attention.

If, for some reason, she had escaped without her phone or the pack, Jack had a secondary trail laid with tiny pieces of that neon pink duct tape. But these were stuck on the roots and rocks and were purposefully easy to miss. As they hiked deeper into the woods and down the hill, Suz felt relief every time she caught sight of one. It told her she was headed in the right direction. Finally, they got to the creek bed – she turned in the direction of the water flow and knew they had two hundred steps to take – adult steps, not first grader-sized steps. But by leading her away from the original trail and markings in this way, Jack had said he hoped that any bad guys would lose their trail or at least be slowed down.

Suddenly, there it was in front of her. Like a mirage after crawling through the desert, the camo fabric that covered the top of their hide fluttered in the wind. The children huddled together for warmth and support while Suz opened up the escape backpack. She pulled out the tablet that Jack had put in the pack and pressed play just as he had instructed her to do. This was as far as his training had gone. And now that she was here, she was at a loss for how to proceed.

Jack's face came up on the screen. "Boys and girls," Jack grinned into the camera, and Suz held the tablet up so everyone could see. "Wow! You are the best soldiers in the world! Look what you've accomplished working together today. You remember me, I'm Captain Jack, I visited your class, and we talked about teamwork. Now we're putting what we learned to the test." Her students had loved Jack. They couldn't get enough of him. Begged for him to come back to their class and still sent their drawings home for him, though his visit had been months ago. Suz had teased him about getting a stint as the Pied Piper. She had thought what a wonderful dad he would be if only he could be around for his kids and not in some jungle, or desert. . . or hospital room.

"First up – we need to pee."

The children giggled. Seeing Captain Jack's calm face worked instant magic on the kids.

"Boys, in just a second, I'm going to ask you to step up to the black line I painted on the rocks in front of the water, point toward the stream, and do your business. Girls, I made you a latrine in the back left of our little hide. Now, this is important. Everyone listen up. When we get scared, our bodies don't always do what we'd like them to do – being cold is very bad, being wet and cold is life-threatening. If you're wet, that's okay. Just let

Miss Molloy know so she can get you dry and warm. Quick, quick. Now, everyone needs to pee. Greenlight!"

And as if they were all trained soldiers, the boys stepped right up to the black line; the girls filed back to where Suz was pointing, and Suz looked down to where Jack was talking to her. "Suz, honey, you've got this far. You're doing great. I'm so proud of you. You can do this." Suz's stomach clenched down, and she stifled a sob behind her wrist. She nodded at Jack's image as if acknowledging what he said. "Go to the back of the hide, and you'll see there is a mat rolled up. Use the knife I taped to the binding to cut the ropes and unroll it. Press pause."

Suz tucked the tablet into the back of her pants and moved to accomplish her task. Her eyes scanned over the boys who were doing up their zippers and heading her way. The girls, having to go two at a time to the little white latrine buckets behind the curtain, were much slower. She sliced through the binding, and the mat unrolled. It was nice- a camo-patterned, vinyl-covered thick foam rubber that would keep them off the ground. Jack had told her, somewhere along the way, that the ground would suck your body heat right out of you, so she knew she should never sit or lay directly on the earth. As the children gathered along the outside of the pad, Suz pressed play to hear what she should do next.

"Suz, there's a pack on your left marked #1. In it, you'll find hot sacks. One per child. Now let the kids see me." He raised his voice. "Hey, guys. Great job so far. Wonderful teamwork. We're all here to help each other and be good friends. I want you to watch me now. Miss Molloy is going to help you get warm. She'll hand you a little packet. This is how we open our hot sack and get in."

Suz held the video up, and Jack opened his sack and got in, pulling it right up over his head. He was demonstrating this exactly where they stood, curling up on the pad that was now in front of them. Suz vaguely wondered who had helped him tape this tutorial. "Watch again while Miss Molloy hands out your hot sack." As the demonstration repeated, Suz handed the tablet to Tad and had him hold it up over his head for all to see.

At the top of pack #1 was a sub-zero hooded ski jacket and a pair of fingerless gloves with a note, "You first."

After she pulled on the blissful warmth of the down jacket, Suz distributed the Mylar-lined emergency sacks. Though the gloves were a relief, her hands hadn't warmed yet. They were blue and stiff with cold, and the kids needed a lot of help, having lost much of their dexterity from rigid, shaking fingers. At the bottom of the bag, Suz found hand warmers.

The video example repeated three times before he said, "Suz, I need to talk to you for a minute."

Suz reached for the tablet and stepped away from the students. Jack lowered his voice to just above a whisper. "Open and place one hand warmer per student at the bottom of the sacks near their feet. They'll last for 8 hours. I've included enough that you can last 2 days if need be."

If need be? What? Suz thought they might be out here for an hour, maybe two – not two days. That took her to a whole different level of fear and stress. She stared wide-eyed down at Jack's smiling face. So calm. Always so gentle and calm.

"I know what you're thinking," Jack said with a chuckle. "But don't worry. It's just an overabundance of caution. I love you and need to keep you and those kids safe. Okay? Now, if everyone is settled down, I want you to get warm too. Remember, they need you functioning. Your health and safety mean their health and safety. I have videos loaded onto the tablet for the kids to watch, very, very quietly. Let them be distracted. You need to listen to the radio in pack #3, so you know what's going on. Click this video back on when you all are hungry, and I'll walk you through heating an MRE."

Jack had truly thought of everything, including the Meal Ready to Eat packets.

He pointed and said, "I need to talk to the kids again." Suz nodded and turned the tablet toward the class, wondering how he knew her so well that he could choreograph this video so precisely that she felt like they were Skyping. It was uncanny.

His voice had been his Jack-and-Suz voice — intimate, loving, protective, a solid team. Now he lifted his volume and sounded more like the lead on a fun-day mission. This was just a great adventure. "Class. I'm really proud of you. But this isn't over yet. To stay safe, we need to stay quiet. Miss Molloy is going to put down the sides of the tent, so it will be a little dark. Take a nap if you'd like. Watch a video but no noise at all. Everyone, seal your lips tight now. Zip them up like you have a secret."

Suz watched as the kids followed the zipping motion Jack made on the screen.

"Thank you," Jack said, confident that they had followed through. "I'm with you guys in spirit. Help will be with you soon. Be good for Miss Molloy, and most of all, be safe."

* * *

IT WAS GETTING dim behind the flaps of the camouflaged hide. The sun set early in February. The trees were already masking the last of what little sunlight glowed through the dove-colored cloud cover. The kids had eaten lunch in the company of Captain

Jack. He talked Suz through heating the meals, then told the kids stories about being a boy in Montana and all the fun he had going camping. Meanwhile, she got everything together and passed out the meals. It felt to Suz like there were two responsible adults in the hide – it wasn't just her and sixteen six-year-olds.

Now it was time to get dinner together before it got too much later, and she'd end up groping around in the dark. Jack hadn't said anything about lighting, but Suz was pretty sure it wouldn't be allowed.

As the children's video came to an end, Suz picked up the tablet to get her next instructions to the moans of the children.

"How about we all take a bathroom break while we can still see what we're doing."

They had heard sirens every once in a while, but now, things seemed peaceful. Again, Suz had to talk herself out of thinking she had hallucinated the whole thing. The children had heard what she had. They talked amongst themselves, speculating about what was happening back at the school. The children all thought it was over. Whatever "it" was. If that were true, why were they still out here?

Suz checked her phone for the millionth time. She had plenty of bars but no reception. Tad said they must be jamming the airwaves in the area. Tad's father was an executive with Lockheed Marten, so Suz assumed that, even if he was six, he knew what he was talking about. It was possible. Suz worked to convince herself *that* scenario was unlikely because a) that would mean this wasn't a freak occurrence where someone lost their mind but an actual strategized, planned, equipment purchased, and implemented attack. And b) Suz thought that the police would probably have some way to unjam them; otherwise, how would they affect communications?

Suz felt herself getting a little nuts as the night loomed closer. Her mind whirled about all the things that could be happening and why no one had shown up yet the way Jack had assured her they would. Sixteen little sets of eyes were on her. Sixteen little kids depended on her. Her decisions would make all the difference in the world. Sixteen human beings would always remember this day, and her, and how she handled things.

At what point did hunkering in this hide with her students make no sense? The radio station said that there was an active shooter event at a local Bethesda school, rescue was on scene. But that was all that she could pick up. She thought if Jack was there, he'd rig something that allowed her to access the police scanners, and she'd know moment to moment what was happening. But Jack wasn't here. He was laid up in the hospital. Sedated. In a leg brace. He wouldn't be riding to her rescue. She was here on her own. She tapped at her phone again, trying to reach Iniquus headquarters. She was met with dead air.

"If you're getting ready to prep meal number two, Suz, I know you're getting worried. Believe me, no one is going to leave you out here any longer than is necessary. Once they see a whole class is missing, they'll have Search and Rescue out with the dogs and their trackers. It's not going to be hard for them to follow a line of twenty students marching through the woods. Stay put. Stay strong. You're safe. Trust me, if it comes to the end of your supplies, I have a plan for that too. Okay? You trust me?"

"Yes, I do."

"Good," Jack continued as if they had an actual conversation. "Now, this tablet is probably losing battery life, but I rigged up a solar back-up in the tree. It's recharging a replacement battery. It's in the bag marked #4. Now, in there, you'll also find an airtight canister filled with chocolate. That's for you. I bet you could use some right about now, sorry it can't be Bailey's – not yet, anyway." He stopped to give her a grin. "I have a treat for the kids in the pack with meal two. You're doing great. I'm so proud of you. I love you so much."

Suz nodded to the screen as his image disappeared. "I love you too, Jack," she whispered.

Just then, a black nose shoved under the hide flap, making Suz jump. Another nose joined besides the first. Both were snuffling hard. The kids scrambled back, some of them giggling. Others had been wound too tightly all day to have any other reaction than fear.

A whistle went up. "Beetle, Bella heel to me," a female voice called. "Suz, it's Lynx. I'm going to lift your flaps up now. Okay?"

Suz supposed Lynx was cautious lest Jack had provided her with some kind of weapon. Jack hadn't. He said that she'd never use it, so giving her a weapon was like arming the bad guys. He was right. She could never conjure a situation where she would harm another human being. Stand in the way of someone being hurt? Yes. Wield a blade or pull a trigger? No. Never.

Suz lifted the flap herself. The temperature had dropped; the fallen leaves looked like they were dusted with powdered sugar. She turned to her students. "I need you guys to sit still for a minute while I talk to Capt. Jack's partner, okay? I'll let you know what's going on in just a minute."

The two women stepped away from blind, and Suz reached out to wrap Lynx in a hug. Lynx's two Dobermans pushed their heads against her thigh for their greeting, too.

"I don't think I've ever been so glad to see anyone in my life," Suz gasped out.

"Ditto. Are the kids okay?"

"They're hanging in there. What's happening up at the school? How is everyone?"

"They have four deceased adults. The principal, a teacher, the secretary, and an unidentified male, we think he was a chauffeur/bodyguard. Definitely not one of the bad guys. He was shot in the back."

Suz's body braced for the worst. "And the children?"

"The kids are all safe and accounted for except for your class. I already radioed that I had you in sight. Sixteen?"

"Yes, I have sixteen. Four of my students were absent today." Suz shuffled her feet. Maybe it was a mistake for her to have brought her students out this way.

As if reading her mind, Lynx squeezed Suz's shoulder. "You did the right thing. Absolutely. No doubt in anyone's mind." She leaned down and whispered in Suz's ear. "They think one of your students had been targeted. Your door was blown in with C-4."

"One of my students?" Suz's brow pulled in tightly. "But why? Who?" She glanced quickly back to the hide to make sure her kids hadn't lifted the cover to watch them.

Lynx stepped forward. "We'd better get moving. We need to get these kids to the trailer. Hot chocolate and some hugs from their families are waiting for them." Lynx said, looking up at the sky. "Dark is coming, and an ice storm is moving in fast."

5

SUZ

5:00 p.m., Monday, February 14th
Mobile Command Center, St. Basil's, Bethesda, Md.

BEETLE AND BELLA danced beside Miss Molloy's first graders as they waddled out of the woods. Suz and Lynx had tucked hand warmers into their clothes and cut their hot sacks across the bottoms and up one side to make them into single lengths that each child could wrap around themselves like they were wearing blankets. They made sure each child had a firm grip on the rainbow rope. Lynx took the lead, and Suz was the caboose. It was five o'clock when they reached the far edge of the parking lot. Lynx had led them to the responders from a direction that hid the view of the school. Suz wondered what it looked like now that the shooting and blasting had stopped.

The children's parents tried to rush to their sons and daughters, but the responders held them back. The police made the adults stand behind a yellow crime tape and wait for the child to be identified on the roster. The parents then had to display identification before the child was released to them and the emergency medical technicians who would give them a once over. The students were all in fine shape. There wasn't a tear on a single face, and only one scraped knee, but that had already been attended to.

A man stepped forward. "Gillian Molloy?"

Suz tilted her head up, taking in the stern face. Suz turned concerned eyes toward Lynx.

"Suz, this is Special Agent Damion Prescott from the FBI," she said. "The FBI was first on the scene today." She turned to Prescott. "Perhaps you could speak to her over at the rescue squads. I'm sure they'll want to look her over and make sure Miss Molloy isn't suffering from any injuries or shock."

Lynx wrapped her arm around Suz, which made Suz feel warm and cared for, but also a little confused. Why was Prescott giving her the stink-eye? Suz reached out and wrapped a hand around Bella's collar. The well-trained Doberman felt like a weapon against–well, whatever was coming her way.

Though the sky was still a gunmetal gray, the responders had set up a lighting system that was bright to the point of being obnoxious. Suz squinted and made her way to the back of an ambulance, where they stuck a thermometer in her mouth and had her slide one hand out of her ski jacket so they could wrap a blood pressure cuff around her arm.

"Well, Houdini," Prescott began.

Suz's gaze shot up, startled by his tone.

"You have some explaining to do." He pulled out a digital recorder.

Suz sought out Lynx, but she was nowhere in sight. Her dogs were gone too. There wasn't a single friendly face around her.

Suz did her best to explain how her class and only her class had escaped. How she and only she was prepared with equipment. And why she and only she had a cache of supplies back in the woods. But Suz had to explain without mentioning Jack. There was no way in the world that Suz was going to pull him into this situation. Looking over Prescott's shoulder, Suz could see the TV crews salivating behind the taped line. Their cameras were focused in her direction. If Jack's name were mentioned, they might try to find images of him to go with their story. As handsome as he was, his picture would circulate over social media and the news sites. His face would become known, and that knowledge would put him in danger. He had protected her. Now it was her job to protect him.

"Look, it's really very simple. I was terrified that Sandy Hook would happen in our school."

"Why? What about your school made you think that would happen here?"

"Nothing about my school made me think it wouldn't happen here. I'm sure the teachers at Sandy Hook felt that such an atrocity could never happen in their safe hamlet either." Suz felt like she was a criminal on the witness stand. "I… I… I'm a teacher. I watched the news and saw that other teachers' only recourse in these horrible events was throwing their bodies in front of bullets to protect their children. And while they are true heroes and heroines, I thought that many deaths could have been prevented had better emergency protocol been in place at the school."

"Protocol? Were you in the military, Miss Molloy?"

"No, I was not. But I do have a substantial vocabulary." This guy's tone was rubbing her like sandpaper. It had been one heck of a long day after one heck of a long night and too many emotions for her to navigate successfully. Her nerves had been stretched to the breaking point. She wanted a hot bath, a glass of Bailey's, and some freaking chocolate. Suz could feel her Scottish blood heating.

Suz took in a deep breath and modulated her voice to low professionalism. If there was one thing she had learned hanging around the alpha males of Iniquus was that there was a tone in their voice that said they were in perfect control. Jack said if you were yelling, you'd lost. She always remembered that with the kids. The worse her students behaved, the quieter and more authoritative her voice became. "I am a well-educated woman. I am a woman who can do research. I am capable of identifying where things are not functioning as they should, and I am equally capable of coming up with alternative plans."

"Plans you kept to yourself."

"Not at all. I asked Principal Caldwell to invite security personnel to develop a whole-school plan and to train the teachers and run drills. He didn't believe this was in the best interest of the children. I thought otherwise. And I acted otherwise. But he certainly knew." Well, he knew that there was a security door brace. He didn't know anything else.

"Did he have this in writing as part of the information that he gave the fire department? That would be an important piece to their safety inspections."

"I can't speak to that." Suz began to wonder if she'd need a lawyer. She wondered what she should be doing and saying or not saying at this moment, and she knew she wasn't in full use of her brain. She should probably cut this short. Suz scanned for a friendly face, but the lights were too bright in her eyes to see past Prescott's shoulders.

"You hiked the children out into the woods where you had

stored provisions. That's quite the preparation. I've never heard of a teacher going to such extremes before."

"Okay," Suz said.

"Okay, what?"

"Okay, you've never heard of anyone doing that before. That has no meaning. No bearing whatsoever on whether other teachers have made their own preparations or not. It simply means that you are unaware." Her tone was ratcheting up. She needed to take a breath and stay in control. Suz felt decidedly not in control and wondered where these questions were leading. She turned to the paramedic. "May I have some water please? Or maybe something warm to drink?" She turned back to the special agent. "Marla Ferris, one of our fourth-grade teachers, for example, has her trunk filled with cans of tuna, bottles of water, flea collars, and dry cat food. She's prepared for finding stray cats. That's where her concern lies. That's what she spent her time and money preparing for. I suppose, in an emergency, the canned tuna and water could help her or those with her to some extent. But for me, my focus was on preventing myself and my students from becoming victims like in Newtown or the other schools that have experienced tragedies. And I believe I did a darned good job. Unless I'm under arrest or some such nonsense. . . I'm cold. I'm tired. And I'm done talking to you for the day. You can schedule an interview for any further information."

With that, she turned from the agent to accept the Styrofoam cup of coffee from the paramedic. Special Agent Prescott was sought out by a man dressed in SWAT tactical gear.

Lynx came up to her side. "Where'd you go?" Suz asked.

"I needed to take a phone call. I had sent a friend to your house to check on things as soon as we heard your class had gone out of the window. I called Jack, and he explained the exfil plan he had put in place. I had the pups with me, so we got to go back and fish you out."

"Then why did someone go to my house?"

"The reporters announced your name over the news, so we thought they might try to access you for an interview, which would be a mistake. You can't tell people about your escape route."

"Yes, I know that. I haven't mentioned Jack."

"Good." Lynx squeezed Suz's arm. "By the time the team got to your place, it seems that the media had lined your street with their vans. My friend picked up your dogs and is taking them to Iniquus, where they'll be safe and cared for. I'd suggest that you'll be more comfortable in an alternative location where no one will bother you. I was given an address where things will be quiet. Okay?"

That meant a safe house. Suz closed her eyes as she took in a shaking breath. "Yes, thank you."

They moved together toward Suz's car.

"Wait. They don't have a key to my house," Suz said.

Lynx merely lifted a brow. Iniquus operators didn't need keys. They could open locks in their sleep. It was child's play. "Prescott looked like he's got a stick up his ass," Lynx said.

"He didn't appreciate my foresight and preparations."

"Hmm." Lynx pulled the strap of Suz's purse from her shoulder and handed the bag over to Suz. "Here, they got this from your classroom."

"What does 'hmm' mean?"

"It means that this might get interesting. I'm going to give my company a heads up, and they'll probably give you some legal support. Before I made that phone call to my friend, an agent removed me from your line of sight while you were interviewed. It's interesting that they wanted you isolated."

Suz looked around. "Where's your car? Do you need a ride?" She reached into her purse and pulled out her keys.

Lynx took the keys from her hands and fobbed open the car. "An ISO took my vehicle and my dogs. I'll catch up with them when we get out of this area," she said, referring to the Iniquus Support Officers whose job it was to make everything run smoothly, whatever was needed. Lynx opened the driver's side door and stuck a foot in. "I'm going to drive your car. I don't think you're in any shape to be focused on the road."

After Suz was settled into the passenger side and pulling on her safety belt, Lynx reached up to adjust her mirrors. "The ISO will help me run counter-surveillance to make sure no one follows you to the safe house. Now," Lynx smiled as she backed out of the parking lot, "shall we run by the hospital first so you can get a well-deserved hug from Jack?"

Suz turned to see Lynx's face. "But Jack was supposed to be released by now. It was out-patient surgery, and he'd only be at Suburban for twenty-three hours. Isn't he at the barracks?"

"No." Lynx reached to put a hand on Suz's shoulder. "I'm sorry. Of course, you wouldn't know. Jack's been having complications."

Suz closed her eyes as fear danced down her spine. "What kinds of complications?"

6

Suz

7:00 P.M., MONDAY, FEBRUARY 14TH

Safe House, Secret Location

WHEN THEY PULLED into the garage that made up the first story of a three-story townhouse, Suz was surprised to find that there was a bag of clothes, a bag of food, and a bag from the liquor store, sitting in the back seat of her car.

"Your ISO bought you some pieces, just yoga pants and sweaters, undies, and pajamas so you could feel comfortable. He went in the back door, got your dogs, and hiked out through the woods. We didn't want anyone to see any of us. And there were a lot of eyes on your place. So, he didn't stay to pack you a bag."

"Thank you," Suz said, reaching instinctively for the bag of alcohol first. She had promised herself a drink since she stood on the ladder outside of her classroom. Lynx gave her a knowing wink. "Jack said Bailey's was your best friend in times of emotional meltdown. I assumed that would be your state of mind. It would be mine." She laughed like this was all fun and games. "Girl! You hoisted sixteen little kids out of a second-story window and hid them in the woods for eight hours. Not a tear-stained cheek among them. That is some kind of awesome. Jack is so proud of you. It was killing him not to come get you."

It didn't sound to Suz like Lynx was fishing for comments, but it must have been noted that Suz had declined to go see Jack. That he was feverish and on an antibiotic drip, and she was dirty from the woods, so it would be better not to drag germs into the hospital, didn't seem like it passed muster with Lynx as a viable argument. Lynx had given her a gentle smile, but Suz had been reading eyes and faces as a teacher for a long time, and she knew that Lynx didn't buy the explanation and was a little worried about what this could all mean.

They walked up the garage stairs into a great room. It had the feel of a hotel to it. The non-descript corporate décor lacked any personal touches. The art on the wall had been mass-produced. It was clean and didn't smell stale. It was fine. Suz noticed that there was heavy drapery on the windows.

Lynx followed her gaze. "Kevlar lined – not that that's going to be an issue for you. But some of the people who have stayed here made it a practice to crawl around on the floor rather than walk upright." She grinned. "It's our policy to tell everyone who stays here. It won't stop a grenade, but it will stop anyone from seeing in, getting a bead, and taking a shot."

"Okay, thanks," Suz said, a little bit at a loss.

"I also have to say that you are in a safe house. This is not a prison. You are free to come and go as you please. It's better not to, though. Every time you go out, eyes will see your face. I'd give this situation 24-48 hours, and something else will peak in the news. Funding and interest will fall off over that time. Okay?" She turned and put a key on the coffee table.

"Yeah, sure, okay."

Lynx checked her watch. "I actually need to take off. I'm working on an assignment."

Suz nodded.

"Last thing, call the Iniquus operator and tell them when you're leaving. I don't need to be in the loop, though I'll stay in touch." Lynx was giving her a hug.

Suz felt numb. She nodded her understanding to Lynx, and Lynx left.

Suz stood in the middle of the living room, wondering what the heck to do next, and how to get her body to do it. She'd start with a bath and a glass of Bailey's.

"I'M FINE. I SWEAR."

"No, you're not." Emma was her best friend since kindergarten. Of course, she couldn't fool Emma. "And you shouldn't be. In the last day, your fiancé was in surgery, you decided to dump him, and you were in a live-shooting incident."

"I'm not dumping Jack. Don't ever say that. Dumping makes him sound like he's at fault or that he's not good enough. The truth is, I have to leave him because I'm not good enough for him. He deserves better than me. He deserves someone who has the stamina and backbone to support him in anything he chooses to do. And I'm not capable of that level of strength."

"*Pshhh*, listen to you."

"I'd rather not." Suz's fingers traced over the shape of the side-table lamp. "I wish I were at home. Maybe I should come to visit? They said on the news the school will be closed for the foreseeable future. Lots of repairs. . . new staffing positions to be filled. God, that's so horrible."

"Coronado isn't a good plan. Too many military types around here. You need to get away from your worries."

"Okay, what's a good plan, then?"

"I'm flipping through some websites. There are some package deals out there. . . here's one. No, that won't work. . . Ah, here's one for St. Martens on the Last-minute Deals site. It includes an all-inclusive resort, spa package. I could swing this. I can use some of my time off and meet you there. Starts this Thursday, the 17th. How about that?"

"Send me the link, and let me take a look at it. Right now, I'm going to pour a second glass of Bailey's and get in bed. I haven't slept since Saturday. And Em . . .? Thanks for talking me down off my emotional ledge. I feel much better now."

"Go. Get in bed. But stop with the Bailey's. You know you're a drinking lightweight – one, and you're done. Get some sleep. We'll hash through all your problems when I see you Thursday in St. Martens. I love you." She paused, and when she spoke again, her voice was thick with emotion. "I'm really glad you're safe."

"Thanks, Em. I love you too."

Suz put the phone down on the table and burst into tears.

7

Petr

22:40 Hours, Monday, February 14th

An apartment, Washington D.C.

"Sir, I have a report."

"Very well," the graveled voice came over Petr's burner phone. Petr had no idea who exactly was on the other end, but the signature growl was easily distinguishable.

"Sir, Pavel and most of the Zoric family were apprehended Friday night. He and Musclav did not play their roles today. We ran into other problems as well." Petr tried to hide the fact that his shaking was making his teeth rattle.

The man on the other end of the line did not appreciate problems, and he tended to make them, and all those who allowed them to happen, go away, quickly and permanently.

Petr waited for a response and, getting none, continued with his report. "Once the communication was received that our team should proceed with the Saints Assault, we began immediately by putting surveillance on the Levinski's home. St. Clair is in Illinois at Navigational Defense, Inc. Their headquarters is hosting an extended fishing and hunting weekend. St. Clair is not expected back until Wednesday." Petr paused again.

Silence met him.

"The Levinski children left Monday morning, much earlier than was expected." He traded the phone from one hand to the other as he swiped the sweat from his palms. "They were accompanied by their driver, who also serves as their bodyguard, as well as the nanny. The father is on a buying trip to Bern, Switzerland – there is an annual jewelry show. The mother left at the same time. As far as we can tell, the parents are together out of the country."

"Good."

The single syllable shut down Petr's thought process, and he blinked several times before he could realign the sequence of events he was relating. "The Levinski children were taken to the pediatrician's office. Then they took the girl and the nanny home. The driver took the boys to school."

"Did you collect the girl at her home?"

"No, sir. We were directed to make no-contact outside of the school, and also, if she is too ill for school, keeping her alive in the next stage might have been a challenge, thereby creating further problems with St. Clair."

"Agreed."

Petr swallowed the glob of phlegm that was choking him. "Nadia and I followed the boys to the school. I walked right in behind them. I shot the bodyguard, and Nadia grabbed the boys. They ran with her easily, thinking that she was saving them, I'm sure. They were put in the van and given a drink dosed with Rohypnol. My last report from the courier is that both boys are still asleep, and they are still about five hours outside of Panama City, Florida. Our boat is sitting off the coast, waiting for them to approach."

"I was extremely displeased to see that the school was not destroyed. The authorities will know that the children are missing, and there will be a national search for them. This will brighten the fears of the Americans, and movement could become difficult."

"Yes, sir. I believe, though, that the authorities might just now—or maybe not even yet–be realizing that the boys are missing."

"How is this?"

"The parents and St. Clair are out of town, as I explained. The Levinski's nanny is French-speaking and has very poor English, so she'll not be watching American media. The daughter, Rebeca, is ill and may not ask for her brothers. And the bodyguard who is in charge of their transportation is dead. His body has not yet been identified, according to news reports. That might take days to accomplish, they've reported. Also, on Mondays, the boys have sports classes, they often eat in a restaurant and do not return home until around this point in the evening."

"Yes, but the boys are still five hours from the shoreline, you said."

"The GPS shows the van reached Jacksonville, Florida, and has already turned west. Authorities will not think to spread their search to that distance."

"You do not think that the authorities are already wise to the children's disappearance? The school would not apprise them?"

"No, sir, Nadia and I walked in with her young son just behind the bodyguard. The boys had not signed in yet. The school believes all three of the Levinski children were absent today. Nadia grabbed the boys, and her young son yelled to the boys to run for their lives. Nadia's son was very handy in getting the boys to believe that Nadia would save them. Also, I should report that there were three other adults in the area. I made sure that no one who saw the incident survived to tell what it was they saw. I removed the identification and keys from the body-guard and drove his car away."

This was met with silence. Petr knew that to babble on with details would not be a wise move. He forced himself to wait. Silently. His bowels cramped.

"So, it was the others who failed."

"Sir, there should not have been a failure. Everything was going according to plan – better than we could have hoped. The gunmen herded the children. The explosive trucks parked against either side of the school, ready for detonation. All was readied."

"What was the mechanism for the bombs' detonation?"

"A cell phone device so that we maintained control should our timing not work out the way we had planned. Since we were jamming cell phone signals to prevent emergency calls, this would necessitate a time after our team evacuated that the jammers were stopped from inside the school, and then our call was made from a distance. To this end, we had a jihadist from the Paraguayan camp who wished to be a martyr. And this is as far as we proceeded."

"Why is this?"

Petr sucked in a long breath, filling his chest to capacity. "We had given ourselves seven minutes from evacuation. At the six-minute mark, our point man, the jihadist, would need to deactivate the jammers. At the seven-minute mark, our phone call was made. The call did not activate the bombs. At first, we believed the jihadist had forgotten to take the pill that would calm his nerves and had gotten what the Americans call 'cold feet.' Or perhaps, he took the medication, and it had affected him in an unintended manner. But this was not the case. The FBI had arrived on the scene. They entered the auditorium, and the jihadist shot himself before the six-minute mark.

"You are sure he is dead?"

"That, sir, I do not know. I can only report what was on the news. Perhaps the Americans have taken him into custody and do not wish anyone to know. It is possible. But doubtful. There were many reporters there watching. They arrived even before the police and ambulances. I'm sure they were counting the bodies as they were removed. And the children, of course, were in the auditorium with him. And this is what they said happened."

"The jihadist is dead. Well, that at least is good news."

"Indeed – though he knew little of the plans and spoke no English, he had heard names and seen faces in the transport. It is better that he is now enjoying his rewards. However, there is an interesting piece of information that was gathered."

The voice on the other end of the line grunted.

"Our team followed the mission plan as if we were not already in possession of the boys. When they got to Caleb's room, the teacher had followed the protocol one expects from American teachers — lights out, door locked, children stuffed into a corner of the room blanketed by the teacher. That door was easily kicked in." Petr sniffed and swallowed, trying to clear his throat, giving himself another moment before he had to reveal this new piece of information. "This was not true of Ari's class."

"Oh?" For the first time, the voice rose in energy.

"Gillian Molloy's classroom was barricaded. The team used C-4 to blast open the doorway. The students weren't in the room. But the door had been secured from the inside. The only other way out of the room was through the windows, and because of the dip in the land, this classroom was effectively on the second floor. The team checked the windows. One was unlocked, and there was a rope ladder hanging down from the sill."

"They knew we had targeted the boy?"

"It would seem. Though, that isn't logical, is it? Why would Ari be protected and not Caleb?"

"Ari was the firstborn of the twins."

"Still, sir, in this culture, the extra caution for one and not the other makes little sense. I left Jones at the school to watch how things transpired after Nadia, and I drove away. Jones reported that a single class had disappeared, and they had had word that a single teacher had evacuated her class to the woods. They sent an operator and her dogs after the children to tell them it was safe to return. It was confirmed that the teacher was Gillian Molloy, and it had been Ari's class hidden in the trees. It seemed odd to me at the time, so I've instructed Jones to keep an eye on where Molloy went following the incident. Jones reported that the people with whom she was driving used a team and counter-surveillance moves to lose a tail. They would have succeeded, but Jones had taped his phone under the woman's bumper, and it was quite easy to get the GPS coordinates. She remains under surveillance."

"Hmph. Here, listen, they are talking about it on the news now. Turn your TV to Channel 13 News."

"Yes, sir, I will call you back." Petr touched the phone to release the call and closed his eyes for a brief moment of respite before he reached for the remote and turned to Channel 13.

"IT'S time for Hound News with Lisa Hassel and Berry Greg — America's number one trusted news team for sniffing out the truth."

Berry slid to the edge of the round couch he shared with his colleague. Lisa sat to his right in a bright pink, skin-skimming, mini-dress. Berry swiveled to Lisa. "Tonight, I smell a rat."

She nodded. "Me too."

"A big fat rat. Did you all see where our reporter caught a rather angry conversation between St. Basil's heroine first-grade teacher and the FBI?" Berry looked directly in the lens so that all of America knew he was talking to them personally. "Does anyone else think it was rather odd? This Miss Molloy – is that her name?" He swung toward Lisa for confirmation.

"Gillian Suzanne Molloy," Lisa piped in. "But she goes by Suz."

"Right, so tonight we find out that the FBI is looking for two children Ari and Caleb Levinski, who are students at St. Basil's school. The children vanished–poof–into thin air." Berry snapped his fingers and flailed his arms about his head like a magician. "We know for a fact that the three Levinski children visited their pediatrician's office early this morning. We know for a fact that the older sister Rebecca was sent home sick with her nanny, but the boys were sent on to school."

Lisa raised her eyebrows then dropped them emphatically as she said, "They haven't been heard from since."

"One of the deceased adults was unknown and wore an empty shoulder holster. His picture was identified by the Levinski family's nanny as the family's driver and bodyguard. He would have left his firearm in the glove compartment since he was on school property. Imagine if this trained guard had been allowed to have his gun with him. He might be alive. He might have protected the school staff. Taken down the bad guys. Saved the children — but for these senseless gun prohibition laws, keeping guns out of the hands of the good guys. . ." Berry shook his head mournfully.

"A driver/bodyguard and a nanny? This Levinski family is very wealthy."

"Multi-millionaires. As are many of the students' families at St. Basil's Prep, which is one of the preeminent private schools in our area. Were Ari and Caleb Levinksi taken by the terrorists? And why?" He paused dramatically. "This Suz Molloy person was apparently Ari's teacher. Now, we don't know for sure if these boys were targeted or if they happened to be at the wrong place at the wrong time. But we do know that Suz Molloy was the only teacher who was able to get her entire class out of the building and hide them in the woods." Berry cocked his head to show his skepticism about this scenario.

"The only one with door barricades. The only one with an escape ladder from a second-floor window." Lisa's eyes danced as she got into the swing of their back and forth.

"The only one with a trail that she could follow through the woods and MREs and hot sacks ready in a backpack." Berry paused and spoke again directly to the American viewers. "Does this smell bad to anyone else?"

"Here's the other thing that strikes me as really odd," Lisa pushed forward, not to be outdone. "The first responders were an FBI SWAT team in full battle uniforms with explosive sniffing dogs and a bomb team. They showed up before a single call went out."

"But Lisa, they said they had actionable intelligence."

"Sure, they did." She nodded. "From inside the school –

from their operator, this Miss Molloy woman. That's what I think happened."

"You're right. The FBI had to have known all along something bad was happening and had planted Suz Molloy as a first-grade teacher in that targeted child's class."

"Was she even really a teacher?"

"Perhaps. . ." Berry strung the word out with a *where are you going with this*? tip of the head.

"I'd bet she wasn't really a teacher but held a fake teachers' license provided by the FBI when they were putting together her cover story."

"Fake credentials are easy enough for the Bureau to fabricate, aren't they?" Berry yanked at the knot to loosen his tie as he got excited. "She was probably posted there to keep an eye on things. Otherwise, how did the FBI SWAT team show up in such a timely manner? – No one could call out for help. The phone lines had been cut, and the cell phones had been jammed. The janitor had sprinted to a nearby subdivision to get help."

"So, you feel sure, Berry, that she was an FBI Special Agent?"

"Let's say she was CIA, operating in the US illegally. She could have been a part of an ongoing sting to take down a Muslim terrorist cell and got word to the FBI to come in and stop things before they got out of control."

"That makes a lot of sense. The terrorists could be Muslim. Has the CIA denied that Molloy's their operator?"

Berry shook his head with pure disdain. "The CIA has been tight-lipped about Miss Molloy's association. They aren't admitting to anything. They're certainly not claiming her as one of their own."

"I thought the CIA and FBI were adversarial even though they're supposed to be working together through Homeland

Security. That might actually explain why Molloy got angry when she was talking to Special Agent in Charge, Damion Prescott. He's kind of a big deal."

Berry considered that for a moment. "What choice did the CIA have other than to bring the FBI in? It's illegal for them to operate in the US."

"That's not entirely true." Lisa uncrossed her legs and crossed them in the other direction. The camera panned down to capture the movement and was reluctant to find her face again after resting the focus on her legs. "The CIA is permitted to act within the US to address the specific areas of foreign intelligence, counter-intelligence, and terrorism. But they do intelligence, not law enforcement."

"So ostensibly the CIA thought their intelligence gathering was more important than those four victims' lives? More important than the potential threat to hundreds of our countries' precious children?"

Lisa's shoulders drooped. "Apparently so."

"Let me get this straight. A CIA officer, using the fake name Suz Molloy, sat on international Muslim terror plot information and, in the last minute, decided to do the right thing and call in the FBI? Called in the nick of time to save most of the students but not in time to save the adults? Seems to me that she'll be facing second-degree murder charges. I would say the St. Basil deaths fit the definition: 'a killing caused by dangerous conduct and the offender's obvious lack of concern for human life'. Is there a warrant already out for her arrest?"

"They don't need one," Lisa replied. "Molloy knows too much. Having all the information she has about the Muslim's future attacks on our nations' children means she's a liability to the United States. Her spilling the beans on what she knows would alert the Muslims that they should stop their plans and make new ones. The government can't allow her to publicly disclose the information. They're trying to protect other schools where like plots are probably being hatched as we speak. More attacks could come any day now. Tomorrow even."

"The Patriots Act says they can scoop her up and imprison her without counsel or due process and hold her as long as they like."

Now Lisa's angry face glowered into the camera lens. "Serves her right for putting our American children in the hands of Muslim terrorists the way she did."

"What do you bet we never hear anything about her again?"

"That would be par for the course. Yet another CIA plot to try to protect the president from being impeached for crimes against American citizens. For being soft — protecting Muslims whose only goal is to take over our great nation and make it a country governed by Sharia law."

Berry shook his head. "Horrible. What kind of woman hands American children over to Muslim terrorists just because the President ordered her to? Hasn't she ever heard of the Nuremberg Trials? She's going to jail for life. Being ordered to commit atrocities by your leader is not a defense."

Lisa pat her hands onto the tight fabric stretching over her thighs. "There you have it, folks. Apparently, our president ordered Suz Molloy to endanger America's most precious treasure, our children." She paused, then a smile lit up her face. "Stay right there, we're going to take a quick break to pay the bills, and we'll be right back to discuss the newest science quackery that's being put out there to convince you that there is actually change happening to our climate."

As the newscasters laughed, Petr knocked back a shot of vodka. How did the American's know about their plan with enough time to plant the CIA officer as a teacher? He quickly dialed his cell phone. “Jones, are you still following the teacher?”

“I am. She’s at a townhouse just over the New Jersey state line. There are no journalists here. It’s quiet.”

“Sit tight. I need to make a plan.”

8

Suz

11:30 A.M. TUESDAY, FEBRUARY 15TH

The House that Jack Built, Bethesda, Maryland

SUZ LEANED back against the headrest in her car and stared at the back wall of her garage. Loneliness was the thick gray that cloaked her, making her feel cold and damp and incapable of not chattering her teeth. Alone. Now that she was going to break it off with Jack, even the friends she had made at Iniquus and the Iniquus support system would be gone from her life.

Yup, alone.

Suz realized she still had her car in gear and shifted to park. Her hand reached out for the keys; her mind was back in sunny California.

She and Jack had been dating for a year—which really worked out to about four months of physically being together because of Jack's deployments–when Jack had proposed. And she had said no. He was a SEAL, of which she was immensely proud. But because he was a SEAL, she had to say no.

Suz had watched the SEALs with their families, and the warriors were excellent fathers—when they were around. Which wasn't much. The women who married those men were strong and independent and could carry the family on their own two shoulders. Suz didn't feel like she was that caliber of woman. She didn't meet the SEAL-wife qualifications for endurance and bravery.

And too, Suz's dad had weighed heavily on her heart when she thought about picking the man who would father her children. The relationship she had had with her dad was very special to her. They had been close, two peas in a pod. One day, he had a heart attack at work, fell down the stairs, and that's what killed him instantly, blunt force trauma to the head. He was gone from her life without a moment's notice. No time to say goodbye. No time to tell him once again how precious he was to her and how deeply she loved him. Just gone and never coming back. Suz couldn't do that to her future children. They deserved a father who was home.

She turned off the ignition and reached for her purse, wondering who had found it in her classroom after she fled and how it had made its way back to her. She was going to have to throw it out; it smelled heavily of smoke.

Get out of the car, Suz, go inside.

She pulled up on the handle and pushed her shoulder into the door.

Suz needed her dad at that moment. She wanted to put her head on his shoulder and for him to tell her that everything was okay. That her heart would someday mend from loving Jack, and she could love again.

"Oh!" Suz gasped aloud. That thought froze her in place. A

stabbing brightness of pain shot through her. That any man could fill her heart like Jack did–how could that be? It seemed absolutely impossible. Yet, she knew, had known, since she had first said no to Jack's proposal, that life as Jack's wife, while he was a SEAL, was not a life she could live. Being an Iniquus operator was almost the same thing. As devastating as it was to admit, Jack would be better off in someone else's arms. Someone who had the fortitude to send her husband off–each time knowing that might well be their final good-bye.

She couldn't live with this level of pain. She was afraid she'd start anesthetizing her anxiety with alcohol or pharmaceuticals. She'd considered it. Yoga and meditation just weren't strong enough antidotes for this amount of angst over this long a time. Yup, that last fear-filled drive to Suburban Hospital, to find out how badly injured Jack really was, ended it for her. Of that, she was sure.

If she wasn't going to be in a relationship with Jack, she had to learn to stand on her own two feet. She couldn't hide out in a safe house under Iniquus protection. Their protection was part and parcel of being involved with Jack.

Suz's eye caught on a bird flying outside the garage door. She was so glad to be home. What would her father say to her if he knew that four people had been shot dead, not a hundred steps from her classroom door and that someone had wanted to hurt one of her kids so badly that they would use C-4 to bypass the spikes that she had pushed into the flooring? Suz slammed her car door shut.

Suz wondered again, which of her students had been the target. She stopped, her hand on the Volvo's roof, her mind brought up pictures of each little face. She considered her kids and their backgrounds and none of them made much sense. . .

Moving zombie-like out of the open bay, Suz was on

autopilot when she fobbed the doors locked. Zombie-like. She let that word roll around in her consciousness as she moved down the sidewalk. It felt like Dementors had sucked her soul right out of her mouth; her body was animated, but she was absent.

Suz was so relieved that the TV crews that had been spotted here by the ISO were now gone. She guessed they figured she wouldn't be going back to this house after Hound News outed her as a CIA officer, and her cover had been blown. That was the most absurd part of this whole experience. Jack would be laughing so hard at the idea. Obviously, Lisa and Berry had never seen her at the gun range, leaning over a toilet, vomiting up her anxiety about the sound and the smell, and the lethality of the weapons. CIA. Ridiculous.

Suz pushed the key into the lock and let herself in. Her house was oddly still without her pups. Someone from Iniquus would bring them back sometime before lunch. She glanced down at her watch as she moved to the couch. *Soon,* she thought and flopped down. She wished her sisters were with her. Suz was so far from her family and friends. They were all in California, which seemed like the ends of the Earth right now.

When Suz had turned down Jack's marriage proposal, and he had listened to her reasons, Jack, being Jack, had developed a compromise. He would leave the SEALs–something that Suz would *never* have asked of him—and take a job along with Striker Rheas, a former SEAL and brother in arms, at Iniquus. Iniquus was a private military support group out of Washington D.C. She would move to D.C. with him and wear her engagement ring on her right ring finger until she felt comfortable moving that ring to her left hand and marrying him.

"Or I decide I still can't marry you." The words hurt to say, and she could tell they hurt Jack to hear them.

Suz had always felt that the phrase was true, "happy wife,

happy life." She also thought it was wrongly interpreted. It wasn't up to the guy to make sure his wife was happy after the marriage. Sure, he should aim to make his spouse happy; they both should. But really, what Suz thought that phrase was all about was that everyone should marry someone who was already happy. Happy with who they were. Happy with how both people fit together, how they worked together. In other words, if they were happy going into a life-time commitment, the chances for a happy life had a much better chance of happening. On the other hand, if a girl abided by the Disney princesses' tropes that they could lead these miserable lives and suddenly some guy was going to swoop in, kiss them, and make things magical and perfect? Whew! That just seemed all kinds of wrong.

Suz believed herself to be a better person than that. A more modern person than that. She had never wanted Jack to be her knight in shining armor. Though he certainly fitted the bill. She pictured Jack in his dress uniform, his shoulder brightly decorated with his ribbons of valor.

Suz lifted her hand and stared at the diamond in her engagement ring. It was clouded and had dirt packed into the prongs from her time in the woods. She let her hand drop.

Jack didn't re-up with his unit; instead, he signed papers with Iniquus. Suz, as her part of this compromise, left all her life-long friends and her family behind. When they arrived in Washington D.C., they were both in pain. It sucked for both of them. But quickly, Jack was back to jumping into hot spots and nabbing hostages from the brink of death, doing what he was trained to do. What he loved to do. And she? Read a lot of books. Took a lot of walks and hot baths. She threw herself into being the best teacher she could be for her students. Making friends here was harder than she had thought it would be.

One night at the extended-stay hotel where she was living—

until she found someplace suitable—Suz had brought up her feelings of isolation. They were discussing some article Jack had read and were speculating on the real chances of an actual zombie apocalypse.

"According to the article," Jack had said, "there are eight parasites that we know turn animals into zombies. There are the drug-addicted ant slaves, and the zombie caterpillars that plant themselves, and there's even a tapeworm that ends up inside of stickleback fish that make the fish leave their schools and swim to the warmer water that is preferred by the tapeworm."

"*Ew*, Jack. That's disgusting," she said, swallowing a bite of her spaghetti with a sudden loss of appetite. "But given that, do you think it's all that farfetched that an invasive organism would animate the dead and make those creatures want to eat our brains?"

The conversation turned into a "What would you do? Who would you want on your team?" debate. Where would they go? How would they get there? And that's when she had started crying.

Granted, she was at a hormonal peak, with killer cramps, coupled with the knowledge that Jack had packed to go down-range into some new hot spot and was just waiting for the call to head out the door – no idea where he was going, no idea when he'd be back, just gone. And she was out of chocolate. But still. It had been embarrassing.

Jack waited for the last of her sniffles and then simply said, "You had thought, and there was a whole lot of emotional energy behind it. I bet that surprised the hell out of you."

He was right. It had. It was a stupid thought. But then again . . .

"If there were a zombie apocalypse – enter any real-possibility disaster situation into that blank—you would grab your go-bag and go. I would be here alone. No family. Surface friends – people whom I just met. So really, would they share their last bite of food with me? What would I do? Where would I go? 'Cause I'm really all alone."

Jack had bundled her up in his arms and whispered against her hair. "Oh no, sweet love, I'd never put you in that position. You're safe." He bent to kiss her curls. "You're part of the Iniquus family –You're on their roster. It's not just sentiment. It's written in my contract. They have emergency protocol – they plan for every contingency. Trust me." He swiveled so she could see his eyes. "You're my priority. Okay?"

Suz tucked her head down against his chest, affirming to herself that it was a bad idea to go beyond a dating relationship with a man whose job was defined by danger; she just wasn't emotionally strong enough. Obviously.

They were still waiting for the call for him to head out the door. And the truth was that very well could have been their last night together, so Suz made a conscious choice not to wallow. She shoved those desperation feelings down deep. She'd have plenty of time to pull them out and roll around in them after Jack took off on his assignment. At that moment, she needed Jack to see she was fine. If he was worried about her, his mind wouldn't be on the mission – and that could prove deadly for him and his team.

"Periods suck," she mumbled to lay the blame for her emotional outburst somewhere safe.

"They do." He kissed the top of her head as he unwound himself from her. "Hang tight for a second. I have chocolate for you in the truck."

Of course, he did.

Suz desperately wanted to call and talk to Jack, to listen to the reassuring warmth in his voice. But he was going to be off-limits now that she had made her decision to leave him. Suz let her eyes move around her living room. It suddenly dawned on her that she couldn't live here anymore. She was going to have to move. Maybe even back to California, she thought, dully. This house, she had often laughed, should be called "The House that Jack Built." His care and hard work had made it the gem that it was. It really belonged to him. How could she start a new life with a new man, living in Jack's house? That thought made her want to sob.

When Jack came back from the mission following their zombie discussion, he invited her for a picnic. She remembered it like it was yesterday. She had worn little copper ballet slippers and a beautiful moss-colored sundress that matched her eyes and let the highlights shine their brightest in her auburn curls. The flowing skirt reached to her ankles, and Suz felt like she had stepped out of a Jane Austen novel. Jack had taken her to a park, and he was full of himself. She couldn't put her finger on it until they had climbed out of the cab, and he pulled a backpack from the pickup's bed.

"We're going to play a game," he'd said.

"What game?" Suz was on high alert. This wasn't Jack's normal vibe. He was. . . excited. Normally, he was very even-tempered and calm; but today, his energy snapped in the air, bright and eager.

"Zombie apocalypse," he'd said. "Remember what we were talking about before I left?"

He held the pack up for her to see.

She stared at it. It looked like a backpack. Nothing fancy or even interesting. It was gray digital camo with what looked like a solar panel clipped onto the front.

"It's one of your birthday presents. We're celebrating your

birthday – though a few weeks late. Sorry about that." He kissed her cheek, then made her put the pack on.

"It's heavy," she complained. This didn't match her mood or her outfit. It wasn't at all romantic. "You carry it, Jack."

"Nope. You can do it."

"What the heck is in here? It weighs as much as I do."

"It's the lightest I could make it – it's 30lbs. I could have gone lighter, but I wanted you to have a power source, so I added that on."

"What?" Suz was thoroughly confused.

"If you were ever in a zombie apocalypse, this is your bugout bag. You can stay happy and healthy for a week on this bag alone. And by then, you could hike out of most situations. The boots make it weigh more right now, but they'll be on your feet in an emergency." He tapped the laces tied to the top handle, draping down the back of the pack.

"Okay, but I don't want to be carrying it today."

"Hang on," he said. He went around to her back, and she could feel him tugging around. A zipper scratched closed. Jack appeared with an odd-looking phone, into which, he explained, he was programming GPS coordinates that she had to follow. "First, you need to find your way to food."

Suz was uncomfortable in the pack and ticked that Jack was hands-free. But Jack was so happy that Suz did her best to be a good sport. Following the arrow indicator on the gadget, they eventually emerged from the trees at a beautiful spot overlooking a picturesque creek where a picnic blanket with pillows and a cooler filled with delicious food had been set.

They had a wonderful lunch.

"You know, I think I could handle an apocalypse if I got to have chocolate-covered strawberries and Moscato whenever I got hungry." She had laughed.

He grinned and took her phone and plugged in another number. "Your next assignment is to find shelter." They left everything from their picnic laying out, which made Suz uneasy until Jack explained that he had texted one of his helpers that they were done, and his buddy would come to pick it up.

"One of them?" she asked.

Again, she was walking through the woods with the heavy pack on her back and twigs slipping into her shoes. The Moscato had put her in a better mood, though. Off she went, down the path, following the arrow on the phone, wondering what was around the bend. Jack's nerves were increasing, and this was so antithetical to Jack that she couldn't help but mirror his excitement, picking up her pace and skipping along the trail.

They emerged at the edge of a neighborhood. The GPS indicated the house at the very end of a cul de sac, surrounded on three sides by nature, the neighborhood stretched out to the east.

She had turned. "Where are we, Jack?"

"Home," he said.

"What?"

"This is your other birthday present." He held up a key.

"But, Jack…"

"I used my Iniquus signing bonus to buy a house for you."

He hadn't asked her if she wanted to live there. She had had no say so. She was conflicted by emotions. It was too generous. Too sudden. Too much. "Mine?"

"Yours."

She turned away. Hers. Not theirs. She'd be alone in that house. Jack, by contract, had to spend nights when he was on assignment up at the Iniquus barracks. Iniquus, like the military, was a lifestyle, not a job. Even though he had his own apartment in the barracks, she wasn't allowed to see it. Anyone that wasn't employed by Iniquus was barred from their secure campus unless they had a darned good reason and an escort.

"Before you go in, I should warn you. It's dated inside. It needs a lot of work." Now he seemed worried. "You decide how you want it fixed up, and I'll do that for you."

"You look overly excited about painting walls and putting down tile."

"I'm going to make it beautiful for you, Suz." He brushed her hair back over her shoulders and kissed her lips, making her tingle right down to her toes.

Her concerns flew away in the breeze.

"You're going to feel at home here. Like you belong. Ready for more?"

"More?" No. She thought she was filled to the brim and couldn't handle more. Really, the zombie bag and the picnic were more than enough.

"You need companionship to keep your spirits up."

Jack raised his hand over his head, and the front door opened. Out waddled two little furballs. Basset hound puppies with tiny little legs and an overabundance of ears. Jack grabbed her hand and pulled her to the porch, where the pups were shuffling around, trying to find a way down the steps. Suz scooped them protectively to her chest, looking wide-eyed at Jack.

"Dick and Jane," he said.

Her heart stuttered. "But I told you that was what I wished for on the first night we met. The night I told you that I wanted—"

"A cottage in the woods with a kitchen big enough to cook and eat as a family, a big dining room – big enough for dinner parties, lots of windows, at least two fireplaces—"

"And a garage," she said.

Jack pointed to the side of the house. "And a garage."

THE COTTAGE WAS PERCHED at the edge of Matthew Henson State Park – it was a 30-minute drive to Iniquus Headquarters on a good day—not that she was allowed to go there, 10 minutes to St. Basil's Prep, and 19 minutes to Suburban Hospital in heavy traffic with a lot of horn honking and arm flailing for people to get the heck out of her way. Though, honestly, she had only made that lone drive to Suburban this last time. Before now, two Iniquus staff had always shown up to give her a full report. One was there to help with whatever she needed help with–finishing a half-cooked dinner and storing it in the fridge, ironing the clothes that she was working on, taking care of Dick and Jane—and the other helper was there to drive her, in her own car, to the hospital so she could get there safely. Jack had said Iniquus had her on the family roster. And they were stellar about smoothing the waters and making things easy for the operators' families.

They won't be taking care of me anymore—time to stand on my own two feet.

Suz let her gaze rest on her 1940's style rotary dial phone. She should call the hospital and see if Jack was released. Suz didn't want him to show up here at the house. She was too fragile. She didn't have the stamina to go through the actual breakup talk right now. She also couldn't pretend everything was okay.

That's when the doorbell rang.

9

Suz

12:05 P.M., TUESDAY, FEBRUARY 15TH
The House That Jack Built, Bethesda, Maryland

SUZ CLOSED the door behind the Iniquus Support Officer. It would be the last time Suz would have their help, but he didn't know that. Before the ISO left, he gave Suz his cell number and told her he was assigned to her and that if she needed anything at all to send him a text. Suz put the number in her wastebasket and reached down to rub the pups' ears. "You two look like you were spoiled rotten."

Dick waddled into the living room and flopped onto his bed.

The guy had handed her a takeout bag from one of her and Jack's favorite lunch spots. Jack must have listed it with her preferences in some database somewhere. Suz put her head in the bag a sniffed the rich, spicy aroma of the Moroccan cuisine as she shuffled to the kitchen with Jane at her heels. Suz hadn't eaten anything since her MRE in the woods. And she had eaten that for the kids' sake. They had been watching her closely. Seeing how she acted. She pretended that everything was A-Okay. But the truth was, Suz was so depressed that the act of chewing and then swallowing seemed too monumental to take on.

The to-go box was filled with couscous topped with chicken and vegetables that had been slow-roasted in a tagine. The side dishes were the apricot fritters with pistachio coulis that she ordered every single time, and *Zaalouk*, an eggplant and tomato salad. If anything could get her eating, this was the meal. Jack must have noted that too. Otherwise, the ISO could have picked up a pizza at Jack's and her go-to "I don't feel like cooking" spot up the street. Truth be told, Iniquus spoiled her.

Suz understood that Iniquus took good care of her as part of their business model. The United States government put a great deal of time and money into choosing and training the best of the best in their special forces operator military programs. There were only but so many retired SEALs, Green Berets, Marine Raiders, and other specialists to be had. Iniquus also had internationally proficient hackers, lawyers, spies, and thieves. The thieves' part she was making up – maybe. Iniquus wanted the best of the best on their payroll so that no matter what emergency sprang up, they had the right person with the right skillset ready to leap into action.

Keeping those skills on the Iniquus payroll and not someone else's meant more than a fat paycheck. It meant a commitment to excellence, a highly sought-after sterling reputation, and a sense of family. The operators never worried about what was happening on the home front. If there was a way to solve an issue, Iniquus solved it — from mowing the family yards to roadside assistance to flying in world-renowned doctors, to...

well, anything that was needed. Suz had never heard of a family doing without – except, of course, for doing without their loved one.

That was the price.

Too rich for her blood.

But that didn't mean she couldn't enjoy this last, and very delicious, Iniquus delivered meal.

Suz decided her lunch needed a cup of mint tea. She got up and put the kettle on to boil. She was a purest when it came to tea making. It was as much about the process as it was about drinking it. She had just turned the element on high when the bell rang again.

"Did you forget something?" She called as she moved toward the front door, threw the bolt, and swung it wide to two men in long black coats.

"Miss Molloy?" The man in front asked. He was tall and thin with wide apple cheeks and pale eyes that reminded her of a shark, cold and emotionless.

She scowled at him.

"My name is Samuel Jones. I need to ask you a few questions."

Jane was at their feet growling, and soon Dick trotted over to sniff at the strangers. Neither seemed impressed. Their barks echoed off the ceiling and bounced off the walls. Basset Hounds were known for being loud, but Dick and Jane were unusually riled. Suz pushed the door to close it. "This isn't a good time. You should call my lawyer and make an appointment." Suz didn't have a lawyer, but suddenly she felt claustrophobic and anxious. These guys needed to go.

Samuel Jones reached out and blocked the door's movement. "You misunderstand," he said in his quiet alpha-male voice. "I am not making a request." He walked in as if he had been invited. As if he owned the place.

The two men stalked into her living room, corralling her away from any exits. "You may call me Jones. Take a seat, please." He gestured to the armchair where Jack would never sit. It had no view of the windows or the doors, and the back was "unprotected," according to Jack. As a matter of fact, the Iniquus team would rather sit on the floor up against the wall than sit in that particular seat. It was the submissive seat. Suz felt her vulnerability quotient ratchet up.

Jones sat in Jack's spot. The alpha place in the room. Between Jones's posture, his voice, and this seating selection, Suz recognized that the man in front of her was of the class of men who killed as part of their job description, and he was here on a mission. For the good guys? For the bad guys? Suz knew from stories told around the campfire by Jack's soldiering friends that there was a whole lot of gray in the world. So even the good guys could act like the bad. In the gray world, classifying someone came down to their motivation, not how they got to the end result. Sometimes any means to the end was necessary. Where did what was happening here in her living room land on that spectrum?

The other man turned the bolt on the door, clicked on the living room lights, then moved to the windows where he yanked the drapes tightly closed.

Jones looked down at the dogs baring their teeth and yapping at him – which was about as vicious as these two sad-eyed, droopy-eared dogs could get—and he flicked a finger toward the second man.

The other man—medium everything, non-descript, monochromatic—who had not yet mentioned his name or spoken, reached into his pocket and pulled a handful of liver-smelling treats. He fed a few to each of the pups and rubbed them behind their ears, making them moan and wag their tails.

Traitors.

He whistled, and they happily followed him into the kitchen, where he opened the door and let them go out.

Suz was wide-eyed at the audacity. Her gaze traveled to the trashcan, where her Iniquus support guy's number lay. She wondered where she put her cell phone. She eyed the antique dial phone next to Jones. Jones turned his attention to where she was looking. He leaned back and pulled a knife from his pocket, reached over, and cut the cord that led to the wall socket.

"What do you want from me?" she asked with a whisper-thin voice.

"We have a few questions, we have a few requests, but it is not really what we want. It is what your little students want that is most important here."

Suz felt darkness slowly drape down over her eyeballs. She felt heat and pressure round over the spheres, blocking out light, then she saw a fringe of brown fibers. *Those are my eyelashes*, she thought. *I just blinked.* Her mind had moved with the adrenaline that spiked through her system into that weird vortex-y place where it felt like her brain opened up and vacuumed in every single extraneous morsel of information. The cardinal who sat in a nest under her eaves let out a call that sounded like a bomb falling. The long whistle came to a momentary halt, then bounced four times on nothingness, each time emitting a short, staccato note. Suz had these thoughts inside her head, but another part of her brain sat just to the side, yelling, "Stop! You have to stop. Something horrible is happening. You need to focus on the important things."

The tea kettles shriek jolted her in her seat. She stared into the kitchen at the high-pitched sound, not knowing what she should do. Instead of making an actionable decision, her brain went to a word she had studied for the GMATs that were required by her grad school: "impuissance, middle English, French derivation – the lack of physical or mental power, weakness." That word did nothing to help her deal with this situation; it simply stated the obvious. Suz's eyes followed the second nameless guy as he went into the kitchen. She heard him lift the kettle, rendering it instantly silent, then he rattled around in there.

Jones snapped his fingers, and the spell was broken. Suz focused over on him, her brain functioning again. Suz hated adrenaline.

Jones had removed his overcoat and draped it neatly on the arm of the chair. She had missed that while she focused on eyelids, and bird songs, and tea whistles. He reached into the inside pocket of his suitcoat, pulled out three pictures, and handed them to her. She reached out and saw that he wore gloves made of thin black leather. They looked odd with his suit coat. It was odd to wear gloves inside her house.

She focused on the pictures. The first one was of Rebeca, Ari, and Caleb Levinski cheesing it up for the camera. The second one was of Ari and Caleb looking like they were asleep in the seat of a minivan. In the third, the boys were squatting in the mud, dirty and wild-eyed.

"Where did you get these photographs of the children?" she asked, not understanding their import.

"The Levinski children have been of interest to us for quite a while. But they suddenly became relevant."

Suz knew the cryptic-speak were code words for something, but she just didn't understand.

"We think that it would be a very good idea for your good

health and that of these children that you cooperate by answering my questions."

"If I can. . ."

"You can, and you will." Jones leaned back and crossed his ankle over his knee, looking perfectly comfortable.

"I'm sorry, let me re-phrase. If I have any information, I will tell you. If I don't have the information, well, then obviously, I can't tell you."

Jones dipped his head left and then right as if weighing her words. "That sounds fair enough." He glanced up, and number two was coming in with a tray that held a steaming teapot and a plate of cookies. He set it on the coffee table and said something in a foreign language to Jones. Jones responded in that same dialect. Suz tried to puzzle out what language they were speaking; it sounded vaguely Russian. That's as far as she got. None of the words stood out as familiar.

The other man left then came immediately back with another tray with her lunch on it. Jones swept an open hand toward the tray as the other man brought it over and set it on her lap. He, too was, wearing thin black gloves.

"Please, it seems that we've interrupted your lunch. Enjoy." He spread his colorless lips in what might have been an attempt at a smile. Suz fought her desire to shudder. She looked down at the stew; she had absolutely no appetite. But to show her good intentions of being cooperative until she could find a way to escape this mess, she offered up her own semblance of a smile and took a bite.

Jones waited for her to finish every last painful morsel on her plate, then he nodded at the other-man. The other-man immediately stepped forward and took the tray.

Jones leaned forward with his elbows on his knees, his fingers loosely interlaced, and his cold-fish stare. "Let's begin."

Suz gripped the arms of her winged back chair. What did that mean? Her mind went to interrogation scenes in movies where the man would take out a cloth and unroll it on the table, revealing his torture tools. She stopped breathing.

"How long have you worked with the CIA?"

The question caught her off guard. She stared at the man as if he were mad. Her brain tried to churn through the situation and what it came up with was a burst of laughter. "What?" she sputtered.

The man turned his head slightly as the other-man handed him a piece of her stationary. He glanced at it. "Dearest Jack." Jones attempted to smile again. "This is your boyfriend?"

Jack! "My ex-."

"You always write dearest to your ex-?"

Suz had trouble holding eye contact with the man. She found herself staring at the stationary instead. "He doesn't know he's an ex- yet. I was writing a letter to tell him."

"Ah, I see. And dearest Jack is also the Captain Jack that your students are speaking of on the television."

Suz nodded and swallowed.

"He set up your great escape. He is a military man, a captain, huh? A special forces operator?"

"He's not a captain, no. I was very afraid after Sandy Hook. . ."

"Yes, this was a very loving gesture, putting into place these plans so you would be safe. He did a superlative job by all accounts. I wonder how he knew what to do? Where he got his supplies. He must be special forces operator, no?"

"He isn't with the military, no." Suz saw Jones tweak his head and knew he didn't believe her. "But he used to be in the Navy. He left the service years ago. That's why they called him

Captain, like the Gordon's fisherman. You know, a guy on a boat."

"A fisherman in the navy? A SEAL then?"

"In his dreams, he is." That was completely truthful, but she thought the bitterness in her words sounded a whole lot like sarcasm, and she thought that was probably how Jones read it. "Right now, he's not working. He's disabled. As a matter of fact, he just came out of yet another surgery. They were trying to fix his knee."

"And yet you are willing to leave the relationship when he is in recovery?"

"I've done all I can. I'm wrung out. I just can't be part of his life anymore."

"You have an engagement ring on your right hand. You planned to marry him?"

"No, he asked. He wanted me to hang on to the ring and think it over. And I decided to give it back and end the relationship. It's on my right hand until I can give it to him."

Jones held out his hand.

Suz stared at the open palm, then realizing what he wanted, she pulled off the ring and handed it to him.

"It is a very large diamond. Two carats? Three? This must be worth more than fifty-thousand dollars."

"I…I wouldn't know."

"How would he get this kind of money, a disabled veteran?"

"Well, the stone was his grandmother's. . . so he didn't buy it. He bought the setting for me. That shouldn't have cost him much." What a weird conversation this was.

The other-man came back and spoke to Jones in their foreign language.

"Come, I have a question for you." Jones stood and opened

his leather-clad palm to indicate the hallway to her bedroom. Those gloves – Suz had been scared for other people's safety, scared for her students yesterday, and Ari and his brother in those photos. Those photos scared her. She was scared for Jack all the time. . . but she had never been scared like this for herself before.

Her bedroom felt too intimate a place, too far from an exit.

She hesitated.

"Please." Jones countered with a slight uptick in inflection, which Suz herself used when she wasn't giving her students any choices.

Jones had placed the engagement ring in his pants' pocket and then swung in to walk behind her. They walked to her closet. She had taken out her suitcase and her summer box of clothes and was packing for her trip Thursday – it was something to do to keep her mind busy on things other than her broken heart.

The other-man pointed to the corner where she stored her birthday bag from Jack.

"This is a go-bag," Jones said.

"It's a zombie bag," Suz countered to her own amazement.

"Excuse me?"

"Do you watch *Day of the Dead* on TV? It's about the end of civilization because there's an epidemic that turns people into zombies. If that ever happened, that's my bag to get out of Dodge and flee the hoards. It was a birthday gift."

"Out of Dodge," Jones said, then turned and conferred with the other-man who seemed to explain the idiom. That meant the other-man also understood English. Suz wondered why he had only conversed with this guy in their language. "Ah, and you packed this bag? Or did Captain Jack?"

"Jack did. As my birthday present."

Jones had her take it out of the closet and open it. She unzipped the top flap that had the solar panels attached, and she lifted it up. There, in various holsters, was a gun, a machete, a big knife like soldiers use, a large canister of mace, and a stun gun.

"You are, as they say, 'loaded for bear,'" Jones commented.

Suz looked up at him. "Who says that?"

"Take the gun out," Jones said.

Suz reached out her thumb and forefinger and slid the gun out of the holster, leaving the pistol on the bag.

"It has a magazine inserted already. Is there a bullet in the chamber?"

Suz looked down at the gun, then up at the ceiling. "'Bullet in the chamber' that means that the slide was racked, and a bullet was pushed up and ready for the trigger." There was a window on the gun Jack had shown her. She leaned over the Ruger and looked down, seeing nothing. She gingerly flipped it over and peered down again. There, just in front of the grip, she could see a little bit of brass. "Yes, there's a bullet there," she said.

"Good. Lift the gun and point it at my colleague."

Suz looked at him and blinked.

"I wish you to point the gun at my colleague. He is here without your invitation. He has, in effect, broken into your home. Lift the gun and point it at him." The growl was a command.

Suz vibrated from head to foot as she sat back on her heels, reached out for the gun, and wrapped it in her fingers. She had to process through the grip. It had been a long time since Jack had tried to teach her how to use it. Her index finger laid on the outside of the trigger guard. She lifted the gun and found the other-man's chest at the end of her sight. Her hands shook uncontrollably, swinging the barrel in a disjointed pattern. She panted, her jaw dropped down, her tongue didn't feel like it fit properly in her mouth.

"Shoot him," Jones said softly.

Suz did nothing but quiver.

"Shoot him." Jones's voice suddenly boomed out with such authority that her brain seemed to want to short circuit her own decision making and hand its power over to the foreigner in her bedroom.

Her stomach dropped. Releasing the gun, Suz raced for the bathroom, where she was just in time to lift the lids and vomit up the orange couscous.

10

Jack

20:30 Hours, Tuesday, Feb. 15th

Suburban Hospital, Bethesda, Md.

"Lynx, have you talked to Suz?" Jack's face looked slightly pixilated over Skype.

"Not since Monday night at the safe house. I've had my nose in this case, trying to figure out where the Levinski children were taken." She was standing in Striker's kitchen at the Iniquus barracks, making a sandwich. She was multi-tasking. Checking in on Jack, grabbing a quick bite, and then a shower. After that, she planned a thirty-minute power nap, then back on the trail of those boys who disappeared into thin air.

"Any luck?"

"Nada. You were asking about Suz. Hasn't she—" Lynx reached out to grab at the wall behind her, her feet widened her stance, and she bent her knees as if she were surfing a high wave and working to maintain her balance. "Holy moly," she whispered.

"What's that, Lynx?"

"Jack, be nimble, Jack, be quick," she muttered like she was casting an incantation.

"The timing on that text couldn't have been any better. Thank you. That jump saved my life."

"No – oh. Holy hell. Your jump off the building was serendipitous." Lynx squatted down on the floor, not even bothering to move to a chair. She leaned her back into the wall and pulled her knees to her chest.

"Are you okay?" Jack pushed up in his bed. "Move the screen, so I can see you better. What are you doing on the floor?"

Lynx pulled the ThinkPad down to her lap. Her face had blanched. "My texting that to you – the timing—that was a stroke of good luck."

"I'd agree. But I'm still not following. You look like you've seen a ghost."

Lynx blinked as she looked like she was trying to get her thoughts to line themselves up.

"Holy moly," she said, again, as the enormity of some discovery seemed to hit her hard. "I texted you my sixth sense warning when it came to me. And you read it as an immediate danger."

"Which it was."

"No. It wasn't."

"How can you say that – the building exploded as my feet hit the car roof."

"The warning wasn't about your being in danger on that building."

"I don't understand."

"Yeah – that's the fricking nature of my psychic *knowings*, isn't it? They don't truly make sense until I'm interpreting them in hindsight. But this I can tell you, that message definitely wasn't meant to prod you off that roof. Just – well, thank God it did. It was a bonus."

"A bonus," he deadpanned. "What was it about then?"

"Someone else – something else. You need to intervene."

"Lynx, I'm really not following you. These pain meds. . ."

"If the *knowing* I heard, 'Jack be nimble, Jack be quick, Jack jump over the candlestick,' was about the rooftop blowing and your jumping, I wouldn't have the warning come up again. It just hit me between the eyes. Hard."

Jack looked at her, stunned. "Jeezus, Lynx! I jumped off a three-story building when I read that."

"I know! I'm sorry. Wait. No. I'm not sorry. It saved your life. So maybe it was a two-for…" Lynx turned her head this way and that as if using an antenna to home in on something. "No, it's definitely not over, and it's definitely not you who's in trouble. You have to jump."

"That's kind of cryptic, Lynx. And I think my jumping days are over, at least in the near future. A couple months until I can actually jump. Do you think this *knowing* is literal?"

"I hope not." Lynx leaned her head back, staring up at the ceiling. "Let's stop and think. What were we talking about when the knowing hit me? Ah, we were talking about Suz. . ."

"Suz? What about her?" Jack's face pushed toward the camera, filling the entire screen.

"I don't. . ." Lynx shook her head.

"Come help me get up. Now!"

"But—"

"Now, or we aren't friends." Jack emphasized the threat by closing the lid on his computer, effectively ending the conversation without a good-bye. Something he never did.

It was less than an hour later that Lynx walked into the hospital room with a backpack slung over her shoulder. She looked exhausted. "Jack, I am so conflicted. I don't know what to do. Here, I brought you a bag, so at least you can cover up your backside."

"Thanks." Jack picked up the bag, hoisted himself out of bed, and propelled into the bathroom on his crutches with his leg locked out straight. He left the door open as he dug through the kit.

Lynx sat with her back to the door.

"What's the conflict?" he called as he leaned into the wall, so he could pull on a pair of boxer briefs.

"Last time you were in here, after your brush with Satan and death, you released yourself from the hospital against medical advice. Iniquus Command was pretty ticked at you, as you'll recall." She turned around to catch his eye, then blinked and quickly turned her head back to the wall, "Sorry," she said, then cleared her throat. "Now, granted, it was for a good reason. You were part of the team that took down Striker's kidnapper, and you helped to save our company. But still, Command warned you against your cowboy behavior. You were told that doctors' orders were the same as orders from your superior, and disobeying them would be viewed as insubordination, which is a terminable offense. If you pack up and leave without some doctor okaying this, you could be fired."

"I can't get Suz to answer the phone. It goes to voice mail. She's not answering my texts." His brace was laying across the sink, and Jack stiffened his muscles to keep his leg straight. He had pulled a t-shirt over his head and was now struggling with his pants. As he grunted and banged into the wall, Lynx moved into the bathroom to help.

"To be fair, every person she's known since birth, and their friends and relatives are all probably calling her to get a direct line on the scoop about what happened at her school. And you heard that she was outed as a CIA officer. Hound News may have it right. She could be in some black site to prevent her from telling the intel we have about upcoming attacks against children." Lynx snorted; she laughed so hard.

"That's not even close to being funny."

"Sit on the toilet. We're going to have to work as a team to get these pants on you." She helped lower him down. "It's Suz. Suz who carries spiders outside and tells them to have a happy life elsewhere. Suz, who sobbed when the stray cat she'd been feeding brought her a dead mouse as a thank you. Suz is . . . like chocolate chip oatmeal cookies and a glass of milk."

Jack tipped his head.

"You know — warm, sweet, healthy to be around but not obnoxiously so. She brings a taste of normality to our lives – we all love her for that. She's good stuff. Solid. And I, for one, look forward to the times I get to see her."

Jack nodded, and Lynx swiveled to catch Jack's gaze. "But I have to be truthful, Suz was acting skittish when it came to talking to you." She had both pants legs up around his thighs. "Suz made up something about being covered in dirt so she couldn't come by the hospital – but it just didn't read right body-language-wise. Since I took her to the safe house, I haven't been able to reach her, either." Lynx moved around to the other side of the toilet and put her cheek on Jack's back, reaching around him for the waistband of his pants. "I do know that she called in to ask for her dogs to be brought back to her place and to tell us she was done using the safe house. Can you lift your weight onto your good foot and get your hips up?"

Jack complied.

Lynx shimmied the fabric over his butt and up to his hips. "Whew. There." She stood up and brushed her hands together. "Okay, that call to Iniquus came in early this morning. Other than that, I don't have anything. It could well be that she just needs some private time to process. Doing what she did at the school, experiencing what she experienced, it's not part of most humans' world. It can deflate you quick, and it takes time. . ."

Jack leaned back to access the zipper and snap. He did them up. "You don't sound like you believe that."

"Something's off. I don't know what. Is it attached to my *knowing*?" Lynx fitted the brace back into place over Jack's gray camo BDUs, quiet for a moment while she aligned and clipped the many closures. "I have no clue – you know that my information system is kind of shitty until I'm looking in the rearview mirror. I feel like a broken record saying this; hindsight makes everything crystal clear." She stood up to find Jack's boots. "I had thought your quick exit strategy off the roof was actually what this had been all about."

"But it's not."

"It's not. That's the only thing I can say for sure."

"I've got to find Suz and talk to her. In person."

A nurse stood at the bathroom door where Lynx was on the floor, tying Jack's boot on his good foot. "Can I ask what's going on here?" Her hands landed on her hips, and she looked thoroughly put out.

"Ma'am, there's an emergency. My fiancée is . . . I have to get to her right now. Can you please help me fill out the papers I need to sign to leave?" Jack turned his husky-blue eyes and his husky-smooth tones on the woman. The combination had rarely failed him.

"The doctor said that *maybe* you would be released this evening. He hasn't gotten to you on his rounds yet."

Jack reached for the woman's hand. Lynx pursed her lips. Jack didn't often use this trick unless he needed it in the field, but it seemed he was pulling out all the stops. He looked deeply into the woman's eyes and said softly, "The woman who holds my heart in her palm is in imminent danger. *Nothing* will keep me from her side. Please, I'm asking for your help."

The nurse pulled her hand free; her entire body stance had changed. With a nod of determination, she stalked out the door.

Lynx rolled her eyes. "I hate it when you guys pull that cheesy, soul-searching romcom crap on women."

"It works, though," Jack said.

"Sadly, true." Lynx pushed to standing. "Hopefully, it will this time, anyway." Lynx pulled out her cell phone. "It's twenty-two hundred hours. Suz'll be in bed. But let me try one more time to get her by phone. Okay? I don't want you to lose your job over a misinterpreted *knowing*."

Jack's phone vibrated on the table beside his bed.

"There, see? I bet that's Suz now, calling to tell you good night." Lynx brought Jack's phone to him.

The screen showed a phone number that Jack didn't recognize. He held the phone to his ear. "Hello?"

"This is Ken Meter, Bethesda PD, trying to reach James McCullen." His voice was loud enough that Lynx heard. She reached over and touched the speaker button, so she could listen to the conversation. Jack cleared his throat; it wasn't often that someone called him by his given name. "This is James."

"Mr. McCullen, your name is listed on Gillian Molloy's DMV records as a person to contact in case of an emergency."

Jack's body stiffened, and Lynx moved to put a steadying hand on his shoulder.

"This is not an emergency, Mr. McCullen. It's just that we responded to a noise ordinance call at Miss Molloy's residence. Her dogs are barking and causing a disturbance. They're in a pen that is set up between her house and the garage with a chain-link roof over the top. And it seems the only way to get to the dogs is through the house itself. Animal control doesn't want to snip through the fencing – it looks like a quality pen. No one's answering the door, and with this weather, the dogs are in physical distress. We thought you might be able to bring the dogs into the house. Get them out of the cold. Give the neighbors some peace and quiet so they can get some sleep."

"Yes, officer, absolutely. I'm about twenty minutes away, but I'm heading there now."

After signing off, Jack looked at Lynx. "She'd never leave Dick and Jane alone outside. Especially in this cold."

"Agreed," Lynx said. "Someone needs to head right over, but I think I should call Panther Force and have them meet me there. You should get back in bed."

"Did you really think that plan would fly with me?" Jack asked.

"No, but I had to try," she said, gathering up Jack's things and heading toward the door.

The nurse scuttled back in with a clipboard in her hand, thrusting a pen in Jack's direction. "I explained everything to the doctor." She held up an infrared thermometer. Standing on her toes, she aimed it at Jack's forehead. "Dr. Newcomb said if your temperature was normal, you could go." The nurse looked at the reading.

Jack saw it glowed red with 99.9F in the window.

"Perfectly normal," she said as she brushed a tear from her face. "Good luck."

Lynx rolled her eyes behind the nurse's back. As Jack reached for the pen to sign the papers, Lynx pulled his pack over her shoulders. "I'll jog ahead and pull the car around to the front door. You go slow. If you get any more broken than you are now, you'll be of no use. Got me?" Lynx gave him a pointed look then headed out the door, not waiting for his response.

THEY DROVE in silence toward Suz's house. Lynx made the twenty-minute drive in fifteen minutes flat. Jack's seat was pushed back as far as it would go to accommodate his leg, but he ended up having to release the clasp on his brace, forcing his knee to bend enough to shut the car door.

He caught a glimpse of his face in the side mirror. He was nearly white beneath his tan. Pain shot through him in waves. His hands splayed out on the console as if he could push the car to go faster. Anxiety rolled off him, and he knew it was hitting Lynx's highly tuned sensibilities hard because she was plastered up against her door, putting as much distance as she could between them.

Jack had been in combat situations for the last seven years, seen his friends injured and killed, been pulled back from the brink himself, anything that a human being could do that was evil and horrific to another – he had seen, but none of it ever felt like this to him. He was a different person, altogether, thinking that something wasn't right with Suz, that she might be in danger. He relished the power of adrenaline surges on a normal day – but today, he was awash in a fear that he had never experienced before.

Lynx pulled up as close as she could to the sidewalk and opened the back door to pull out Jack's crutches.

"We're here!" she called over to the officer who seemed to be getting an earful from the antique lady who stood in slippered feet and a robe in the twenty-degree weather, her hair done up in pink plastic curlers.

Jack reached for the crutches that Lynx extended to him, and he jerked his head toward the officer.

Lynx turned and went to play diplomat.

Jack pulled his keys from his pocket and made a beeline for the front door. On the way, he noticed the garage was open, and Suz's car was parked where it normally was parked. The front porch light was off – something that Suz never left unattended when she was at home. The interior lights were on, but the drapes had been pulled tightly closed.

None of this was normal.

Jack wished Lynx had brought him a sidearm. He felt naked as he twisted the key in the lock. He stood at an angle next to the door frame when he pushed the knob. It was a habit that had been drilled into him over years of clearing buildings in hot spots in case someone inside was watching and waiting and willing to take a sucker shot at whoever pushed that door open. Standing on the front porch, Jack let his eyes scan the entranceway. Normal. He turned his gaze on Lynx, which she picked up immediately and turned to look his way. He tipped his head toward the interior.

Lynx rubbed a hand down the old lady's arm, wiggled her fingers in a good-bye, and turned to jog his way. Along the path, he saw her reach into the conceal-carry pocket on her jacket as she hustled up beside him. He let her take point as she buttonhooked into the room, cleared the corners, and he hopped in behind her.

Through the dining room and into the kitchen, they progressed with practiced moves. Lynx opened the side door so the dogs would come in, and they'd stop their barking. Dick and Jane were up under Jack's feet, quivering with cold and excitement to see him. Lynx continued checking the house.

"Clear," she called from Suz's bathroom. Then walked back to the kitchen. "Don't move anything you don't have to, Jack. Something's off in here."

"Besides a distinct lack of Suz, what did you pick up on?"

"Her computer is booted up in the office. She has a suitcase sitting outside of her closet that she's been filling from a summer box that she pulled out. And her engagement ring is sitting on her bed on top of a letter that says only, "Dearest Jack.'"

Jack jerked toward their bedroom, the crutches clacking along the wooden floors. Sure enough, there was her lavender stationery with his name written in Suz's curling script across the top – Dearest Jack —and nothing more. And there was her ring. He reached out and lifted it to his lips. It was cold. She hadn't worn it recently. What would make her take it off?

He hadn't seen her since he left on his mission. Had only received confirmation that she was headed to the hospital via text. Then he was in the operating room. She hadn't visited him since he was awake. He thought he hadn't seen her because of St. Basil's. But that made no damned sense. None of this picture did.

Lynx had followed him as far as the second bedroom, where Suz had her desk and bookshelves and wall of plastic rolling drawers where she kept supplies to put together art projects for her kids. Lynx called back to him. "Her computer isn't password protected?"

"No," he said, standing in the middle of their bedroom doing a slow scan for things out of place. True, he was only here when he wasn't on assignment. But it felt like home to him. His things were in the drawers. His shampoo was on the shower rack. . . but somehow, right then, he felt like he was no longer welcome, and it shook him to the core. Jack wondered if the medications they had been giving him at the hospital was messing with his system. The sensations he was experiencing physically and emotionally weren't things he had known before. He cleared his throat. "No, that's her house computer. She hated the extra step of logging in."

"Well, I'm in her account history. Her last email is to Emma Todd,"

"That's her best friend in Coronado," Jack called back, staring at the engagement ring, hoping for a clue about what this all meant.

"Suz sent Emma airline information. According to the email, she's leaving Reagan International Thursday morning. The departure time for zero-eight-hundred hours. That would explain the warm weather clothing. Maybe she wanted to get out of town what with Hound News trying to make her into public enemy number one instead of a hero."

Jack moved to the office door. Cold brushed over him. "She's going home then?"

"No, she's going to St. Marten's. They're going to meet down there. She and Emma. Or that's what it says here in the email. Ten days at the Warm Breezes All-Inclusive Spa and Resort. Look, they get unending food and drinks. This looks like fun. Probably exactly what she needs, a Pina Colada on the beach, her best friend, some sun. Good for her."

"It doesn't explain anything. The dogs. The drapes."

"I'm. . . huh, here's something interesting. She went on Travelocity earlier today at 14:29 . . . She purchased two tickets to Brazil."

"Brazil? What? From St. Martens?" Jack tried to squeeze his large frame into the overcrowded room, so he could see the screen.

"No, from out of Reagan, they're landing in Brasília, and then they have another leg to Foz do Iguaçu."

"When?"

Lynx tapped at the computer. "Uhm, looks like she should already be in the air over the Gulf of Mexico."

She turned the screen so Jack could see it better.

4:40 PM – 7:35 PM

Washington (IAD) – Miami (MIA)
American 2536 · Boeing 737
Average legroom (31")
Often delayed by 30+ min

9:10 PM – 5:45 am (+1)

Miami (MIA) – Brasília (BSB)
TAM 8043 · Boeing 767
Above-average legroom (32")
Overnight flight

"BUT HER SUITCASE IS HERE." Jack went back to her bedroom and checked the top drawer, where she kept her passport and her emergency cash.

The cash was there; the passport was gone.

He called her phone again, desperate to talk to her.

The sound of a thunderstorm rose from the bathroom sink. It was sitting under a picture of him that was lying face down on the counter. "Her phone is here," he called out. He looked at the text history. The last one she had sent out was Suz letting him know she was on her way. That was Sunday before his operation. He opened her phone history. The list of incoming calls was long. Outgoing, she had called home to her parents, her sisters, and Emma, Monday evening. She had called Iniquus, Tuesday morning at 09:46 hours. She hadn't called him.

He didn't know what to think of that.

He looked down and saw both lids were up on the toilet as if a man had taken a leak. But when Jack looked in, there was a splash of goo near the rim that looked like vomit that hadn't been swept down with the flush. Jack touched her toothbrush. It was wet.

Jack went back to Suz's closet and checked her suitcases; they were both there. She had been packing her green case, her bikini, some shorts, and sundresses. This made no sense. He looked down at the empty spot next to her shoe tower. Her zombie bag was gone.

"Lynx, come here. I need you to puzzle something through with me."

Lynx rounded the corner.

"Her bug-out bag is gone." Jack pointed to the empty closet corner.

"Okay, this is getting strange." Lynx moved over to stand where Jack had pointed. "Here, move out of my way." She put her hands on his elbows as he jostled sideways. Then she turned, and to his eye, it looked like she was pretending to reach into the closet and heft out the bag. She stepped over the suitcase, around the box of summer wear, and mimed flipping the bug-out bag onto the floor. "She would have had to adjust her grip here." Lynx squatted down, feigning the bag was in front of her. Her gaze scanned the area, she put her cheek on the floor. "Here we go."

Lying flat on her stomach, she reached under the bed and pulled out stray items: a lighter, matches, a machete, a Leatherman, lithium batteries, a KABAR fixed blade knife, eight filled magazines, and the Ruger LCP .380 that Suz swore she would never touch. "Not even to stop a pudding-headed zombie from chomping on my leg," Suz had sworn. Jack thought that if that zombie was chomping on his leg or on Dick and Jane, she'd probably change her tune. But there had been no reason to press her. He'd just stowed the weapons in their various holsters attached to the front flap of the bag for ease of access.

Mace and a stun gun were the last two things Lynx pushed into the open. "What do all of these things have in common?" Lynx asked as she shimmied her way back out and came to her knees.

"Things she can't take on a flight. Things she could use to defend herself. . ."

"It looks like she took her go-bag to Brazil."

"What the hell?" Jack stared down at the assortment that Lynx had pulled into a pile. His mind ran through the items he had stowed in the bag. "Is there a SAT phone under there?"

Lynx pressed flat on her belly and pushed herself all the way under the king-sized bed. "Do you know a Samuel Jones?" she called out from underneath.

"No."

"That's the name listed as her traveling partner," Lynx said, squirming back out. "She kept the SAT phone? That's good, right?"

"She may not remember she has it. It's in the pocket behind the solar panels, plugged into a charger. It's not readily obvious that there's a pocket there. You'd have to know about it to find it."

"She won't have much battery life if the pack's been sitting in the back of her closet."

"Yeah, but since she's pulled it out, maybe it's gotten enough charge that I can pick her up on GPS." Jack was tapping at his smartphone while Lynx continued her slow process of looking for clues.

"It was brief. But there was a ping around 16:00 at Reagan International. It looks like her zombie apocalypse bag was heading out of town."

"We don't know that Suz was with the bag. Or the phone was with the bag, for that matter. Maybe Suz changed her mind on a whim and wanted to go to Southern Brazil."

"You think she left the country to fly to Brazil with a guy I've never heard of before, without telling me she's going, when she has plans to meet Emma in St. Marten's in two days for drinks and giggles?"

"Okay, devil's advocate. If Suz was taken against her will, and without any obvious signs of an intruder or violence, one would speculate it was a professional. Why wouldn't the professional clear the history off the computer? Or, for that matter, take the computer with him or them?"

"Because her name and passport would be registered with the airlines, so what did it matter? It would be traceable."

"It did matter. No one would have known she was gone until she didn't show up in St. Marten's, and Emma called to find out what happened – that would be Thursday. They'd have a two-day lead. And then there would be time to get the police motivated and the paperwork – warrants etc. into place. If they took her, they weren't concerned about time. And honestly, if there was a bad guy involved, they wouldn't have left these weapons loose and available to grab. You gave her some pretty high-end hardware to just kick under a bed. They don't need money, or they'd have taken the weapons. Her engagement ring, her jewelry, her cash, it's all here." Lynx raised her brows. "A hostage situation where they don't care about taking her money or covering their direction? What kind of person would do that?"

Jack shook his head. "Nothing that's running through my head makes any sense. But I've been mainlining pain killers. This is your deal. You're the puzzle master. What do you think happened?"

"Surface information says this was just what she wanted to do. It was her decision to go to Brazil. The only thing that stands out as truly odd is her dogs, to be honest."

Jack leaned his weight into the wall and pinched at his lip. His eyes scanned the room. His mind scanned the details. "She didn't take her phone."

"That's odd thing number two – unless she was fed up with people calling her about St. Basil's and being in the CIA."

"That one worries me. You told me in the car that they had targeted the Levinski kids in relationship with their grandfather. What if the bad guys believe she really was a plant? They'd think this house was part of her cover story. They might just try to find out how the CIA knew to put an officer in place. They'd try to break her. And since she has no information to feed them, she wouldn't be able to give them anything. But they'd perceive that as a highly-trained skill level – expert level with SERE training and a stint at torture school. They'd peel back her psyche, trying to find information that doesn't exist."

Lynx's face was serious. "Yeah, it's crossed my mind."

"The alternative is she went on vacation to see a waterfall. Which is, at this moment, what I wish more than anything. Even if it were with a guy named Samuel Jones. And even if that

Dearest Jack letter with the engagement ring meant that she'd finally had enough. I just want her safe and happy. Gone to see a waterfall. . .is that what *you* think's happening here?"

"I'm leaving the doors on my hypotheses open. Things are rarely what they seem on the surface. This could all be a setup, so it looks like Suz wanted a vacation. It does look like she was breaking up with you to be with this other guy. Would Suz do that? It's not the Suz I know. But people do weird things under stress. The dogs. That's my sticking point. So, to answer your question, what I think is that we should take the computer to Iniquus and get Nutsbe involved. If the bag was at Reagan, maybe we can find some CCTV footage. According to the ticket's itinerary, she had to have landed in and taken off out of Miami. If she were in trouble, there would have been plenty of opportunities for her to get help. I mean, they process you individually through security. All she needed to do was say, 'Help me.' Right? Surely there's a simple explanation."

Jack's face hardened. "You don't believe that for a second."

Lynx let out a long exhale. "No. I don't." She turned her gaze on Jack. The concern he read there was a sucker punch.

He had worked hundreds of operations where innocent people dangled on the other end of a bad guy's line. Happy endings were actually pretty damned rare. Pulling someone out of a hellhole didn't mean they were put together the same way anymore – mentally or physically.

"Iniquus computers have Suz's biologics. The computers will be able to pick her right out of the databases. Then we can see if she was there and the body language between her and this Samuel Jones person. We can do a background check on the guy. Standing here isn't getting us closer to an answer." Lynx held up a card. "Suz's ISO contact card was in the trash. I'm going to give him a call and have him take charge of the dogs and secure the house, ask him what he saw when he had contact."

Jack nodded, his face grim. He maneuvered to the bathroom and reached for a fever reducer. He stared into Suz's medicine chest. "That's damned odd."

"What's that?" Lynx moved to see what Jack saw. "Her medicine cabinet is empty?"

He stared at the empty shelves. "Looks like she cleared it out."

"What does she normally keep there?"

"The usual OTC meds, thermometer . . . tampons, Q-tips. Medicine cabinet stuff."

"We'll add that to the list of odd things to consider."

As they moved toward Lynx's car, Jack knew in his bones that Suz was with the bag, and she was headed to Brazil. He knew that she went against her will or her dogs would be in someone's care, not shivering and howling pressed up against the house for warmth on a sub-freezing night. Who had her? What was their plan? How was he going to get her back?

11

Lynx

00:03 Hours, Wednesday, February 16th

Panther Force War Room, Iniquus Headquarters, Washington D.C.

"Give it a minute to think." Nutsbe pushed his rolling chair back from the computer and meandered over to the coffee station.

"I appreciate you doing this for us," Lynx said. "I know it's not a direct line to the Levinski kids, but this is Ari's teacher who's acting one-eighty to her normal character."

"And you think this might give us a direction?" he asked, tipping the sugar until a broad stream poured into his cup, turning the black coffee into liquid candy.

That'll give his overtaxed system a jolt. Lynx reached for a container of coconut water. She'd been drinking so much coffee that she could feel her hair shift. "When it comes to those kids,

I'm out of breadcrumbs. They haven't been able to pry anything out of the Zoric clan. The whole family lawyered up. None of them has any interest in turning State's evidence. I think they're more afraid of internal forces than external ones at this point."

Lynx glanced around at Jack. When they arrived at Headquarters, his skin had been bright pink and slick with oily sweat. He had wobbled on his crutches even as he had rushed down the corridor with her scuttling behind him. There was no way in this world that Lynx could catch someone his size if he were to suddenly keel over. She had threatened that she wasn't going to do another damned thing to help him if he didn't lie down while she worked. Jack refused to go back to the barracks but did allow an Iniquus medic to bring over a rolling gurney and an IV. They had dimmed the lights, so Jack could get some rest. Lynx suspected the medic put something for pain and sleep into the antibiotic cocktail because Jack's mouth hung open, and his rhythmic snores filled the room.

Mr. Spencer, one of the owners, had already sent his PA down to get a copy of Jack's hospital release. Lynx wondered why they were here and working at midnight and how Spencer had become aware that Jack was in the building so quickly. Neither here nor there, it wasn't getting them any answers. She was just happy that that nurse at Suburban was willing to bend the rules to help Jack since nothing would have held him back. But now Lynx was worried about the repercussions for Jack's well-being. Jack had been running a fever since his surgery, and that could be very dangerous.

The computer dinged.

Nutsbe sat in front of the screen and rubbed his hands together, lacing them, and turning his palms inside out like a pianist, stretching his fingers, getting ready to play. "First up, Samuel Jones. He is traveling on an American passport. It was newly issued a month ago, no previous passports, no overseas travel. . . Samuel Jones is thirty-two. Self-employed, non-specified consultant. US Tax records for the last two years only. He has a Northern Virginia address. He rents. No car. A Suntrust bank account . . . seven thousand dollars in savings. Sixteen hundred in checking. Bank-issued Visa – no balance. Yup, this is looking like a false identity. No fingerprints on record. You may be on to something here, Lynx."

Lynx sent a glance back over to Jack. He hadn't moved.

"This is his passport photo."

"Can you put it up on the board?" When Samuel Jones's picture showed up on the screen, Lynx walked over to stare at it. She had gone through all the Zoric files and had committed their faces to memory, this one she didn't recognize. "Can you put the picture through the system and see if this guy's on anyone's watch list?"

Lynx continued to stare at Jones's face as Nutsbe *ratatat-tatted* the keys. When quiet filled the room, she turned back to him. "Do we have anyone in Brasília? A contact? Someone who could get eyes on? Actually, her end destination is Foz do Iguaçu."

Nutsbe's eyes widened. "No shit?"

"Why 'no shit'?" Lynx felt the cold flush of adrenaline hit her system. The way Nutsbe had said that, it certainly didn't bode well.

"It's one tough region. Bad things happen down there."

"Bad things happen everywhere," Lynx countered.

Nutsbe slowly swung his head back and forth. "Not like this, it doesn't."

The computer pinged, drawing their attention back to the screen.

"Here we go. . .There she is. . ."

LYNX ROUSED JACK. She hated to do it, but she had sworn on all that was holy that she would wake him when they had footage at the airport.

His eyes sprang open, and he wore a sheen of guilt under the sweat. "I fell asleep," he mumbled, the medication still working hard in his system. Jack rubbed the heels of his palms into his eyes. "I'm up. I've got this." His eyes were bloodshot and glassy. He definitely didn't have this.

Lynx shoved his crutches under his arms and went around back to act as a flying buttress to counterbalance him as he hopped a step.

Nutsbe looked up. "Hey, man, lay your ass back down. There's no need for you coming over here." He pushed a button lowering one of the screens.

Jack lay back down, and Lynx swiveled the gurney and popped up the backrest, so Jack could see clearly. A grainy CCTV image was frozen in place with Suz front and center.

12

Jack

00:57 Hours, Wed., Feb 16th

Panther Force War Room,
Iniquus Headquarters, Washington D.C.

"This is Reagan International's front entrance," Nutsbe explained.

Suz had changed her clothes out of the yoga pants and hoody that Joe, her ISO, had said she had been wearing with the black ballet slippers she had on during her great escape from St. Basil's. In this picture, Jack saw her taking her zombie bag from the taxi driver's hands and thanking him. She had put on a pair of the BDUs stored in the bag along with a t-shirt, an all-weather jacket, and her hiking boots. New. Never broken in. Clothing he could never imagine her actually wearing. While he had packed the bag in all seriousness, he had given it to her as a joke. Her taste ran toward the romantic and feminine. She preferred long, flowing dresses. That she had been dressed in all black on Valentine's day – with no makeup, pants, and turtleneck instead of the pretty pink dress she had modeled for him before he left. . . what did that say? Something. It looked like she was in mourning.

She pulled the zombie bag up and fumbled with the straps that buckled around her waist and sternum. The way she held her posture, Jack could tell she hadn't adjusted the lengths correctly, and the bag sat too high on her hips, making her lean forward to counterbalance the weight.

She was alone. In one hand, she had a piece of paper. In the other, she had a black object.

"Cell phone in her right hand?" Nutsbe asked.

"Looks that way," Lynx responded. "Must be someone else's. We have her phone."

"Could be a burner phone to give her instructions," Nutsbe said, his fingers flying over the keyboard. He tapped enter and the screenshot, while pixilated, showed the screen of a phone and text messages.

"Any way to read that screen?" Jack asked.

"Sorry, man, that's as tight as I can get."

Lynx moved over to the whiteboard. She noted:

- Not visibly constrained
- No visible handler
- Has phone access
- Dressed for the outdoors

THE VIEW SWITCHED BACK to Suz as she hiked to the ticket counter to check her bag in. She had nothing but the paper and the phone in her hand as she moved to the security desk.

"The check-in lady was pretty blasé. It didn't look like Suz passed her any kind of 'help-me' message when she was showing the woman her ticket," Lynx said.

Suz now entered the security section. There was a collective holding of breath. This was the spot to get help, with the phone on the conveyor belt, her boots and jacket in a bin, and no possible way that it wouldn't be detected if she were wearing a wire as she raised her arms for the x-rays. *Come on, Suz.* This was the time to explain that something weird was happening as she stood in a protected machine where she spoke one on one with an armed guard. *There's no better time than this. . . take this chance, Suz. . . tell them you need help.* Jack pushed his thoughts out there though he knew full well that this was hours and hours ago, and whatever had happened was a done deal.

Suz moved on through like everyone else moved through. She gathered her things, checked her paper, checked the phone, went to the bathroom, went to the shop, and bought a large bottle of water with money that was in the cargo pocket on her thigh. So many opportunities to get help. She took none of them, and Jack knew that this was all being noted by Nutsbe and Lynx.

After Suz paid for her water, she went to the gate that said Miami. Time passed with Suz sitting alone, staring straight ahead. Nutsbe sped up the video feed.

"They called seating," he said, shifting it to natural speed, again. "She must have a first-class ticket because she's in with the first ones loading."

"Suz can't afford first-class tickets. Did this go on her credit card?"

"Yup. On the Travelocity site. But you're right, the tickets she bought were first class where her flight to St. Martens was commuter class," Lynx responded, walking to the board.

- Sat alone at gate
- First-class seats
- Boarded alone
- No purse

"All righty then, ready to see what happened in Miami?" Nutsbe focused down on his keys.

"Wait," Lynx said. "Can we watch the other passengers board? She bought two tickets."

They watched the black and white images of the slow process of boarding. A few of the men had hats on their heads. From what they could see, no one who looked like Jones was in the line. But not everyone turned in the direction of the security camera.

Jack turned to Nutsbe, "Do you have any descriptors on the guy? Weight, height, hair color?"

"According to the passport, he's five-eleven, hundred and sixty pounds, brown hair, blue eyes, no distinguishing tattoos or scars. His name and facial biological markers are churning through the system. Hopefully, we'll get a ping and some identification beyond the Samuel Jones name soon. I sent a request up to IT to see if they couldn't get hold of the passenger lists and see if he checked in. I'm not a good enough hacker to do that here. I have the CCTV because we already have their security link on file."

Lynx leaned down and quietly caught Jack up on what he had missed while he was asleep.

"Do we have someone down in Brazil who can get eyes on? We still have a few hours until they land."

"Lynx already asked that. I sent out an inquiry. This isn't a contract case, so it's a low priority. Logistics hasn't gotten back to me yet, and I doubt they will, until after zero eight hundred hours. They're running a skeleton crew at night unless they had a heads up, and Command called them in for emergency action. It's our new protocol while we get our feet back under us from the Hydra attacks. Once their crew clock-in, though, you know how they are — they've got fingers in pots all over the world, US agencies and foreign. I'm betting they can pull something out of their hat."

"Along that line, let me see." Lynx pulled Suz's computer over and typed to pull up a screen with the itinerary for Brazil, "Suz has another stop – it's not a straight shot."

7:30 AM – 9:05 am

Brasilia Intl Airport (BSB) – Guarulhos Intl Airport (GRU)
Flight 3578
TAM · Airbus A320
Layover GRU Guarulhos Intl Airport1h 30m

9:40 AM – 11:10 am

Guarulhos Intl Airport (GRU) – Cataratas Airport (IGU)
Flight 3559
TAM · Airbus A320

"11:10 HOURS THEIR TIME. They're an hour ahead of Washington, so 10:10 hours our time, and that's the point where we lose track. That's our time frame for making contact," Jack said. "Lynx, did she schedule a hotel from the Travelocity site? Is there any clue about what she's doing once she hits the airport?"

"Here we go." Nutsbe clicked away at the keyboard, and a new CCTV stream showed up on the screen. "She's getting off her flight and walking to her new gate." The image jumped as he used the feed of one camera and then another as he followed her to the TAM gate. Her walk slowed to almost a crawl. She stopped completely and gazed around her. Her shoulders sagged, and she moved to the seats, choosing a chair next to a tall man in a dark-colored coat with wide apple cheeks showing under his Homburg-style hat.

"He looks very European businessman-like," Lynx said. "Did you see that? Go back a couple frames, try to get the image down to her face, please, Nutsbe."

The image spun down to take in Suz and the guy beside her. "This is as close as I can get it and still keep things recognizable," Nutsbe said.

"A little farther back. Take it to where she moved to that seat and sat down." Lynx stood up and walked to the screen, so she could point. "That's it. Now slow-mo. Okay, good. Suz walks in and sees the guy, recognizes him, walks over toward the only open seat, which happens to be next to him, but she's determined not to look at him. See? Her eyes are everywhere except on the man. She sits down and crosses her legs away from the guy, swivels her hips to turn her belly button toward the exit – the belly button is a body language indicator of where a person would like to go. In this case, she wants to go back to where she had walked from. She lifts her right shoulder. That's a protection gesture – a block. He's typing something into his phone. . . Her phone buzzes. . . she looks down. She hates what she reads. Did you see that her eyes squint and her head sways back? That's a momentary short circuit of the nervous system. It happens when someone gets bad news. No way to see that message?"

"None," Nutsbe responded. "That guy was on the first leg of

the Suz's flight. He was one of the first off. She was one of the last off."

"Same guy as in the passport photo?" Jack asked.

Lynx got up and walked toward the screens, her focus moving back and forth between the two images. "Bottom of the face seems to match, but it's hard to tell with the hat on." She came back to sit next to Jack.

"I'm being fed another piece of information," Nutsbe said. "The DOD has a satellite in the area. It hasn't got a long window. It'll be in range until 14:11 hours her time. Then we go black."

Jack's eye was twitching. "So, we can see where she goes."

"I'm making the request now." Nutsbe typed rapidly, then took a sip from his mug, wiping his mouth with the back of his hand. "I'll do my best. If she stays on the streets, we can follow her. Once she goes into a building, maybe a garage, and gets in a car? We'd lose her for sure."

13

Suz

11:00 A.M. WEDNESDAY, FEBRUARY 16TH

In the sky over southern Brazil

"YOU ARE A VERY HONEST WOMAN." Jones had said back at her house as she brushed her teeth after vomiting up her lunch. "Not your words as much as your body language. You hide very little with your body."

She held her curls back and looked at him out of the corner of her eye.

He ran his tongue predatorily across his teeth then his gaze slid down her body.

Was he sizing her up sexually? *I just vomited in front of you.* Suz quickly looked away, spitting toothpaste into the sink.

"Your words are not as honest. You prevaricate with your words. The term is correct, yes? Prevaricate? Your words might be true, but their conveyed meanings are not. I have been playing games with humanity for a very long time. You will find that I am not a man who is easily fooled."

Suz turned her attention out the window of her first-class seat and wondered how she was going to pay off the credit card. Jones had insisted she pay. *The least of her worries*, she reminded herself.

One good thing came from her vomiting, Jones knew she wasn't with the CIA, at least he said he did. That was good. Yes, hard to think that a real CIA officer wouldn't have snatched up the gun in her bedroom, shot both men in the head, and asked questions later. She wasn't someone who could do that. The thought of harming someone – her thoughts went to Jack. Yes, breaking up with him would cause him pain. But he'd live through it. Breaking up wasn't in the same realm as being shot.

Suz's ears popped as the plane began its descent somewhere in southern Brazil. They were here now—the last leg of their journey. Suz wondered if it were possible that somehow Iniquus had pulled a rabbit out of their hat and would already be standing outside the airport, waiting to shake her free of her nightmare.

Did she want them to?

She hadn't found Ari and his brother yet.

Jones said they were ill. They needed care. Their deaths would not only be a tragedy for young lives lost, but the purpose they served would be lost as well. The children were stopping some geopolitical horror show, according to the man who hadn't taken off his leather gloves since he walked through her front door. She was sure that how this man defined geopolitical disaster and how she did were two very different things. In fact, Suz had no idea what that could mean. No idea how she became a pawn on this chessboard.

After she had failed — or passed; she guessed it depended on one's point of view — the gun test, Jones had gotten on his phone and had conferenced with someone. "Ah-no, Ah-no," he had said over and over, but it seemed some kind of affirmation rather than a negative. She wished she knew where these men were from. The Levinski's were of the Jewish faith. Could that be Hebrew?

Jones had played a video of the boys. They were damp and crying, lying in the mud. The noises that rose behind their wails sounded like something off a survivor show when they dropped the guy into the Amazon. She reached into her limited South American geography knowledge-file and thought the Amazon ran across northern Brazil, and that wasn't where their plane tickets were taking them.

The plane hit a section of turbulence, throwing her off balance. She gripped at the armrests to keep from touching Jones, who sat beside her.

She couldn't guess why Ari and Caleb ended up as hostages. She did know those children were better off with her than without. She had said during Sandy Hook that that was the kind of person she thought she was, a teacher who would throw her body in front of a bullet to save her kids – and here was her chance to prove it.

Or. . . when they deplaned, she could run. This was it. Her last chance to stay safe. She could tell the passport officials. She could make a joke about bombs or smuggling drugs in her bra, and they'd take her to an interrogation room. . .

"After you move through customs, you will walk outside and get a cab. You will go to this address." He typed something into his phone, and she felt the buzz against her thigh, indicating the information had arrived in her text messages. Their phones were supposed to be on airplane mode, but Jones had not allowed that.

The phone the other man had given to her was monitored both by whom she contacted and by GPS. She wasn't to try anything funny, or the boys would suffer – it was not the captors' intention to harm the children; they, in fact, needed them to be well. But the children weren't being held by men with nurturing instincts or skills. And the place they were held had not been set up with the children's comfort in mind. Any word that she was a problem would mean that she would not be allowed to go and care for them. He made it sound like it was her idea to go to them instead of her being some weird kind of hostage herself.

Suz knew that in the US, Amber alerts were going out for Ari and Caleb. The emergency information had been broadcast over the airport sound system in Miami. Authorities were looking up and down the East Coast. Amber alerts - they didn't have such things for adults. Had she even been missed yet?

She knew that Iniquus contractually thought of her as one of their own. She didn't think that these leather-gloved men had made the connection. And her ties to Jack and Iniquus – not yet broken – led her to believe that they'd have Lynx's keen mind and Strike Force's amazing skillsets all rolled out to affect her rescue. She merely needed to go to the children and help them as best she could and wait. Jack would come for her. No. Jack couldn't come for her; Jack couldn't walk. Someone would, though, surely. Not Strike Force – they weren't in the country. And not Lynx – she wasn't a field operator. Someone though. . . surely.

And then she remembered how Jones had set up the house to make it look like she was leaving Jack and going with Jones on an impromptu vacation. Would Jack read it that way? That she left? Scooted out of town with another guy?

Jones had made a mistake. One mistake. When they left, her dogs were sleeping in the sun. When they woke up, they'd cause a riot with their barking. Eventually, someone would try to shut them up. Her ISO would probably stop by – they'd see even before Jack was released from the hospital that she had disappeared.

Unless. . . Suz had never left her dogs outside when she was away from home before. She had been surprised they hadn't barked – or gotten up. Maybe the treats the other-man was giving them were poisoned, and her dogs were dead, and the other-man would simply return and dump their bodies in the woods around her house. Then everyone would think that she had made babysitting arrangements for her dogs as she went off on her new adventure. That thought slammed into her so hard that her body hit back on the seat and the guy behind her, who had rested his drink on the tray, now wore his scotch-rocks. The flight attendant quickly mopped him up and then checked on her.

"Sorry, I panic when I land. It was my nerves." Suz's skin buzzed as adrenaline electrified her system. She pushed her fist into her sternum to counter the pain that radiated across her chest, and she wondered if a twenty-five-year-old in reasonable physical health could go into full cardiac arrest from fear alone. Why would Jack and his teammates think this kind of thing was fun? And they didn't even have the luxury, most of the time, of walking out the plane door and down some steps – they were leaping out the back at thirteen thousand feet or fast-roping from the open door on a hovering helicopter. Suz stared out the window again. Strike Force was probably doing just that, sliding down a rope on some continent she could only guess at, already busy on a mission.

Her plan had been to be the beacon that led the rescuers to the children. Maybe she was heading to the children to help them, and no one was coming after her. Maybe she was just handing herself over to the bad guys. Should she try to escape now? They'd move the kids. They'd be even harder to find. Was she even heading toward the children? She had leaped with only one eye looking. And now, with both eyes open, she could see the chasm was a heck of a lot deeper than she could have ever supposed. So deep that she couldn't even see the bottom.

The wheels squealed as the rubber bit into the macadam, and the brakes fought to stop the forward momentum. They rolled to a stop. Suz sat still, her fingers tightly laced in her lap. Up until now, she had been following a known sequence of events. Now she was going to be thrown into some situation that she was pretty sure she lacked the ability to navigate.

For all the touting of his ability to read humans, Jones seemed to be missing that Suz's system was winding up for a full-blown panic attack. He turned toward her and said in a conversational tone, "When you get through customs, you will take a taxi to the address I sent you. Check in to the hotel for two nights, and I will send you a text with your next instructions."

"Uhm, okay."

CHE LAGARTO STUDENT HOSTEL looked reasonable, Suz thought as she climbed out of her taxi and paid the man in the Brazilian real that Jones had handed her on the plane. She had been afraid that he was going to dump her in some slum somewhere. She was to be traveling as a university student. She was to use her real name but speak to no one unless absolutely required to. She would be watched.

Suz made her way inside. She wasn't sure what she would do about language barriers.

"Hello, I'm Gillian Molloy. I have a reservation."

"How do you do, Miss Molloy? Let me check. Yes, room for two." The elderly man looked toward the door. He spoke English clearly with a trill of the "r" and an elongation on certain syllables that made his sentences sound like song lyrics. "Your friend is here?"

Suz looked toward the door. Two in my room? "Not here yet. I'm not sure when to expect . . . my friend." Male? Female?

"No problem. Do you have a credit card?"

"No, only cash."

The man frowned.

Suz swayed from foot to foot. What if she wasn't allowed to stay here without a card? Where would she go? She had to follow her instructions exactly.

"This is okay. You look like a very nice young lady."

"Thank you." Suz's voice was full of relief. He caught her eye, and Suz thought she had probably revealed something that she wasn't supposed to have. Her phone buzzed, and she looked down:

Ask the man where to go to buy sight-seeing packages. Then ask him how long the

Zoo Bosque Guarani is open today.

He knows I'm talking to a man. He's watching me. Suz fought to not turn her head and search for Jones. She focused on the key that was extended to her and reached out for it, eyes forward. "Can you direct me to a place where I can sign up for tours?"

"Simple, you must go to Itaipu Visitors Reception Center. It is 12 km from downtown. Ask any taxi driver. He will know how to take you there."

"And the Zoo Bosque Guarani?" Suz chewed on the words as they left her mouth. She was sure that her pronunciation was unintelligible.

The man tipped his head. "You plan to be with your friend, no?"

"No. I mean, maybe. I kind of do my own thing."

"This is not the place for that. Not even for two. It is much better for you to travel with others around you in a group. The Zoo is but 200 meters up the street. I do not suggest you go there."

"Oh?"

"First, it is quite sad. Most of the animals are gone. Those who remain." He shrugged his shoulders. "They are not as well cared for as one would wish. It is not a beautiful example of conservation. The Zoo is poorly kept. Dirty. There is really no reason to go there. And certainly, no reason to go there alone." He had a grandfatherly feel, and Suz could see a gentle smile under his bristly gray mustache. "Now, I can put you safely in a taxi and send you to the tourism department. They can set you up with plenty of interesting things to do and see while you are here. I suggest the dam and, of course, our waterfalls. Also, it is a great pleasure to visit the biological sanctuary. They have a walk – it takes several hours, and you get to promenade right out with the animals. They sit there on the path. Very docile. Very lovely. The animals are being helped since before you were born when they built the dam."

"Thank you, and somewhere I might get a bite to eat?"

"In the morning, you will eat with us. Our breakfast is the reason that we have won awards for our little hostel. Fruits and breads, and juices, delicious."

Suz hated the feeling of eyes on her. It was like ants crawling under her clothes, making her itchy, making her want to squirm. She wanted to get to her room and shower. And then finish her tasks. Maybe they would take her to the children. She offered up an impatient smile.

"But out?" He shook his head and tsked his tongue. "You should not go alone. You are if you will forgive me, obviously not familiar with this part of the world. It is very dangerous alone."

She was already up to her neck in danger. It felt that way, like Jones's hands had wrapped around her throat and held there. He wasn't squeezing. Yet. "Thank you. Then perhaps somewhere the taxi could deliver me?" This guy seemed really kind. Suz hoped to make an impression on him. When—*if*—Iniquus came after her, she hoped he would remember her and confirm that she had been there. Ah, but there was the two-person reservation. This might just confirm that she ran away on a mini-vacation with some guy. Suz felt the sting of tears in her eyes but didn't wipe them away. She didn't want the gesture picked up by Jones or whoever was watching her, and she saw that the desk manager had remarked of them.

"Safest? Eat while you are at the visitors' center."

"Thank you again. And you can get me a taxi?"

Her phone buzzed: A half-an-hour. Go to the tourist center.

"I'll be ready in a half-hour."

"Yes, Miss."

Who was watching her and from where? Suz pursed her lips. The back straps of the zombie bag bit into her shoulders as she climbed to the third floor and shucked off the weight, locked the door, and went into the tiny bathroom. *What the hell have I gotten myself into?*

14

Jack

11:50 Hours, Wed., Feb. 16th

Iniquus Headquarters, Washington D.C.

"Jack, Suz's ISO is on the phone. He wants to know what the dogs' vet's name is."

"Is something wrong with Dick and Jane?"

"When he went to pick them up this morning, he found a pill pocket with medication in it on the kitchen floor. He's looked around and can't find a prescription bottle or a bottle of vitamins anywhere. Do you know the name of their vet so he can follow up?"

"The dogs will eat anything you hand to them. Suz doesn't use pill pockets."

Lynx stared at him for a second, then she got back on the phone. "Hey, that's an important piece of evidence. Can you bag it up and bring it in? It needs analysis in the forensics department. Ask them to identify what the name of that medication is, please."

She paused as she listened.

"That's great," Lynx said into the phone. "Thank you. Can you tell them this one is a high priority? We're working a hostage situation."

When she slid her phone back in her pants pocket, Jack caught her eye. "You believe that, don't you? That something is going on, and she's at risk? You don't believe that she's running around with some other guy behind my back?"

Lynx didn't answer right away. She scraped her teeth over her bottom lip. "That's not how I line up my thoughts," she said after what seemed to Jack like a monumental pause. "If I categorize things, then evidence lines up to support that evidence. That's how a human brain works. I counteract that by not coming to conclusions. Right now, I can say we have a lot of concerning information. It's my job to figure out what that information means."

Jack knew intellectually that that was not only the right way to view this, but it was the view that would get them where they needed to be the fastest. But he just wanted her to say it out loud – "Suz would never leave you, Jack. She loves you too much. The only thing that would make her go away with another man was brute force." But even as he had those thoughts, he knew that there was the distinct possibility that that wasn't true.

Suz was lonely here in D.C. He was rarely home. She had given up her whole lifestyle to give their relationship a chance. And it was love alone that made her come to that decision. She loved him, but she hated his job. He loved his job, and he also loved her. It had been a huge debacle in their relationship. They had talked long and hard about it – about male brains and how he compartmentalized and acted on what was in front of him. When he was on a mission, he still loved her, but his thoughts were on the mission and not on her. That was the honest truth. Hard to hear, he knew.

She had a woman's brain, not compartmentalized. She braided all the threads of her life into one piece of rope. She thought about him in everything she did. He didn't want that for her. He didn't want her to worry about him every minute that she couldn't see him, but that's how humans were wired in general, and Suz in particular. Lynx said she often felt that way about Striker, but her years of meditation practice helped her to better focus on other things. The last time he and Suz had had a fight about his job, Jack suggested she take up meditation. . . that hadn't gone over very well.

He wondered if his trip to the hospital made that rope that she had braided fray. If she'd finally had enough and decided to cut the last of their ties. Done. Was she done with him? Was he seeing what he wanted to see and not the truth? He'd have to depend on Lynx. She, at least, had her head clear of pain meds.

"Man, after this satellite goes dark, I'm headed to bed." Nutsbe cut into Jack's thoughts. "I'm locking my door. I'm going to sleep eight hours with my noise cancellation cans on my ears. And I'm going to hibernate. There would have to be an earthquake measuring at least six on the Richter scale to get my ass up." He yawned noisily. "Here we go. I've got a green box on a female exiting the airport. Zooming in. Target acquired." He tapped on the keyboard, and the image of Suz came up on the screen. She had her zombie bag strapped to her back. She had the phone in her hand.

"Look at that," Lynx said. "She's scanning the overhanging roof along the door." Can we get a split-screen of CCTV?"

"I haven't been able to hack into that system. But I see what you're seeing. She's trying to get her face on someone's camera."

They watched as she queued up in the taxi line. As she climbed into a cab, Nutsbe placed a green square over the car, and the computer program followed its satellite image through the city. Traffic was heavy with lunchtime gridlock. Jack was impatient. He didn't want the last image of her to be her car sitting in traffic. He wanted to see where she was going to go. The cab pulled up to a building in a better part of the city. Nutsbe tapped away as Suz got out and went through the front door.

"Che Lagarto Student Hostel," he said. "What do you want to do next?"

"Let's hang out and watch until we lose visual. Mark who goes in and comes out. See if she goes anywhere else. Do we have anything new about boots on the ground there?"

Nutsbe tipped his wrist to check his watch. "We should have heard back by now. I'll make a call."

Jack glared at the satellite image. Nothing happened. They stared at the street in front of the hostel.

A medic knocked at the door. He came in and checked Jack's vitals, made notes, and hung another IV bag.

Jack caught his arm. "Antibiotics only. You can give me a Tylenol or something for the pain. I've been fighting against your brew since you jammed that needle in my arm. I need to be functioning."

The medic unhooked the IV. "Yes, sir, I'll be back in a few minutes."

"Oh, and hey, can you get those antibiotics in pill form? I need to be ambulatory. I can't hang out here with a drip."

"I'll tell the doctor, and let him figure that out, sir."

When the door shut, Lynx came over for a quiet powwow. "Ambulatory, why?"

"I'm heading down to Brazil."

"What? No way in—" Lynx's sentence was cut short when Jack squeezed her arm.

Nutsbe had hung up the phone. "Israel has a Mossad unit near Ciudad del Este, Paraguay. They're sending an operator over the border. I gave them the address of the hostel. And I gave them your phone as their contact point, Jack. Lynx, you're the backup."

"Israeli Special Ops? There must be some terror cell activity going on down there," Lynx said.

Nutsbe typed and then read from his screen: "Ciudad del Este has long been known as a hotspot for terror activity. The TBA—tri-border area—of Brazil, Paraguay, and Argentina has been a base for Islamic terrorists. From the TBA, terrorists have plotted and carried out attacks in the Americas. The groups that work out of the TBA include Al Qaeda, Hezbollah, and Al-Jihad, among others."

"What attacks are we talking about here?" Jack asked.

Nutsbe ran his finger down the screen. "1992 bombing of the Israeli Embassy in Buenos Aires. The bombing of a Jewish community center a few months later."

"1992. This information seems like it might be past its sell-by date," Jack said. The idea that Suz might be caught up in a Middle Eastern terrorists' cell sent his mind to places he couldn't afford for it to go right now. He needed his focus front and center.

"Hmm, 1995 Osama Bin Ladin was in Ciudad del Este. I'm not seeing fresh intel in that direction. They do have a huge Muslim population living in gated communities down there. Lots of Arabic speakers–I can work on getting into some intelligence reports that aren't in the public domain. Just the presence of a Mossad unit tells me things are jumping down there, though."

"One of their operators is headed toward Suz?" Lynx asked.

"Affirmative," Nutsbe said as his attention was drawn to the screen. A taxi drove up to the hostel and was parking.

The satellite imagery showed the front door swing open and Suz walked out sans backpack. In her hand, she carried the phone, but that was it.

Nutsbe put a green square on the taxi, and they followed it about twenty minutes through town. "Did you know your fiancée was CIA?"

"She's not CIA."

"I thought I saw your hand in her escape and protection of those children. I was laughing my way all the way through the Hound News report. And I was thinkin' that was gonna be kinda shitty for her because there are gullible people who would believe those clowns. I watch that channel for entertainment value. Who knew Hound would get it right? I searched for her in the database. Is she black ops? What's her real name?"

"She's not CIA," Lynx said.

"If you two say so." He grinned as he went back to scanning his computer.

"Come on, Suz, get there already. We're going to lose you," Jack muttered under his breath.

The cab pulled up to a sidewalk. A large white building loomed in the distance, past walkways, and green expanses. It looked like a government building. Suz climbed out of the cab and smiled at the driver. With that same smile plastered across her face, she walked down the sidewalk. Once again, her gaze scanned slowly along the roof, then she reached for the door. The screen flickered and went black.

"So, you're still contending this woman's not a CIA officer?" Nutsbe asked, shaking his head as he stood.

"Not CIA," Jack and Lynx said in unison.

“Sure.” He snorted. “And I’m a fairy godmother. I’m gonna grab some shut-eye. Don’t call me, even if the whole world is imploding. I’ll leave the computer up.” He moved down the hall as the medic came in with a bottle of pills and handed them off to Jack.

Lynx waited for the guy to leave before she asked, “Okay. What do you want to do next?”

15

Suz

2:30 P.M., WEDNESDAY, FEBRUARY 16TH

Itaipu Visitors' Reception Center, Foz do Iguaçu, Brazil

HAD she been on vacation and not on a mission, Suz would have loved being here at the Itaipu Visitors' Reception Center. She repeated the thought to herself. Then she played it through again a third time. *I'm on a mission.* That word surprised her. She wondered how people could walk by her and not know that she was effervescent. Not in a happy ebullient way, but in a fizzy, disoriented, overwhelmed kind of way. Her thoughts pushed to the side by the bubbles of hysteria that churned through her psyche.

The text that had come during her taxi ride had said: **You are a tourist. Enjoy your day.**

As if. . .

When you get out of the taxi, smile. When you thank the driver, smile. Smile as you walk into the complex.

What is all that smiling about? she wondered. Opening the door and moving with the flow of visitors into the open space.

It's almost 3:00, I should eat, she told herself, and her stomach mutinied. She leaned, shaking, and sweat-covered against a pillar. She hoped that she was alone – that no one was watching her. She hoped she wasn't somehow messing anything up now that her plastic smile had fallen off her face. She didn't feel alone. Real or made up, she still felt like someone was watching her every move.

Her eye caught on the cafeteria sign; she shook her head. Suz decided to go to the orientation film, instead. A dark room was what she wanted.

SUZ WAS the last one to leave the little theater. She would have stayed and watched the documentary again had the clean-up man not shoo-ed her toward the door with his broom. Now, she found herself standing in line for tickets. She glanced over the offerings and tried to decide which would be the less painful to undertake.

Under normal circumstances, she would have wanted to do everything. Today, she didn't want to do anything except find those boys. If she and Jack were here to explore, this would be fascinating. But right now, her legs were rubbery, and her vision blurred. Nerves for sure, but some of it also had to be that she hadn't eaten anything that stayed with her since the MRE lunch on Monday. This was Wednesday. She had to eat. Maybe some juice. Something. She couldn't help anyone if she fainted.

She snagged a bottle of papaya smoothie before joining the bus tour of the dam. She could sit, and the bus was air-conditioned, which was good since the air was heavy with moisture and heat. She moved with the group outside under the multi-color striped awning. Thirty-five degrees Celsius the clock read. That was somewhere in the nineties, she thought. She side-stepped to the very back of the bus, where she unscrewed the top of her bottle and began to sip slowly at the unctuous juice. She'd be beside the bathroom if things didn't go well.

The tour would last only two hours. It was two hours when she knew, *hoped*, she'd be alone. They could track her on the phone GPS unless she slid it into someone else's bag surreptitiously, and she disappeared. Called for help. Made a collect call to Iniquus. "I'm here in southern Brazil. Come and find the children." But she didn't know if the children were here or not. They could be anywhere. She might just be the bait to pull attention in the wrong direction. Instead of helping, she could very well be the person who thwarted their rescue.

Suz closed her eyes and let that thought blanket over her. Wow. It all came back to chess.

Jack was a master at the game.

She despised it.

He thought it was fun to try to outguess and outmaneuver; she didn't like to play games. Any games. She liked the win-win mentality, where everyone got to be happy. When she asserted that point, along with a "why can't we all just get along?" Jack would smile at her. Suz interpreted that smile as "endeared by her naiveté." She hated that he looked at her like that. It made her feel childish, like an ostrich with her head buried in the sand. Jack would sometimes ask her how she could live in a sunny little bubble when she knew what he did for a living. It wasn't a challenge or put down. He seemed genuinely confused. It was probably the same confusion she felt at why he did what he did for a living.

Yes, she knew what he did for a living. She knew that he shot people dead without a second thought. Not a single qualm. She knew he jumped onto ships in the middle of the ocean to kill pirates, with his bare hands if need be, and free hostages. He bombed buildings where terrorists sat at their tables, drinking tea and planning on exploding school buses. He tracked genocidal maniacs into the jungle, where they enslaved women and got little boys hyped up on drugs and had them fight. Jack was the mechanism by which she was afforded the luxury of innocence.

His work, the work of men and women like him, allowed her to sleep safely. What was that quote he used? Yes, George Orwell. . . "People sleep peaceably in their beds at night only because rough men stand ready to do violence on their behalf." It was a luxury she hadn't understood until now. And that seemed silly because, so far, nothing bad had happened. She took a plane ride; she had sat down to take a bus ride. And she was barely up to the task. What was going to happen if she was called on to be Jack-like? She stared at her lap. She couldn't imagine

16

Jack

2:40 P.M., WED., FEB. 16TH

Panther Force War Room,
Iniquus Headquarters, Washington D.C.

JACK AND LYNX were alone in the Panther War Room.

Lynx looked him over, and she obviously didn't like what she saw. Jack ran a hand over his week-old scraggle of a beard, brushed his palm up over his hair. It had been a while since he'd gotten a cut. It was long enough now to comb his fingers through. He was sweating and probably stank. Inside and out, he was in rough shape.

Lynx moved to the computer. "I wish we had Deep here. There isn't a computer system in this world. He can't crack. I'd like to see what happened in that building. Any idea when our team's coming in?"

"I was going to ask you the same."

"Okay, here we go. I have an address. She's at *Itapul Tourismo*. According to their website, they have a tour of the dam, an astronomy hub, a biological sanctuary, a panoramic tour of the waterfalls, and a catamaran on the lake. Looks like she's on tour."

Jack shook his head. "I don't know what to do with that."

"That makes two of us," Lynx said, turning to the board to list the new addresses and findings. "I guess we wait until the Israelis have a chance to take a look-see."

Jack took over Lynx's spot behind the computer to find the next flight from D.C. to Brazil.

Lynx waited for him to finish. Without even looking her way, he said, "You're going to start in on me, and I wish to hell you wouldn't." He entered his card information into the computer, then printed his ticket. "I have to grab my go-bag. My flight leaves at 16:20 hours." He lifted his gaze to make sure Lynx was on board with the plan. "I need a ride. Whatever that damned medic juiced me with is still in my system."

Lynx looked like her cogs were whirring. From experience, Jack knew to let her work herself through the process.

He unlocked his knee brace and bent his leg as far as it would go. Sweat beaded on his forehead and the muscles in his face tensed, even with the pain meds swimming through his system.

"What the heck are you doing?" Lynx squatted in front of him and put her hands on his leg to hold it still.

"I can't go after Suz with my leg stuck at 180. Help me get it bent."

Lynx pulled her hands away from his shin. "No way."

Jack's gaze hardened. "With or without you, Lynx. I think you can make this easier. But if you're uncomfortable helping me, it's not a problem. I'm bending my leg and going after Suz."

"You can't walk, Jack. You should be in the hospital."

"It's Suz."

"Yup. It is. And you don't know what's going on with her. But you do know better than to go into an unknown situation without a team. I'd go, but I'd be next to no help. I'm not trained for that kind of thing."

"I've got this."

"Yeah, you do. You've got an infection. You've got a fever. You've got an open surgical site. You've got a brace. You've got a leg that won't bend. You've got—"

"Got it," Jack cut in.

"Take someone with you. Get Titus to lend you a couple guys."

Jack paused. "I'd have to go through Command," he said very quietly. "I have no clue what's happening other than it's not right. Let me check it out before I get Iniquus involved. If I'm getting dumped – I don't want to start an Iniquus mission to find that out. I need to protect Suz, even if that means protecting her privacy and dignity. Let me get eyes on, get some sense for what's happening."

Lynx wore her heart on her sleeve, something he liked about her and something he disliked about her. Right now, he didn't like what he saw. It looked damned close to pity.

"Let's wait for a sit-rep before you jump on a plane," she said quietly.

"You know that when things go down, it's always time-sensitive. Boots on the ground are what make the difference. I have to be there if she needs me. If she doesn't? I can always put my butt back on a plane and fly home."

"And if she's in trouble?"

"I'll let you know what I find out. If she's at risk, I'm not going after her on my own. I'll need help. I'm not stupid enough to put either Suz or myself at risk."

Lynx didn't look like she was buying it.

"I have some contacts down there," he said cryptically.

"Contacts like locals? How come we didn't reach out to them when Suz was deplaning?"

"Local contacts whom I can only approach in person. And we couldn't approach Suz while she was deplaning because we don't know what the hell is going on. This is not Suz. She's being run by someone. You know that, right? And it isn't a CIA handler."

"Of course, it's not. Suz couldn't possibly—*argh*. Shit." Lynx grabbed at her head.

Jack reached out his hand to steady her. Lynx lost focus, and her skin blanched then brightened to pink. His brows pulled together. "You okay, Lynx?"

"A *knowing*. It was a doozy, too." She panted.

"Jack be nimble?"

"Just 'Jack, be quick' this time."

"Exactly. It's time to jump." He reached out and grabbed his ankle in his powerful hands; grimacing with pain, he eased his leg back until it bent.

Lynx held her hands out — her fingers splayed as if to halt what he was doing. – "Jeezus, Jack, that's weeks of PT work. Stop! You're going to destroy your knee."

17

Suz

10:00 P.M. WEDNESDAY, FEBRUARY 16TH

Che Lagarto Student Hostel, Foz do Iguaçu, Brazil

SLEEP.

Suz stared at the phone text. *Sleep*? By command? Was that possible? She turned her light off and lay on her back under the white cotton sheet, dressed in a fresh pair of underwear and t-shirt she had found rolled up tightly in her zombie bag. She had rinsed today's clothes as best she could and hung them over the shower rod in the bathroom.

She didn't have a clue what she was doing. She wondered if Jack ever really did. Jack went to various SEAL schools and specialized training. They helped him do the technical stuff. But his job wasn't all technical; some of it was more finesse. He had to convince locals to give him information, help him, and to shut up when necessary. Did the military teach him how to maneuver through all that? Probably not. But Jack had an aptitude for people. Suz had an aptitude for people too, little people. She liked kids best. Grownups were much harder – they carried baggage and agendas. Maybe that's why she had had such a hard time fitting in since her move to the East Coast.

At home in California, she was with her friends that she'd had since her grade school days. Five steadfast friends like fingers on a hand. Suz had read a psychological study somewhere that said you can't have more than five good friends at a time. And she had felt re-affirmed about her tight circle when she had read that.

Her friends didn't want her to move. They had probably been right. Suz flipped over onto her stomach, balling up one pillow to put under her hip and another under her head. If she'd stayed in California, she wouldn't be here now in stinking Brazil. But her heart would still be broken since Jack wouldn't be there. He'd be swimming with the SEALs somewhere far from her.

What did she think she was doing in Brazil, playing at Jack's job? When she saw the video of the kids, her first instinct was to help. She had immediately agreed to go. But lying there in the dark with sounds of cars puttering down the street and the distant whine of sirens and gunfire, Suz knew that she had agreed because she had been terrified. Two men had burst into her house. Both men towered over her. Both men had obvious skills. Both men wore gloves, even when they had taken off their coats. Surely, if someone was careful enough not to leave fingerprints anywhere, they were careful enough not to leave witnesses either.

It had never been said. It was never even implied. But the gloves were a signal for sure that she either followed along or would suffer the consequences. By flying down here, by aiming to help the kids, Suz was prolonging her life, at least for a little while. She thought about what Jack had always told her about living on the sharp edge of survival, the colors were brighter, every nanosecond was significant. Suz didn't feel that way. All Suz felt was fear. Fear, to her, was a cold gray place.

Suz didn't think she'd ever be able to fall asleep. For all she knew, this was her last night on Earth.

WHEN HER PHONE ALARM RANG, and she discovered that it was morning, Suz was hugely surprised. She had slept eleven hours straight. It was nine o'clock on Thursday morning. She was also surprised at how hungry she was. The day before, all she'd been able to get down was the bottle of juice. Today, her stomach insisted on something substantial. She hurried to dress in yesterday's clothes, now dry and stiff. She hoped the manager hadn't packed up breakfast yet, and she could still grab something down in the common room. She scurried down the stairs, wondering what today would hold. The phone buzzed.

Finally up? The text read.

Suz glanced up the stairwell and didn't see anyone.

The old man from yesterday is at the desk. You are to engage him in conversation. Tell him about your day yesterday and that there was so much to see, you plan to go back. You are planning to stay to see the dam lights. Be specific about this point.

SUZ TREMBLED at the buffet table as she lifted the fruit onto her plate and tried to spoon the eggs. What was their plan? She could be a red herring. She could be there to draw attention away from where the children actually were and to have people spend resources and time on her rather than actually finding the children. They could be taking her to the dam to make her disappear. That seemed unlikely. Why would they go to this much trouble? They could have put her in a car back in Maryland, driven her to a boat, motored her out into the International waters of the Atlantic, and thrown her over the side. Done deal. This whole taking four separate flights to get to this particular place, it was too specific. She could probably scratch the top two off her list. Not a herring — red or otherwise.

Maybe she was actually here to care for the children. How improbable was that? Why would they take her and not someone else? Someone local and convenient? The thing her mind kept coming back to was that they needed someone the boys knew to keep them calm and safe, and eventually if what the bad guys wanted to have happen happened, she would escort them home safe and sound. The other and much more horrific thought was that she was there to witness the negative outcome of the kidnapping and be sent home to share what she saw. Like the teacher, Christa McAuliffe, heading out into outer space so she could translate the experience for others. She died in the explosion.

Suz thought back to the house and was pretty sure that when the foreign men had walked in, they had actually believed she was a CIA officer. A few minutes with her would dislodge that idea from anyone's thought processes. She was about as far from operator material as one can get. Then, they were trying to figure out Jack's role. They seemed to let that go pretty quickly once she had said he was disabled and in the hospital. Did they let it go too quickly?

And why were they laying this odd trail—what Lynx would call breadcrumbs—for people to follow. *If* they were indeed following her? Suz took a bite of a blueberry muffin. She was sure on a normal day that it would be delicious, but she had lost her ability to taste, and it was like chewing a sponge. She didn't know fear could do that. If Iniquus was following her, what would they see? Suz scrolled back through the texts on the phone to read her directives, looking for a clue. She didn't watch crime shows on TV. She didn't watch much TV at all, and her taste in books was more Regency than modern. Elizabeth Bennet would never have faced this kind of thought process. Suz didn't feel equipped to think this through with any kind of accuracy.

But her eye did catch on the smile text.

WHEN YOU GET out of the taxi, smile. When you thank the driver, smile. Smile as you walk into the complex.

WHO WAS she trying to fool with a smile at the taxi? Not the driver. He was only paying attention to getting her where she needed to go, taking her money, and moving on to his next paycheck. Not the people at the ticket counter; it said nothing about smiling at them.

Smile as you walk into the complex.

Someone who would be watching her on the walk from the taxi to the building. Who would do that? No one could get out in front of her from the States. They'd have to figure out where she was going – that was easy enough to do. Jones had made her leave her computer open on the page where she had purchased her tickets. Then she was staying at a hostel and going to a tourist attraction. It looked like a vacation. A vacation where she smiled. Who was she smiling for? She had scanned the roofline for security cameras all along her path, hoping that some camera would pick up her face, and someone could at least say she had been there on a specific day and at a specific time.

Smile as you walk into the complex.

That was really odd. Suz couldn't figure that one out.

She looked down and what had been a heaping plate of food was empty. Again, she was surprised. Her body seemed to be on autopilot, and that was a good thing.

YOU ATE WELL, now go and speak with the old man.

WHERE WAS THIS GUY? Suz got up and deposited her plate and utensils in the bus bin. She wiped her mouth and fingers on a napkin and put that in the trash. Now she was out of stalling tactics. She moved over to the desk manager.

"Hi," she said, wishing she knew what was going on and what piece of information she might be able to slip to this man that might be helpful if someone was coming after her. She had no idea. She stammered along, talking about the impending rain. Yesterday had been muggy; the weight of the clouds, oppressive. But today looked like the skies wanted to open into a deluge.

"It is an odd time to come to Brazil – the rainy season. The most heat. Prices are better. There are few visitors, so competition is aggressive. You are a student? You are traveling in February?"

"I took a semester off. I'm listed as an education major, and I'm just not sure that that's what I should do with my life."

"Travel is the best way to find yourself. I agree that you have made a good choice by traveling. Just not here in this city," he said pointedly. "Your friend has not yet come?

. . .

YOU ARE MEETING YOUR FRIEND; can you have their key please? You will be getting in late from the dam lights.

HOW COULD HE SEE HER? Hear her? She closed her eyes for a moment. "Oh, I'm headed back to the tourist center like yesterday. We'll meet up there. Can I have the other key? It might be late when we get back. We want to see the dam lit up at night."

The man tilted his head and considered her, then slid the other old-fashioned metal key toward her.

YOU'RE TAKING off early in the morning. What time will someone be at the desk?

SUZ REPEATED the question for the man who now leaned back against the cupboard and watched her through squinty eyes.

She rolled her lips in and blinked back the tears that burned her lashes.

"Six in the morning. If you leave sooner than that, just slide the key into the slot here." He pointed to a small hole cut into the top of the counter.

Suz knew he was wondering what her story was. She wanted to tell him something. Pass some kind of message. If only she could figure out how the person on the other end of the phone seemed to see what she saw and hear what she heard; maybe then she could find a way to circumnavigate their system and leave word that she wasn't on vacation; she needed help. She needed Jack. But Jack was in the hospital.

Emma would be flying to St. Martens. She would be there alone. Emma would try to call to figure out where she was, probably sometime tonight. When she didn't answer her phone, then Emma would call Jack's number. Jack's number was for emergencies only. Would Emma read this as an emergency?

Jack would send an ISO to the house to check on her. She wouldn't be there. Then maybe Lynx would be called in. Surely, Lynx would look around and find where Suz had hidden her phone under the picture of Jack after Jones had put it upside down in her bathroom. Would that be enough of a heads up that something was wrong? Her purse was there. Her car was there. It had been a lot more than twenty-four hours since she had been seen by anyone. Tonight was the first time Suz had reasonable hope that people would be worried about her.

Jones made it look like she had gone on vacation. Suz hadn't mentioned her Emma trip to Jones. She had explained her suitcase of summer things away – she was getting rid of some clothes that didn't fit anymore. But others would see she had planned two vacations at once. That was weird, wasn't it? Maybe that was enough to raise an eyebrow and some concern. Emma would be panicking.

There. She was doing it again. This was why she was always frantic about Jack's safety. She'd have no information about where he went or what he was doing. None at all. So, what would she do? She'd chew on all the possibilities. Chew all the meat from the bone, then chew on the gristle that couldn't be broken down anymore. Ruminating. Hashing through. Rehashing. He tried to convince her that she'd never know more by turning over the same stones. She knew that. Of course, she knew that. It didn't stop her mind from whirling. She so wished she had a crystal ball and a means of reading it. Not knowing even the most basic of facts upped her anxiety. Jack said she should meditate — learn to quiet her mind. That conversation had gone badly.

Somehow, Suz had come to the conclusion that thinking about Jack kept him spiritually, if not physically close. Her worry painted him with a protective coating of love, like shellacking her dining room table protected it from water rings. Her thoughts went to dark and scary places where he was concerned because that was his playground. It was a kind of sick act of love to fear for his safety while he was downrange, some kind of heart-shaped self-flagellation. A prayer. He hated that for her. He didn't like how it polluted their relationship.

It had become a habit—a way of life.

And Suz was done with it.

No stone left unturned. Since she had walked out of her house and sat in the back of Jones's car, that's all she'd been doing, looking for answers when there were none. What was happening was happening. What she knew was minuscule. She could guess. She could speculate. It didn't make a darned bit of difference to what was happening here and now. Her mind should be "mission specific" like Jack's. Eye on the prize. What was the prize here? Ha! That was going to start her speculating again. It was like that show on TV she watched as a child where you could pick door number one or door number two. The players didn't know which door to pick or even if they wanted what was behind either.

WALK OUT THE DOOR. Get in the cab. Smile. Wave goodbye.

SUZ DID as she was told, but there was no effort and no conviction in her actions. The guy hadn't moved from his scrutinizing stance. As she shut the cab door, she saw him reaching for the phone. A tiny spark of hope flared that he'd be calling the police to go check her out. *On what grounds?* She asked herself. If this was the dangerous place he kept telling her it was, would the police care that a tourist was acting weird? She let the hope-ember die. Tonight, she pinned her chances there. Tonight, people might start looking for her – no way anyone would get down here before the weekend. Who would Jack send? The team was downrange, and Lynx wasn't field qualified. Would Jack try to come on his own? The man couldn't even walk. . . See? Doing it again. She should be paying attention. Her thoughts should be mission-specific. She told herself again.

When Suz looked out the taxi window, she didn't recognize where they were. This wasn't the same route she had taken yesterday. She tried to talk with the driver, to ask him where he was taking her – he either didn't speak English or had been told to ignore her. Suz didn't know a single word of Portuguese.

They arrived at the river. The driver made scooting motions with his hand. She held out some money, and he shook his head. He brushed his hand through the air again. More emphatically this time. It read very clearly as *get the heck out of my cab*. She skootched across the seat to the curbside and climbed out.

A woman on a yellow blanket, sitting under a tree, motioned her over. "Suz, hello."

Suz moved slowly in the woman's direction. Her eyes scanned the area. She felt asthmatic – functionally unable to process air. Her eyelids stretched wide. As she moved closer to the woman smiling and beckoning her, Suz saw her zombie bag leaning up against the tree.

How did they…?

Somebody probably picked her room lock and brought the bag out the back door while she was at breakfast. The doors didn't seem flimsy, but she had seen Jack open doors for her when she had forgotten her keys in less time than it took her to use a real key. She had known all along; she was dealing with formidable people.

GIVE the woman the two room keys and take the pad and paper.

SUZ READ THE TEXT, then fished the keys from her pocket and handed them out to the woman. The woman, in return, handed her a small pad of paper with a kitten on each pink page and a Bic.

WRITE THE FOLLOWING: **Thank you! We had a fun stay. We've decided to head to Rio on our next adventure. I appreciate all the information you gave me. You were right, though. The city didn't feel safe. Suz Molloy**

SHE WAS HEADED TO RIO? She wrote what the text had asked. The woman took the phone and the page and compared the two. She put the note in an envelope with the two keys and licked it shut.

The woman handed her some money folded in half.

Suz opened it up and looked at it. It didn't look like the real she had been using.

The woman raised her arms over her head as if she were stretching.

A motorcycle stopped at the road and beeped its horn. Suz was standing at the edge of the yellow blanket, wondering what she was supposed to do.

The woman pointed toward her pack then toward the motorcycle. "Go now," she said. The words sounded like they had no meaning to the woman, just sounds that she was repeating. "Go now," she said again and nodded her head, then pointed to the motorcycle.

Suz pulled her pack on; she moved toward the man. He was dirty, his hair slick with grease. Suz lifted her leg and swung onto the seat behind him. The weight of the pack pushed her into his wiry body. She didn't know where to put her hands. She rested them on her knees. He gunned the engine and shot out into the traffic. Without thought, she reached around his chest and held on for dear life. They moved over the bridge. *Ponte da Amizade,* the sign said. Lots of traffic. Lots of people. There, at the end, was an official-looking building. Suz looked back over her shoulder. She recognized where she was from a map she had studied yesterday at the tourism building. Suz had just left Brazil and was heading over the river that bordered Paraguay.

So far, Suz had left a trail. For the first time, she was being directed in a way that would thwart anyone from following along. If anyone asked, the desk manager would indicate she'd be back at the tourism building today. And tomorrow, they would think she was having an adventure in Rio. If they showed pictures around, people might recognize her from yesterday – yes, they had seen her. Would they think to check in with the border guards in Paraguay? This was bad. Off-grid was bad. She'd heard enough stories to know that for sure.

Suz's brain was spinning now like the car tires that rubbed way too close to her calves. Would Iniquus care enough about her to come after her? They'd gone after Lynx when she disappeared – but Lynx was one of their own – and Suz was peripheral. Maybe the FBI or CIA? Would they go after the children?

Wait. They had no idea that she was being sent to care for the children and keep them alive. All they'd have was … nothing.

The motorcycle kept up with traffic and did not stop. She did not get a stamp on her passport. No official would know she was in their country. On this side of the bridge, it was Ciudad del Este. She had been warned by the hostel manager not to go there under any circumstances. And she had promised him she wouldn't – and yet, here she was.

As traffic slowed, Suz panicked. She planted her booted foot on the macadam and shifted her weight to swing her other leg free. From here, she could easily jog back across the bridge to Brazil. The motorcycle guy turned his head in her direction, slammed an elbow into her ribs, pushing her back into place, and zipped forward, lacing through the traffic jam at breakneck speed. Now all Suz could do was hold on for dear life.

18

Jack

13:07 Hours, Thursday, Feb. 17th
Foz do Iguaçu, Brazil

Jack checked his watch as he sat down on the bench outside of the old mission church. He had stowed his bag in a locker at the bus station five blocks east. His crutches rested propped up beside him. He popped open his bottle of antibiotics and knocked two back. He swigged from his water bottle then repeated the process with some Tylenol. His knee was on fire. Lynx was probably right. Bending his knee should have happened over time with professional help. He bent it to about 50% of what had been his normal angle and then straightened it back out a few times, trying to calm the biting edge of pain. The swelling felt like it had increased on the plane. The flight attendant had been helpful in bringing him ice packs. Jack tried to imagine that there was an improvement.

His phone buzzed with a text:

Lynx: Got info from forensics. Acepromazine — a doggie tranquilizer was in the pill pockets. They took blood samples from Dick and Jane. Trace tranq in both dogs. Know anything about that?

Jack: **Nada**

Lynx: Think I should try to contact this Emma person?

Jack: Tough call. Wish we knew what was going on. – Jack hesitated before he typed any more. It might give us more information if we hang tight and see if she calls me to ask about Suz. See if she's in a panic. I hate to do it to her, though.

Lynx: Those were my thoughts, but I wanted that to come from you.

A MAN in a polo and loose-fitting cotton pants came up and sat on the edge of the bench. He pulled out a pack of cigarettes and lit up. Jack slid his phone into the back pocket of his jeans.

The man spat toward the gutter, his saliva arching through the air and landing with precision.

"The rain clouds look like they want to beat the hell out of us," Jack said in Arabic.

The man snorted mucus up his nostrils and spit again. "The same every day. Rain. Let's walk."

They moved down the street, the man flipped to English. "That a fake injury or are you really nursing that knee?"

"I wish it were fake," Jack said.

"We put eyes on your POI," he said. POI was the speech they used to distance themselves from talking about human beings. POI—person of interest—PC—precious cargo. Those little psychological tools kept them from getting emotionally involved. Emotions in these types of circumstances were usually a bad thing. It made one stop and assess, to second guess when first impressions and action should rule.

Jack picked up eyes from a building up ahead. And more from a car at the corner.

"Those your people keeping watch?" Jack asked.

"Have to be careful."

"Agreed. Just checking in. Mind telling the guy with the scope to drop the barrel a couple inches? I need my brains to think through this problem."

The cigarette guy pulled at his ear, and the glint from the glass moved out of sight. "So, who were we looking at?" he asked, turning his head left then right, sweeping his gaze over the neighborhood of boarded-up apartments. "CIA? FBI? Why is she down here?"

"She's a schoolteacher. We don't know why she's down here. We thought you could help us out with that."

"The US is tracking its schoolteachers now?"

"We have a couple of kids missing. We need to ask her a few questions."

"She's the perp?"

Jack squinted at a guy in the car, trying to decide what his hands were doing. "No, she's a puzzle piece."

"Her actions say she's a tourist. She went to the dam yesterday. She slept at the address you gave us last night. She's spoken to no one who isn't busy doing their tourism jobs. She left this morning in a cab."

"Do you know where she went?"

"To a point. First, tell me about these children. About six years old? Boys? American speakers?"

"You've seen them? The boys?"

"We had our eyes on two boys, and they disappeared. We had

followed a mark to his normal pickup spot. We expected a high ranking official. Instead, we saw two sniveling kids."

"Do you have photos?"

"Too dark. Too dangerous."

"Could be the kids we've got missing. And if they are, they aren't high ranking officials, but they could make a high-ranking official jump."

The guy nodded. "The boys came in on the Brazilian side and walked the bridge with our mark, a Hezbollah trainer. We hoped they would lead us to their camp. We know that Hezbollah has something planned. Lots of chatter – nothing concrete. When they came off the bridge, there was a car waiting on the other side. They loaded up and disappeared into the traffic. It's hard to keep track at night."

Jack nodded. "Why are you guys in town?" Jack asked, slowing his gait before he crossed over the alley, giving himself time to assess.

"We believe they have a farmer who grows suicide bombers as his cash crop."

Jack pulled out his phone and opened his photos. "Is this the woman you saw?"

"Affirmative. That's her. She's not dressed that way, though. She's dressed like a soldier – camo pants, olive t-shirt, Bates Defender zip boots. If she's special forces ops, she's doing a crap job at incognito. She couldn't look more like a soldier if she was fast roped off a helo into the middle of the square. She's getting attention with her get up and her red curls. Pale skin sticks out in these parts."

Jack took that information in. He scrolled forward on his phone. "These the boys?"

This time the man took Jack's phone in his hand. He reached up and scratched his shoulder – a signal. A man in a car got out and walked over to them. They both looked at the photos and discussed them in Hebrew. The second man lifted his chin and went back to his car.

"Right size, right age, right coloring. When did they go missing?"

"Monday morning, taken from their school around zero nine hundred eastern standard."

"Right time frame. They came in early Tuesday morning well before dawn."

"So, they're training for suicide runs down here. Where's that?"

"We haven't found their camp."

Jack stared at him hard. The guy had information; he just wasn't willing to share. "You're afraid I'll mess up your operation?"

The man stopped and held Jack's arm to keep him from moving forward. "We have a mission to accomplish, and the outcome is much bigger than the lives of two children – as sad as that is to say."

"The children's well-being might very well have national security implications. Their grandfather is on the Senate Arms Committee, and there are several votes that are coming up with which he has major political sway. It could change the whole dynamic in some of the old Eastern Bloc countries and change the temperature in the Middle East. We believe the children are being leveraged to change United States security policy."

"News of the children's deaths reaching the US population would take away this power."

Jack took that information in and processed it. "We don't know what the desired outcome is and which policy is being influenced. In fact, we don't have any idea who took the children. According to the grandfather, they have heard nothing, and there have been no demands."

"The Americans know that the children were kidnapped?"

"They know the children are missing. There's a difference. We have something called an Amber Alert. It went out up and down the East Coast. A school was attacked, St. Basil's. Four adults were killed, one of the assailants committed suicide in front of an auditorium of kids. Two trucks with explosives were set to detonate on either side of the school. Their detonators failed. That information has not been released to the public."

"The school's attack hasn't played on the news down here."

"Any chance you're missing some people from the cell you're watching?"

"I can find out. Do the Americans believe the live shooter at the school was staged simply to get to those two boys? It seems extreme."

Jack's eyes scanned the horizon as they came up near the river. "Ever hear of St. Mogila's School during World War II?"

The man stopped walking. "That would be a very bad set of circumstances. That's what's being considered? Then the shooters failed to see it through properly. Certainly, if that is the case, the Americans are better off if the boys are dead. The boys are better off dead, too."

"Americans don't think that way."

"Israelis don't either. But sometimes it is best to be pragmatic."

Jack wiped his hand across his mouth and sniffed. The air smelled like hot dog crap. "Let's take that right off the table. We don't know if this is a chess game that's trying to force us to move a particular piece. Sacrifice a Bishop to trap the opponent's King. What if, for example, the politician recuses himself or steps down from the chairmanship? Perhaps, that's exactly the end goal. Perhaps, they have the next in line already over the fence about something. Maybe they have him reaching into their deep pockets. Since we don't know, the best strategy at this point is to rescue the children and return them to their parents. If anything happened to the kids, we don't know what detonator fuse was lit."

"If the Chairman stays in place with the children absent, the reporters would explain this to the Americans. His actions would be scrutinized."

"I think you have an old-school view of our journalists. Now, there are many who are more about entertainment than holding people's feet to the fire. The children who are missing are not taking up any vital time on the news shows. The pundits are fighting about gun laws and second amendment rights. They want to know why the principal wasn't armed, why the secretary couldn't reach under her desk and pull out an AK and take down the bad guys before the school was shot up. The nuances of geopolitics are too difficult to get off in a sound bite. The media doesn't even try."

"Your chess analogy is sound reasoning. The terrorist groups have, by necessity, become extremely savvy strategists. And this woman, the teacher, she is trying to infiltrate the terror group who took the children? If these are the right boys, I'm surprised she made it here so quickly. I'm also surprised that she isn't trying to blend in."

"The woman is my fiancée." Jack's voice was so quiet he wasn't sure his counterpart could hear him. "We believe she is being manipulated by the terrorists. She's wearing the clothes that were packed in a bugout bag I gave her one year as a birthday gift. I think she grabbed it on the way out, and that gear is all she has with her."

"Digital print backpack? Solar panels?"

"Exactly."

"Someone handed that to her just this side of the Friendship bridge."

"When was that?" Jack's whole body tightened down.

"10:40 hours. This morning."

Jack's jaw locked, thrusting his chin forward. "Do you still have eyes on her?"

"No, my friend, that we do not. She took a taxi thirty kilometers to the north, to Refugio Tatí Yupí. The taxis can only go 10 kilometers into the park, then the passenger must walk the rest of the way. We saw the taxi exit without a passenger."

"You left someone there to watch for when she comes out? Is she there now?"

"This is personal. I understand that. I'm very sorry to tell you that we doubt very much that she will ever come out again. Walking into Refugio Tatí Yupí is like walking into quicksand."

19

Suz

Somewhere Close to Noon, Thursday, February 17th

Yati Tupi, Paraguay

Suz had stepped out of the taxi, bewildered. The taxi driver had done some wrangling with the guard who stood at the entrance sign –a long piece of wood with white painted writing. Three brightly colored orange cones stopped cars from entering. She wasn't sure what that was about. It didn't seem like a very popular place. Suz didn't see any other cars around. Finally, the taxi driver gave the guard some cash; the gatekeeper, in return, pulled one of the cones aside and let them pass. The cabby drove for about ten minutes and then stopped at the side of the road. Suz stared up the wide dirt road and saw nothing. She looked back over her shoulder and saw nothing. She was alone on the road without witnesses to what would happen next.

The driver exited the cab and went around to pop the trunk.

No matter what happens, Suz thought. *I will fight him. I'm not letting him put me into a trunk.* When he slammed the lid and walked around with her backpack in his hands, hysteria floated out of her chest in a bubble of craziness, and she found herself laughing until her eyes streamed.

When she was under some semblance of control, she found the driver standing by the car saying something to her. When she finally opened the door and crawled out to stand next to him, he thrust her bag into her hands. He was miming to her. Suz got the impression that this was as far as he could drive, that she needed to walk around the corner. He took his index and middle finger and twiddled them back and forth to look like legs walking, and it was kind of sweet and kind of unnerving. Suz focused on getting her backpack on in order to keep the next bubble of hysteria packed into her chest. She nodded and gave the man some money. From the look of a windfall on his face, it was too much money, but Suz didn't know anything about Paraguayan money. It looked like brightly colored Monopoly bills to her.

She moved around the corner and immediately saw the one-story tourist building painted white with a green roof. She approached slowly, waiting for a text. None came. She stood outside the door, waiting. None came. Big fat droplets of water began to fall, and even under the overhang, Suz was getting wet. She decided to go in.

Here, a man approached her and caught her under the elbow. "Man" might have been a stretch. Suz didn't know what to make of the guy. His teeth were crooked when he smiled at her. A forced kind of smile that twitched at the corners with a wrinkled nose, like someone had handed him a bag of dog doo, and he was obliged to carry it. He was very thin, she thought, young. Very young. She wondered if he was still a teenager. At home, she would have guessed sixteen or seventeen years old. His eyes looked old, though. "No English," he said. She recognized the lilt of his accent as someone who spoke native Arabic, but that was as far as she could guess.

He motioned her to the educational information along the walls, and they both pretended to be interested. They finally made it over to a counter where the refuge's offerings could be arranged: bike tours, horse tours, walking tours. A crash of thunder boomed overhead. Suz couldn't imagine going out in this weather. The desk operator wagged a finger at the pictures, then pointed up, and as if on cue, the sky boomed again—a text buzzed against Suz's thigh.

She pulled out her phone: **Show this to the woman,** it said. What followed were Spanish-looking words. Suz was kicking herself for the years of French that she had studied that were serving her no good at all. Suz handed the phone over, the worker read and then pointed to a signup sheet for a walking tour. *Excursión* that sounded like excursion. . . it might mean tour. The woman typed a message into her phone and handed it back to Suz.

You will wait for the rain to stop and then go with the guide.

What if it didn't stop? Then what?

As if reading her mind, the next text said: **Instructions will follow.**

. . .

Suz swung her head around, wondering how this texting-person always knew exactly what was happening. He wasn't spying on her through the camera. After she realized that she had been carrying the phone in her left hand all the time, she had been careful to put it in her thigh pocket. That hadn't seemed to have made a difference. Suz moved over to a low couch, pulled off her bag, and sat down.

The boy scowled as if she should not have moved without his permission.

Suz ignored him.

Instead, she dug through the outer pockets of the bag.

Jack had packed them by hierarchy, he had explained. Each thing in the bag was important, but the things she would need first were in the outside pockets.

What she needed was a first aid kit with moleskin. Her new boots had rubbed inch-wide blisters in rings around her ankles. Each step was agony. She pulled off her boots and doctored her skin. She carefully wrapped her pants' leg over her ankles, folding the extra fabric to cushion her, then put the boots back on.

That was the way Jack wore his pants in the pictures of him in the jungle.

After a short time, the rain stopped, and a man dressed in long pants and a long-sleeved shirt, despite the oppressive heat, called her name, holding up two fingers to indicate she and her newfound friend/guard should come. Two other adults and three children were called, as well, and they all headed out the door behind their guide. They climbed on a tourist bus that drove them about thirty minutes back into the forest, down a road to a path.

The path they followed was wide and comprised of rich earth, muddy from the shower. There were some small puddles and a few rivulets, but it was easy hiking. While the path was wide enough that they weren't brushing against the foliage, the broad leaves on the trees dripped down on them.

Suz reached around and found the rain poncho that had been stashed in the right-hand pocket. It was a large military issue poncho that was designed to keep men like Jack dry. For Suz, it was much too long. She ended up holding it up like a ball gown as she moved behind the guide, listening to what he was saying about the history of the area and their conservation in English(ish), and then a repeat in Spanish.

"We have classified thirty-nine species of mammals such as jaguars, wild boar, capybara – which are the world's largest rodents, anteater, wolves, and tapir. Paraguay also has a large population of crocodiles in our waterways. As you enjoy your time in Paraguay, please be aware that there are dangers in our waters. The carnivorous piranha, for example, is common." He lifted his eyebrows for emphasis. "Here at Tatí Yupí, we have classified two hundred and forty-seven different kinds of birds and twenty-one reptiles. Perhaps today we will be very lucky and see a boa constrictor. They like to drape their bodies in the tree limbs.

Suz's eyes widened, and she looked up. What's that? Boa constrictors hanging in trees like Christmas tinsel?

"Boa constrictors are non-venomous snakes that kill their prey by squeezing and constricting until their dinner is dead." The guide was walking backward and using his hands to demonstrate. "Boa constrictors are around three meters in length – so around nine feet." He looked pointedly at Suz, the only American, as he said that.

She offered him a wan smile.

"And weigh about forty-five kilograms or one hundred

pounds." He turned back around, and they moved farther along the path.

The nature walk was supposed to last three hours and loop around. Around the one-hour mark, the group was taking a break sitting on logs that had been placed on either side of the path. Suz pulled out her bug spray and was dousing herself as the mosquitos came out with the approach of evening and found their little group by their exhalent. Without thinking about it, Suz held out the spray to the man/boy who was with her. The scathing look he gave her made her shrug and pack the spray back in the side pocket. Sure, manly men didn't need bug spray. She hoped he had his shots. Then she briefly wondered what kinds of diseases the mosquitos might carry – dengue fever and zika. . . His problem. Not hers.

A text buzzed, and she pulled her phone from under her poncho.

YOUR FRIEND DOES NOT FEEL WELL, you will turn around and walk back to the parking area to get him home. Thank your guide for the tour. Tip him with one pink bill. Head back to where you came from.

HER "FRIEND" looked just fine. Here she was again, having to make the decision. Did she follow through? Did she ignore the directive? Once again, she realized she was seat-of-the-pantsing this thing, and she'd have to rely on her gut. Her gut said she needed to get to those kids. She felt like they were near.

Suz walked over and spoke with the guide. The guide said that the bus could take them back and would return in time to pick up the other family. The guide grinned, accepting the money, and hoping all would be well. And off she moved with the guy.

They walked for about ten minutes when the guy slowed his pace. His eyes were on the ground, searching. She saw it before he did. At the side of the road, three rocks were stacked.

She stopped beside them, reaching under her poncho to lift the backpack straps off her shoulders. They had rubbed her raw through the t-shirt material.

Thirty pounds, Jack had said. Minus the weapons.

Weapons were metal; they were probably pretty heavy. But last night, she had gone through the bag a little and remembered there was a water bladder incorporated in the design.

She had filled it with water. Thank goodness she had filled it with water. But water was heavy. Probably heavier than the weapons that had been left behind. She pulled the hose from the clip on the strap and ran it to her mouth, and drank down a gulp. It tasted like plastic. She clipped it back in place quickly, so she didn't feel compelled to share with the guy. Suz felt very protective of her water.

The guy's eyes swept back across the path, and this time he saw the stack. He motioned to her as he moved into the tropical forest, kicking the stack as he went. The guy had a compass out and was following in some direction right through the foliage. After a few paces, he picked up a couple of short sticks. After searching around, he found two more. He handed these off to her. They began walking again. Suz realized the sticks were to use in holding back the dense foliage. Just a few paces in, and already Suz was exhausted.

An hour later, she was ready to drop to the ground and sleep with the capybaras. This was by far the most physically grueling thing she had ever done in her life. The rain had started again. The earth began sucking at her boots. As she lagged behind, the guy would turn and hiss at her—literally, hiss.

There were no animals. No birds. No lizards (thank god). She could hear them, though, in their mad cacophony of trills and squawks. The eyes she had felt on her by whoever was instructing her over the cell phone had nothing on this. This was beyond spooky. As she moved farther and farther into the dense forest, her mind was back on the pictures in the educational building of all the terrifying animals that breathed with her amongst the trees.

The silent one with his disdain for women – or maybe just for her – walked ahead, moving vegetation out of the way for his passage, sometimes letting it snap back at her. She thought she sensed some glee from him when she would yelp in pain. She felt like her pain was his pleasure. If she had done something to rile this boy up and make him want to hurt her, she couldn't imagine what it was. But she decided to try to keep herself quiet. Sometimes a bully just thrived on getting the desired outcome. When that response wasn't forthcoming, the bullying stopped. That's the way it worked at her school – it's not how things were working here in the Paraguayan forest.

When they left the main tourist trail, Suz wondered why this guy didn't use a machete to hack his way through, then realized they were trying not to leave any trails. At first, she was careful to leave guideposts herself, reaching out and bending branches the way she had read that Indians sometimes did when they were taken from their villages – so their scouts could follow and find them. Suz thought if her marks were frequent enough and visible enough that she could get herself out of here. She was losing hope that they were headed for the boys. She wasn't sure what lay at the other end of their hike, but she thought if they meant to just kill her, that could have happened an hour ago, and there would be no way that anyone would find her body. If they were even looking.

Would they be looking? Suz started the loop that would take her through her speculations of what could be. The same kind of speculations that filled her with anxiety that then turned to a low burning rage when it came to Jack. And then it hit her like a smack across the face, the irony. Oh, the irony. "Irony is the hygiene of the mind," which was a Bilbescoe quote Suz had used to answer an essay question to get into Stanford undergrad. Why the heck they were asking high school seniors about irony was beyond her. Back then, the biggest irony in her life was that when she was dead tired, she was too tired to sleep.

But now. . .now irony was slapping upside the head.

Suz had been angry. Yes, furious. She had to own it. Suz had been angry because Jack kept choosing "other" than her. He chose his missions. He chose the kidnapped victims. He chose the law. He chose his brothers in arms. He kept choosing "other" than her. She was *angry* because she wanted him to be hers. Living in their little house in the woods, living the life that had always been painted for her since her childhood – a husband who comes home from work and scooped the children up in hugs, pecked his wife on the cheek, and they all lived happily ever after. She wanted her happily ever after – though, wow, to put it in those terms seemed very 1950s Disneyesque. Her little "Leave It to Beaver" world.

But Jack insisted on being in danger, and danger meant he could die. She'd never get to see him again, never get to tell him she loved him in person again, never get to make love with him again. That sudden and horrific loss, well, she had been through something a little like that with her dad. She didn't think she could survive it with Jack. So, she fought to keep him safe. To keep him nearby.

And now she had decided enough was enough, and she needed to let him go. Go and be himself. If she didn't have the details, eventually, she'd stop worrying. He needed to live his life away from her. She needed to open that space he had been living in to welcome some other man in and be hers. Suz felt as she laid it out in those words to be monumentally selfish.

And then, here was the irony piece.

She knew back at her house that she was in desperate trouble. She very well could be killed by Jones and the other one. Hence, she decided to go along with their "request" that she go and care for the children. It was an odd request, very odd, and she wasn't going to try to work her way out of that maze again. She had gone along. And she continued to go along. She had had a gazillion opportunities and ways that she could have escaped and gotten aid. She had taken none of them because there was a shot that she could find the children and help them. But in that script, there was always a "Jack" coming to their rescue. Her Jack was incapacitated, but there were others who were rough and ready, willing to go into dark, damp places like this, willing to put their lives on the line for strangers.

She needed one of those people now.

Yes, they were humans and not characters. They got hot and hurt, and . . . died. How horrible would that be if someone died trying to help her? These rescuers were humans with relationships – mothers and fathers, sisters and brothers, maybe even wives and children if not lovers and would-be fiancées. The person she wished would come for her would do so while someone else was feverishly praying that they did not come for her. Like she had wished Jack would just stay home and take a policy job with the government or something.

That wasn't actually irony at all. What it was was hypocrisy.

She was a hypocrite.

Jack came after people like her. Saved their lives. Pat them on their backs, and off they went to follow their destinies, big or small. Then he came home and painted her bathroom. Built a dog pen for Dick and Jane. Grilled steaks on the grill and told all his friends what a lucky man he was to have such an amazing woman in his life.

Suz felt the conviction that she felt long ago when she first said no to Jack's marriage proposal. There were women built on stronger frames than she was. Women who were physically strong, mentally strong, and emotionally strong. Suz shared their intellectual strength, but that was such a small slice of the pie. Jack deserved someone better than she.

20

18:30 HOURS, THURSDAY, FEB. 17TH

Foz do Iguaçu, Brazil

JACK HAD MADE his way to the Friendship Bridge, watching the dark waters churn along the shoreline. His phone buzzed. He moved to a private place to talk as he pulled his cell from his pants pocket. He glanced at the readout. Lynx.

"Hey there. I'm late getting this intel to you. I was on the interrogation team to chat with Pavle. We didn't get anywhere. He just stared at us for a few hours. But I wanted to let you know what's new here. First off, our systems haven't found any intel on Jones. When I get the green light from you, I'll take this to Iniquus command, and we can expand the search to all databanks."

"Hold off for now," Jack replied.

"We picked up the SAT phone from Suz's pack."

Jack raised a victory fist. "Is it still pinging her location?"

"Negative. We had a trail crossing over the Friendship

Bridge between Foz do Iguaçu, Brazil, and Ciudad del Este, Paraguay."

"Copy that."

"The trail travels 3 km north of Hernandaria on the Supercarretera to Saltos del Guairá. From there, it went to a place called Refugio Tatí Yupí. I did some research on it. It's another tourist spot."

"And you lost her there?"

"The phone. I lost track of the phone. Remember, we don't know if she is attached to the phone."

"Our Israeli friends had eyes-on when she entered the Tatí Yupí gate."

"They didn't follow her in?"

"Entrance requires paperwork and IDs. They had someone waiting outside the only exit until the refuge closed for the day, which was an hour ago. She didn't come back out." Jack's hand wrapped around the back of his neck. "I hate to ask you. I really hate to ask this." Jack had trouble forming his mouth into his next words. "Are you picking up anything psychically? Is she. . . is she alive?"

"Jack, I know you're freaking out. I know that her not exiting those gates seems like a really bad thing, but there are other options besides her being hurt – or worse."

"Options like what?"

"Okay, you said she has a reservation for tonight at the hostel. This refuge is on the dam. They have buses that go up to the dam for tours. The Brazilian tourist department has buses that are up there too. It could very well be that she took the tour of the dam to see the night lights and planned to go back over to Brazil via the dam."

"She had her zombie bag."

"She had to have had it, or we wouldn't have picked up the

SAT phone. It could be that she left her gear back at the hostel, and she's carrying the bag with her journal or art supplies, or to carry the souvenirs she wants to bring back. Another scenario is that she's staying at the dorm there at the refuge. Or camping. Both are possibilities there."

"Now, you're reaching."

"I just want you to remember, conjecture isn't fact. Okay?"

Jack sat on a rock, wishing for an ice pack to cool his bulbous knee. He reached for the water bottle in his day pack, tipped back two more pain meds, and didn't reply.

"Okay, well, the good news is we located her even if briefly. The bad news is that it's going to be next to impossible to pick up on anything if she's still in the refuge."

"Because?"

"The forests there have trees that exceed a hundred feet in height. It has canopy cover and only small walking trails, over a very limited section, that allows the tourists to hike beside the waterfalls. Off-trail, you're looking at almost six thousand acres of protected lands. So, a little bigger than Connecticut."

"Government protection?"

"Apparently."

"So, not private ownership."

"No. It's the government – and I don't have to tell you that the graft system is a way of life down there."

"Any luck finding your breadcrumbs with the boys?" Jack asked

"Nada."

"My contacts said they saw two young American boys being walked across the bridge."

"Why walked?"

"It seems the guards are only stopping cars here. You can

walk, bike, motorcycle. . . so if they wanted to get the boys across without official knowledge, it couldn't be in a vehicle."

"Did your contacts take photos?"

"Too dark, they said. Before you ask anything else, that's all they had. It was just interesting timing, the boys on the bridge." Jack took in a deep breath. "What's going on in the states with the political landscape? You have any interface with St. Clair?"

"He's got a Secret Service detail that's on him like flies on the proverbial honey. He refuses to recuse himself from his chairmanship. Certain people are antsy about it. They think that the boys' disappearance might have something to do with grandpa's job title. There's talk that this might be a tiger kidnapping scenario where the boys' safe return is promised after the successful completion of X, Y, and Z. Finley and the FBI and Black and the CIA are holding that information very tightly to their chests. They aren't showing their cards to anyone."

"Because?"

"They don't want to start a precedent in this country to allow our politicians to be manipulated in such a way. It would be impossible to secure every lawmakers' family members. But a few people are making waves, wondering if the kids' disappearance might have a direct effect on how St. Clair's votes are being influenced. Right now, the official line is that there are conspiracy theorists everywhere."

"In this case, they'd be right. Did Hound News bring it up?"

"No, they're still going on about how everyone would be safe and sound if the bodyguard had had his gun on him and not in the glove compartment. Of course, everyone's skipping over the fact that he was shot in the back. They found the guy's car burned out in New Jersey. Guess what was in the glove compartment?"

"His gun. So, the big story hasn't hit the airwaves yet?"

"No, but our computers are tasked with pinpointing it if it does. The Secret Service is stepping out of their normal role and 'protecting' St. Clair but not saying why. I believe the president wants to know who is contacting the senator. Now here's something interesting I've seen on some of the security tapes Finley's brought in. St. Clair is shadowed all the time by his right-hand aid. Thursday, that aid changed."

"Who is it now?"

"No. You misunderstand me. I mean, he *changed.* This guy is suddenly looking like a shock victim. Like someone who is caught in an alleyway with gang bullets flying, and he doesn't know where to run. He's functioning on high octane anxiety. I pointed it out to Finley for a follow-up, and guess what's missing from his house?"

"From the aid's house? I can't imagine."

"His wife. She hasn't shown up to work, and the aid called to make an excuse for her. Family emergency. We have nothing in the way of concrete information."

"But the FBI is looking into it?"

"They are."

"And you have a theory?"

"It would be an interesting play. We know that, indeed, it was a tiger kidnapping ploy. With the school bombing fail, too many eyes were on St. Clair. They couldn't reach him to communicate. What if they just layered on another tiger kidnapping? They pick up the aid's wife. The wife ostensibly goes somewhere to help some family member, while in reality, the bad guy makes the aid into a go-between informing St. Clair how to act to keep the boys safe."

"Seems like a simple solution to their problem."

"Simple is often the best solution. I need you to be checking in regularly. Are you settling in for the night?"

"Right now, I'm headed over to see a bud of mine. He's ex-SRR, British special forces, and runs a cover for freelancers coming through. He'll be able to get some hardware for me. Hopefully, he can put me up while I'm down here. I don't want curious eyes on me, especially if I'm keeping odd hours or coming in, not looking like someone who belongs in polite company."

"Copy that. How's the knee?"

"We're not going to talk about that."

"Okay. I had a *knowing*. Should we talk about that instead?"

Jack stared over the choppy waters and drew in a breath. "More jumping?"

"Looks like you cleared that hurdle. This time I got a rhyme. I can't remember hearing it before. I had to look it up."

"Shoot."

"The rhyme goes: Jacky, come and give me thy fiddle if ever thou mean to thrive. Nay, I'll not give my fiddle to any man alive."

"And what part did you hear?"

"That last bit 'I'll not give my fiddle to any man alive.'"

"Damned straight. Not gonna happen."

21

Suz

7:10 P.M. THURSDAY, FEBRUARY 17TH
Refugio Tatí Yupí, Paraguay

THE LOWER THE SUN SET, the denser the swarms of mosquitos grew.

Suz reached once again into the side pocket where Jack had put the readily at hand items – a button compass, bug spray, a box of Tic Tacs so her breath wouldn't smell like the un-dead who were chasing her (that earned Jack a swat), a whistle. . . Suz fingered the whistle. This far from any other tourists, Suz didn't think that anyone would hear her if she used it. Groups of three. That, according to Jack, was the international signal for help. Three of anything: light flashes, signal fires, blows on a whistle, rock taps on a water pipe.

She hadn't known that.

Who learned those kinds of things?

It could well be that other nationalities spent some of their school time teaching their students how to signal for help in the event of a disaster. Did the Paraguayans? She doubted it. They'd hear the whistles and ask their guide what strange bird made that noise.

She wasn't trying to be rescued, she reminded herself. She was supposed to be the rescuer. Yes, that last thought was laughable.

They had, at some point, arrived at a trail. It was as wide as a single foot tread and divided the forest like a part in a hairline. It moved in and around trees so tall that Suz couldn't see where they ended in the sky and so wide that it would take two or three people reaching hand to hand to encircle them. It was loud. Hauntingly loud. The foliage all around her was filled to brimming with noises and vibrations, yet she did not see a single animal.

Suz was dead on her feet. Her back burned with the exertion of carrying her pack. When they reached the path, the guy pointed to the sky with a frown and mimed hurrying. She got that they didn't want to be in the forest in the dark without reaching their destination. As Jack would say, "copy that." He set the pace at a jog. Suz was obviously not in the same shape as this guy, and she was carrying her pack. But fear that he'd just run on without her and she'd be left in the middle of the forest that night… well, arriving almost anywhere seemed like a better end.

She was hungry. It had rained off and on that day. She just kept the poncho on the whole time, draped over her sack. It was like a sauna underneath it, and she was damp with sweat. The cotton from her clothing rubbed her raw at inconvenient places, like the lines of elastic under her breasts and along the legs of her panties. Bet Jack never thought of *that*.

The humidity levels had been high since she landed in South

America. And in the back of Suz's mind, there rested stories about jungle rot and other horrors of being too wet for too long.

The man-boy had pulled a small flashlight from his pocket. He could see as they moved through the darkening forest. She could not. After her third fall, he finally put her hand on his shoulder, so she could step where he stepped, though it looked like it cost him – according to his grimace, he was loathed to be touched by someone like her.

Suz was on the verge of collapse. Emotionally, physically, spiritually, she had little left. She focused on lifting and placing one foot and then the other. Her head too heavy to support. She let her chin drop to her chest. She moved forward, looking at the guy's heels, so it was a surprise to her when he stopped.

There, in the middle of the forest, was a man-made clearing. Around the perimeter ran a tall chain-link fence. It was maybe twenty feet high, Suz would guess, topped with the looping kind of razor wire used on prisons. Her mouth went dry. *What the . . .*

The guy turned and smirked. He reached under his shirt, producing a gun. With the barrel trained on her, he reached into the pocket on her thigh and pulled out the phone—a fat lot of good that would do him. Suz scoffed. She had checked it under her poncho periodically, and there had been no bars since they had left the tourist center. So, no loss to her.

The man-boy lifted and dropped his brows and nudged her toward the gate where a guard was posted with an AK rifle. Suz recognized it as what Strike Force carried. There were tents on either side of the gate entrance and an open expanse where she could see a glimmer of the sky. In the twilight, there was no other movement. The three of them stood there, looking at one another.

The air was heavy, oppressively humid; it weighed down on Suz's shoulders along with the pack and made her sway. She locked her legs to hold herself upright, then remembered that was a quick way to make yourself pass out. She bent her knees again and now felt like she was falling over. Still, they stood and stared at each other.

Movement suddenly caught Suz's eye. A tall, thin man in dark clothes slid forward, under each of his hands, he gripped the shoulder of a young boy. Suz ran forward and grabbed the fence. "Ari, Caleb, it's me, Miss Molloy. Oh, thank God."

The boys tried to bolt to her, but the tall man had them pinned in place.

Another man walked up behind them and moved toward the gate. He unlocked the padlock. Suz turned and saw that her guide had stashed his gun again. As soon as the gate opened, Suz rushed in and gathered the boys in her arms. They clung to her tightly. Their silence worried her. They were hot. Even for a day like today, they were hot. Suz cupped Ari's chin and tried to peer at his face in the dim light leftover from the day. His skin was pink, and his eyes glassy. She could see a headache thrumming at his temple. She pulled his head to her stomach as she checked on Caleb. He looked equally miserable.

"These children are ill," she said. But she already knew that. Jones had told her as much when they were still at her house. She asked if she could bring some medicine with her and when he said, "you have ten seconds to grab what you need," Suz had walked to her medicine cabinet, held out her shirt as a receptacle, and scooped all of the contents off the shelves. She had stuffed the bottles and vials and boxes into the space that was freed up when the weapons were removed from the backpack.

Suz looked up as big globs of wet fell on her head. The sky rumbled then opened as a torrent fell on them. She quickly pulled her poncho over the children's heads. "Where should I go?" she asked, scanning the tents that stood out as black against a purple and green background. The man who had brought the children out walked to a tent, lifted the flap, and gestured in.

Moving up the step, Suz and the boys climbed in. It was empty except for what looked like a heater in the center. Suz shucked off her poncho and backpack and moved over to turn the temperature up high. It gave the tent a little light. Suz was shaking from head to foot. Exhaustion. Fear. Excitement to see the boys were actually at the end of her trail. Her body was short wiring.

The boys crowded close to the stove, their knees to their chins, leaning on each other.

"Okay," Suz said. "Okay." She blinked. "Okay," she said again. No. Not okay. What should she do? "Is this where you've been staying, Ari?"

He nodded.

"Is there food and water?"

He shrugged.

"Okay." Water. There was plenty of water outside. She moved over the wooden planks that made up the base of the decking that kept them well off the ground and opened the pack, and pulled out a cooking pot and a clean t-shirt. Holding the t-shirt in a loose ball, she reached out from under the tent fly, bringing the cloth in and squeezing it into the pot repeatedly until it was full. She pulled a cup from the pack and made each boy drink several servings. She drank straight from the pot. She couldn't afford to get sick too.

The rain would come, and the rain would go, but maintaining a supply of water was imperative. Once they had all drunk their fill, Suz pulled her camel reservoir and funnel to the side of the tent, and there she worked to fill the water bladder. It would hold half a gallon – two liters. That wasn't a lot for two sick boys.

"Ari, honey, can you talk? Can you tell me what happened?

How did you get here?" Anything the boys could tell her might give her better insight into how to get them back out.

"Rebecca got sick, and we went to the doctor."

"She's at home now. She's okay," Suz reassured the brothers.

Ari and Caleb nodded, sad-eyed.

"The doctor said we were okay to go to school. Mr. Cummings drove us. When we got there, a bad man shot Mr. Cummings, and a woman grabbed our hands and said we should run," Ari said.

"We got sleepy in the car." Caleb picked up. "When we woke up, we were at the beach. There was a boat."

"A boat? Were you scared?" Suz asked gently.

"I was too sleepy to care. You?" Caleb looked at Ari. Ari nodded.

"Were you on the boat for a long time?"

"I don't think so. You?" Ari looked at Caleb. Caleb shook his head.

"Where did the boat take you?"

"We got out at a boat dock, and we went on a plane. The plane took us to another airport."

"And then what happened?" Suz asked, topping off the water bladder and turning the cap on tightly.

"We drove in a car, then we walked across a long bridge, then we got in another car."

"That's a very long day for you. You must have felt tired." Suz filled the pot again and moved to put it on the heater to warm so she could clean the children.

"We slept a lot along the way. But I was still really tired. You?" Ari asked Caleb. Caleb nodded.

"Do you remember where the car took you?" She reached in her bag and took out three meal replacement bars, and gave one to each of the kids. They ripped the paper off and ate hungrily.

So did Suz. She wanted to give them another. She wanted another herself — or maybe all of them in one big munch-fest. But Suz wasn't sure how long she'd have to make her meager rations last.

When they had licked their fingers clean. Suz tried again, "Do you remember where the car took you?"

"It stopped in the middle of a road. There was a man with a four-wheeler, they put us in the back, in a wagon thing, and they drove us here and put us in this tent."

"I see. Do you know how many nights you've slept in this tent?"

"Two," Ari said.

"One," Caleb said.

They turned to each other. "Last night, we were here."

"And the night before," Ari said.

"Nuh-uh, that wasn't a night that was just a little dark, and then them guys moaning outside," Caleb countered.

"Yeah, you're right."

Them guys moaning? Suz was too exhausted to take in much more information. She decided to wait until the morning to get more details. "And they didn't give you a blanket or anything?"

The boys shook their heads.

"Okay, let's see if we can't get more comfortable."

Suz vaguely remembered Jack telling her some basics of staying alive with the things in the bag, but this had been a joke gift. A zombie backpack, for heaven's sake. She hadn't really been paying attention to the contents of the lecture as much as she had paid attention to her teacher, how vivid his blue eyes were. How broad his shoulders were. She had watched his hands and had thought about how much she loved his caresses, how his hands warmed her skin with their broad expanse. She loved his callouses. She loved how he made her feel precious. She loved him. Just deeply and thoroughly loved him. But hated the fear that went along with loving him, she tacked onto the end.

Suz pulled out a ground tarp. It was lined in reflective material. Jack had said to use it to reflect heat away or reflect heat toward her depending on the situation.

They needed heat.

Though the day had been unbearably hot, the night temperatures were dropping quickly.

Suz looked around. Jack had said over and under for heat. She reached back in the pack and found a roll of bank line. Stuck inside the spool was taped a razor blade.

Jack had shown that to her and said, "One is none, and two is one." Like that should mean something to her.

She had nodded because who cared? There wasn't going to be a zombie apocalypse.

Though, this situation seemed apocalyptic to her now.

She used the razor to carefully cut stretches of cord and then used those in the grommet holes to tie the tarp up to the side of the tent. Now it had a base along the flooring to reflect heat up and a side to reflect the heat from the stove. She couldn't figure out a way to get it over their heads.

Next, she pulled out a large roll that wrapped inside the top of the bag. She pulled the bands off and was surprised and thrilled to find they were no-slip hair bands. Suz took a moment to pull her hair into a knotted ponytail.

She looked over at the boys. They stared at her with glassy eyes.

Suz had thought that she was unrolling a ground cloth to put another layer between them and the wood floor that felt slimy to the touch, but she discovered a vent with a screw top. When she unscrewed the cap, it released its vacuum, and the vinyl backed cloth became an air mattress. Not terribly thick – but enough to get the kids' little bodies farther up off the moist planks. "Tada," she said like she had done a magic trick.

That earned her a couple of weak smiles. Suz needed to take their temperatures and get some fever medicine in them. Get the mud off them and help them to feel restful. The dark circles under both boys' eyes worried her.

Suz pulled out a little cylinder pillow. One end was held together with a drawstring. Jack called it a "stuff bag." "You don't roll your sleeping bag, Suz. You just stuff it in." Suz opened it up and pulled out a limp sad rectangle of cloth.

Jack said, "After stuffing, it needs fluffing." He'd made her repeat the phrase. He tickled her while she did. By the third repeat, she had been giggling so hard her eyes were streaming. And he had kissed her and looked into her eyes with such conviction.

Love.

Love had shone back at her.

Suz cleared her throat as she stood up and started shaking the sleeping bag in the air, hoping it wasn't too humid to get the down fluffed up and warm. The movement helped hide the emotional pain stretching across Suz's face. She might not ever get to see Jack again.

Wow.

That thought almost put her on the ground.

She was in enough trouble here. She had to push her longing away.

This zombie bag is everything "Jack," Suz thought. Keeping thoughts of him at bay was going to be impossible.

By the time she got their bed made, the water was warm on the stove. She used a small cloth to wash the boys. She dressed them — one in a hoody and the other in a fleece jacket. Suz pulled on a fleece vest and zipped it high.

She took the boys' temperatures; both were over a hundred. She had them drink again. "What do you do when you need to pee?" Suz asked.

"I haven't needed to pee," Ari said. "You?"

Caleb shook his head.

Well, that was something. Hadn't needed to pee? Had they had nothing to drink? "Do you need to go now?"

Caleb nodded, then tapped his brother. "You?"

Ari nodded.

It was still raining. Suz walked the boys to the corner of the tent and lifted the flap. "Can you kneel down and get all the pee outside the tent?" They did, and the rain washed it quickly away, but Suz wasn't sure how she was going to cope with her own needs.

That particular strategy wasn't going to work for her.

The boys got into the sleeping bag and pushed over. It was a queen-sized sleeping bag – she guessed that Jack had planned for Suz and him to share body heat in whatever horrible scenario he had conjured up that would have her using this bag—so plenty of room for all three. She took her poncho, now dry from the heater, and tucked it around the sleeping bag at a bid to keep the humidity off.

Jack had said on the tablet, cold and wet were deadly. Suz stopped to wonder at the marked difference in temperature between day and night. It was pretty extreme.

The boys fell almost instantly asleep.

Suz worked at filling the water bladder again, filling the pot, and warming it on the stove so she could clean herself. Suz had never felt so disgustingly dirty in her life. She washed their clothes in the rain and hung them up to dry over the heat. Opening her boots wide, Suz turned them so the heat could get deep inside. Though they had done a pretty adequate job of keeping her feet dry, stories of jungle rot resurfaced and turned her stomach.

Her immediate chores done, Suz sat in a fresh pair of BDUs and stared at the red glow of the propane heater. She wondered how often they filled up the tanks. Was she wasting resources? She peeked out of the front flap and saw that all the tents glowed softly with the heater light, and so she decided not to turn it off.

The rain stopped as suddenly as it had started, but the drip, drip, drip continued. Now the night was filled with other noises. A jaguar screamed somewhere in the forest, and Suz thought that the fence served not only to keep them in but to keep other things out.

Here I am, she thought. Exactly where I wanted to be. Here with the kids. Here to help these children. It was a weird journey to get here. Now, what am I supposed to do?

22

Jack

19:10 HOURS, THURSDAY, FEB. 17TH
Ciudad Del Este, Paraguay

JACK TOWERED over the pedestrians as he moved down the street in the Taiwanese section of the city. He couldn't make out the words written in Chinese characters. He was relying on his GPS to get him where he needed to be. He pushed through a glass door and then through a beaded curtain to get into the main bar area. Chairs were stacked on tables, and a man pushed a mop over the floor. The worker hadn't yet cleaned the spot where Jack was walking. His boots held then released with each step, making squishing, sucking noises as he paced forward.

Behind the bar stood a heavily tattooed Englishman, slicing lemons. He glanced up as Jack approached.

"Mac?" Jack said with a grin.

"Son of a bloody gun." Mac moved haltingly down the counter and around the end of the bar, grabbing Jack into a hug. "Ah, it's good to see you, mate. How've you been keeping?" He backed away and lifted his chin to look Jack in the eye.

"You're taller than I remember," Jack said.

Mac laughed and reached down to point at his feet. Titanium legs showed beneath the man's cargo shorts. "When they blew my legs off, I got me a new pair. The doc said I could be any length I wanted, so I went from what you Yanks would call five-eight to six feet tall. I tried for a little taller than that, but Doc said I'd look like I was wearing stilts. The birds dig it, though. It's true what they say," he slapped Jack in the chest, "tall lads get the girls."

Jack laughed. "Hey, I could use something to drink. You open for business?"

"Grab yourself a stool, and I'll snag you a cold one. Put some hair on that girly chest of yours, heh? So, what's with the leg? Why're you hobbling on crutches?" Mac moved behind the bar.

"Eh, flesh wound. I use the crutches for sympathy. Nice place you've got here," Jack said, taking in the pictures of naked girls that had been pulled out of men's magazines and taped to the walls. Dancing poles dotted the open space, and there were lipstick and handprint stains on the walls.

"It's shite, but it serves its needs." Mac pulled a beer from the fridge under the bar and popped the top off before setting it, frosty cold, in front of Jack. "How do you find yourself in the armpit of the world?"

Jack took a long swig, relishing the way the carbonation cut through the grit and pollution that tickled his throat. He looked around to see where the cleaner had gone. Seeing him working on the other side of the room, Jack pulled out his phone. "I need some intel. I have one, possibly three missing persons in the area."

"One maybe three, huh?" He reached out. "That's Suz," he said. "You still with her?"

Jack didn't know. Was he? "She was spotted going into Tatí Yupí but not coming out."

"That happens with an alarming frequency." Mac rubbed at his chin. "Panthers and the like make quick work of bodies, and the bones get spread around." Mac put both hands on his head. "Bullocks. That's not what I should have said. It's just . . ."

"I've heard about its reputation. I'm not clear on what's going on down here. I'm trying to catch up with Suz."

"You said maybe three."

"Two boys. Here." Jack swiped the phone to reveal a recent photo of the twins.

"Her kids?"

"The one on the right is her student. There was a high-profile snatch and grab at their school."

"Zero details," Mac said and put his hands up.

"There's another guy that we think is involved, Samuel Jones. Got anything on him?"

Mac reached for the phone again, and he scowled at the photo. "Yeah, I know him. That there is Simon Zoric. Slovakian. His family has ties to the Russians working in the area, and by extension Hezbollah. Most of their finances pass through the financial systems down here."

"Any ideas where I can catch up with that guy?"

Mac popped his eyebrows.

Jack tipped back the last of his beer and put the empty on the bar.

"Another?"

Jack shook his head. "I'd love another, but later." Look, I need work equipment. Do you think you can hook me up?"

Mac nodded. "Normal kit?"

"In this part of the world, will normal kit be enough?"

23

Suz

4:30 A.M. FRIDAY, FEBRUARY 18TH

Somewhere deep in Refugio Yati Tupi, Paraguay

THE SOUND of haunting music filled the tent. Beautiful, eerie chanting backed with awakening fauna. It must be very early. Suz went over to the tent opening, and, standing to the side so that she could not be seen, she looked out.

A large tarp was spread on the ground, and men approached with prayer rugs in their hands, slipping off their sandals, and moving into neat rows, six across and six deep. One stood in front. They were dressed in olive drab harem pants and matching tunics, shemagh cloths covered their heads, they were thinly bearded and seemed, like the guide who brought her here, to be very young.

Standing at the edges of their prayer rugs, they chanted

together, "*Alla o Akbar*," their hands up in front of them. They crossed one arm over the other, everyone moving in a choreographed spiritual dance. The men stood silently, though they moved their lips, reciting their prayers beneath a periwinkle sky.

Suz shifted silently to the other side of the slit. From this angle, she could see that there was another tent beside hers and then the fencing. Obviously, this place was secret. Obviously, these men were Muslim – Suz saw no women except herself, no children except the sleeping Levinski boys. She could see straw dummies strung up on ropes draped in clear tarps. On the far side of the camp, away from the line of tents, firing range bullseyes were attached to the fencing. There was no berm behind them to catch the stray bullets, but then again, out here, the stray bullets would sail for a time and then hit one of the massive trees. Suz wondered about that for a time. Guns made a great deal of noise. They must be very far into the forest, very far from people for no one to hear and investigate. She wondered if the trees muffled sound or augmented it. The forest was very loud. All the time loud, except when the rain came down in torrents. And that had its own loudness.

Suz needed to pee. She scanned what little she could see, and she didn't see anything that looked like a latrine. She wasn't sure she was brave enough to leave the tent and move into the open and disrupt the men at prayer. They were now prostrate on their mats.

She went to the back of the tent, where she had the boys kneel the night before. She untied a knot, lifted the corner, and slipped outside, jumping to the ground. She moved as close as she dared to the fencing, dropped her BDUs to her ankles, and squatted down, wiping with a Kleenex. She was glad that here the land slid downhill away from their tent. She stood and looked at the fencing. If she were to escape with the boys. She'd have to get past this fencing.

She looked up. The concertina wire was daunting. Beyond daunting. Undoable. She slunk back to the tent and crawled back through the hole. She went and checked the boys. They both seemed to be in the deep sleep that came from pure exhaustion. She had broken a Tylenol in half and used her finger to stick the pill down each boys' throats since she had no liquid or chewables in her medicine cabinet. Their fevers seemed to be down. She needed to ask the boys what the doctor said about their sister.

The men were still at prayer. Suz undid a tie at the back of their tent at eye level so she could stick her face through and consider the fence. Tall. Even if she could climb it and could come up with a strategy for how to get over it, she knew that she couldn't get the boys out that way. Getting her class down the rope ladder had been hard enough for the kids to do, and running away. . .she had learned lessons about that too. Ari and Caleb were small and slight for their age. Not clumsy, but not athletically gifted either. And sick.

A man was outside of her tent. "Molloy. Here," he commanded in barely-there English. Suz opened the tent flap and stepped out. His eyebrows raised to his hairline, his eyes wide in shock, quickly replaced by fury, he slapped her across the face, knocking her off the one step. She flailed and was able to right herself before she fell into the mud. He reached over and grabbed her shoulders; Suz stood frozen, not knowing what right-action to take. "No," he spat and gestured up and down her body. Then lifted her by the elbows and threw her toward the tent opening.

Suz scrambled inside, thoroughly shaken. She looked down at what she was wearing. BDUs, combat boots, a t-shirt. Standing two feet back from the tent slit, she focused on the men, moving away, their prayer rugs rolled up under their arms. They were covered in drab olive. She thought back to St. Basil's and her student Layla Kalb, she wore western-style clothes, but her mother wore clothing that covered all her body except for her hands. Her head was wrapped in a flowing hijab.

Suz realized that her clothing wasn't sufficiently modest.

She went back to the pack and found a shemagh that Jack wore when he was in the desert. It was basically a huge bandana. That would help. She draped it over her head. She needed something for her arms and elbows. Moving things around, Suz found out a pair of silk long johns rolled tightly and fastened with hair bands. She tugged the bands off.

"Molloy. Here," the guy yelled. His impatience was palpable.

Suz's cheek stung from where he hit her. Suz cast her eyes around for a quick cover-up and pulled the poncho from over the boys, and yanked it on. Only her face showed as she exited the tent again.

The guy scowled at her, then walked away. She thought maybe she should go with him. Suz moved to walk beside him; he looked down at her.

"No." He pushed her back behind him on his left. He glowered.

She was to follow behind as a subservient; to him, women weren't equal and shouldn't walk side by side with a man. Suz took a deep breath in and tried to think about how she had seen Middle Eastern women present themselves, so she could pattern her behavior.

Suz remembered an evening on her back deck around the fire pit. And Striker was telling them a story about Kabul. He had noticed that even though the people had been freed of the Taliban culture, the women still walked the requisite five steps behind, and to his eye, it looked like even farther back than before. He asked a local woman why this was. She bowed her head to hide her grin and said, "Landmines."

The guy stopped moving. She stopped moving. Suz was standing before the man she assumed to be the commander of the camp. "Molloy," he said, pointing at her. He patted his chest, "Salib."

Suz couldn't tell if that was a first name or last name. She stepped forward. "Salib," she repeated.

"Boys good?"

"No. Boys not good," She shook her head for emphasis.

He scowled.

"The boys need a doctor. Medicine." Suz tried for the simplest phrases.

He scowled again. He pointed. "You. Medicine." Then he pointed to his back, pretended that his hands looped through straps, leaned over, and took a few paces. He raised his eyebrows as if to ask if she understood.

Before she could answer, her eye caught on an enormous snake that was coiled into the concertina wire on the fence behind his head. Her eyes stretched wide; she had never seen such an enormous snake outside of a pet shop vivarium. Salib followed her gaze. He pointed to other points along the wall that also had snakes, then flicked his finger. "Word?"

"Snake," Suz said. "Snake," she repeated, drawing the word out.

"No snake." Then he moved his finger around to point at the enclosed area. "No animal. Fence."

Suz looked at the ground. This guy was nuts. This was, after all, a chain-link fence. Perhaps it kept out bigger animals, wild boars and the like, and maybe even gigantic boa constrictors like the three she could see dangling and decaying in the concertina wire, but there were plenty of animals and snakes that could slide through the holes.

"You, girl," Salib said.

Suz didn't know what to say to that.

"One girl," he said, holding up a single finger.

This time Suz understood. One girl. That was going to create problems – well, it had on occasion for Strike Force when they were traveling with a female soldier who would do the security checks on Muslim women and talk with them away from the men. Men were not allowed to address another man's wife. And they certainly weren't allowed to pat a woman down. What would this mean for her? Suz waited patiently.

He pointed to the latrine that she could see at the far left-hand corner and then wagged his finger at her.

Suz made a face that she hoped said, "Well, what am I supposed to do?"

His eye scanned over the area. If Suz was guessing, she'd say it was a little bigger than half a football field with the housing along one side of the fencing and various training areas throughout – obstacle courses and strength training areas. She wondered how they had cleared such a big swath of land. From the amount of rust on the metal, she'd say this place had been around for a good long while. But then again, with the amount of moisture in the air, it was hard to tell. The wooden planks that created the steps up into the various tent slabs seemed worn down and cupped. She'd guess it had been here well over a decade. Nothing was new or in great shape.

They had been standing there for quite a while. Salib stroked his beard, and Suz could tell he was at a total loss for how to handle the situation. Suz wondered if she should help him out with a solution or if that would be considered dishonoring. He was staring at the padlock on the front gate. He shook his head.

Looking at her feet, Suz said, "If I may," in what she considered a subservient voice. She felt his focus shift back on her, and she raised her eyes. "Men. Pray. 5 times each day." She held up five fingers, then repeated the crossed arms and bows that she saw this morning. She raised her eyebrows.

"Yes," he said with a tilt of his head.

"You pray, I go wash." Suz pointed at what she thought was a shower tent on the other side of the main gate. Then she pointed at the latrines stuck in the corner. "You pray. I go."

Relief flashed across Salib's face. "Yes, we pray. You go." He pointed as she had done. "Yes." He waved his hand at her. "Come." He moved away.

Suz followed five paces behind. She was in their world here. It would only help her if she tried to assimilate. They might trust her more. Watch her less. Hit her less.

They moved toward the corner of the camp that was on the other side of the main gate, where the showers and latrine were situated. He opened the tent flap on the longest/largest of the camp tents. It sat in a second line in front of the showers. The men were eating their breakfasts. He yelled a command into the tent. They responded in unison. He turned and yelled toward the showers and the latrine. No response came from either. Salib nodded. "Come."

He must have been making sure the way was clear. He showed her a large reservoir that contained water. Above it, a large tarp had been strung. Like a funnel, it would route the rain waters down into the opening at the top of the tank. A stack of buckets sat on a chair to keep them from the mud beneath. Salib picked up a bucket and demonstrated how to fill one with water. He dramatically shut the faucet, then checked it, and shut it some more. "Important," he said and raised his brows.

"Yes." Suz nodded, making sure the spigot wasn't dripping

when this was the camp's water source was incredibly important. She tried to convey that message with her eyes.

In the shower tent, one reached up and emptied the bucket into a contraption that then poured the water over you slowly. Suz looked up. Gravity fed, this device was high up off the ground. Suz reached up to see if she could make it work. She was about six inches too short. Salib screwed his lips to the side in thought.

There were five stations on either side of the tent. At each one, a bar of soap had a hole through it and was tied by a piece of rope to a hook. Salib hung up the bucket on the hook and demonstrated washing hands and face. She nodded. She could make it work. No towels. No mirrors. No shampoo.

As the water ran from the gravity device, it poured between the planks to the ground underneath. That caught Suz's eye. She wondered if thirty-seven men showered each day. And didn't they wash before they prayed? That was a lot of wash water. It had to go somewhere.

Salib motioned to her and exited the tent. He walked to the latrine. Here, he called again. Again no one responded. It was interesting that it didn't smell bad. One side of the tent was lined with a long bench; holes were cut into it. It was close to the ground, which would necessitate squatting like she had earlier. Behind each hole was a plastic grocery bag. Each contained a roll of toilet paper.

He pulled out a roll and looked it over carefully. Then he made his hands into a spider and raised his brow.

Spiders in the toilet paper, *awesome*. Suz's face must have shown she got it because Salib nodded as he put the toilet paper away.

Next, Salib pointed to a plastic bin in the corner. He

unscrewed and lifted the top to reveal a bag of garden lime. There was a scoop hanging on a hook alongside.

He pointed again and caught her eye, so she knew what he was saying was significant. "This," he said, holding his hand up like he was cupping some up. He held his other hand up in the same way. "Water," he labeled the other hand. He brought his hands together and then made them explode back from each other. He shook his hands and grimaced in pain. He raised his eyebrows. Did she understand?

Suz repeated the gesture then said, "No water." She lowered her eyes so as not to seem immodest. She thought *lime is a dangerous alkaline.* She knew that from her gardening. Water and lime might just be something she could use along the way. Could she get thirty-seven males subdued like that? Suz let the thought go as quickly as it bubbled up. There was *nothing* she could do to subdue thirty-seven armed men.

Salib scooped up the white powder with the plastic dipper and dumped it in the hole. Smell control.

He pointed at her, then the latrine. He pointed at himself and the door, then crossed his arms over his chest, miming that he would stand guard.

"Uhm, okay, thank you," Suz said.

Salib went out.

Suz did her thing, fighting with the poncho the whole time. She wiggled her fingers in the bucket of wash water, thinking that was darned unsanitary, and went to the door. The latrine and the shower looked like the only tents with doors.

When she went out, Salib walked her to the mess tent. He handed her a plate and held up three fingers. She held a metal dish out to the server, who put three hard-boiled eggs on her plate, one each for her and the boys. She looked around. That was all that anyone had. No wonder these guys were so thin. And angry. Low blood glucose would do that to the kindest of people. None of these men struck her as particularly kind, to begin with. She hoped the other meals were more substantial. She pulled the plate under her poncho. The rains were falling again, though not as aggressively as last night. She followed the commander back to her tent, keeping a discreet five paces behind.

24

Jack

10:23 HOURS FRIDAY, FEB. 18TH
Ciudad Del Este, Paraguay

JACK STOOD in the street surrounded by the cheap construction of inner-city high-rises designed to shelve too much humanity in too small a space. It was a world of gray and brown with flecks of color — red and blue, a bit of yellow. Jack didn't like that the windows were filthy with pollution and covered with curtains. He couldn't see if there were eyes watching him from inside.

Late-model cars, more rust than shine, cruised past him down the narrow street.

He had dropped wireless, magnetic earbuds into his ear canals and wore a necklace communicator so Base could hear him.

The city was bustling. Pedestrians wove in and out amongst the umbrella-covered vendors that grew like mushrooms along the sidewalks. Here and there, people would shuffle into the mud-covered streets, merging with the slow-moving traffic to get around a squabble or a beggar.

All around him, Jack heard Arabic spoken. He picked up no Spanish or Guarani or even Portuguese. He was deep in the Arabic community.

As Jack moved down the street into position, he walked through pockets of air, putrid with rotting garbage.

He slipped past sweaty bodies that ripened with the day's heat.

Finally, Jack took up a place against a pillar that held up an overhang.

A low rumble slid overhead, but from here, he had no visual on the sky and couldn't tell how close the storm had surged. Jack hoped they could achieve their objective and get the hell out of Dodge before the skies opened. Everything became more dangerous in the rain.

His newly acquired Sig P226 was stuck in his belt at the small of his back, hidden by a loose-fitting buttoned shirt that seemed as popular here as it was in the Middle East. He had his back up Glock in an ankle holster above his boot. He had two extended mags of ammunition in his pocket and a KABAR folding Mule knife on his belt. If everything went smoothly, he wouldn't need to use any of them.

Jack had left the crutches at the safe house. He didn't have time for them anymore. Wearing the same kind of baggy pants that he'd spotted on the locals, Jack hid his brace from obvious view. He didn't need a red flag waving in a bull's face.

Kick me here. I'm vulnerable.

This was a Mossad action; he was just along for the ride. Glad to be. They were picking up a guy they knew to be a logistics guy for Hezbollah. He was also known to be in regular communication with Simon Zoric. Jack's intel from his British pal was what got him a ticket to this show. *"Cheers, mate,"* Jack whispered under his breath.

The Mossad unit was worried about something. That was an interesting piece of information. Specifics behind their concerns weren't part of their conversation with Jack — not part of his need-to-know. But they did reveal that this guy had a connection to the cell activity that they had lost track of. The cell that might have produced the dead Jihadist back in D.C. It wasn't a straight line to Suz. But if the dead terrorist had been trained in this area, it was possible that his cell had the boys. And Suz.

Over his comms, Jack could hear the undercover say, "*As-salāmu ʿalaykum.*"

"Wa ʿalaykumu as-salām," their mark responded.

Jack glanced to his left, where Ruth had parked in a beat-to-hell van from the seventies, providing another pair of eyes and their exit strategy.

The unit had him positioned out front. They had an operator somewhere covering the back of the building. They also had satellite support and a commander on the comms. The chances of grabbing this guy were pretty good. They just needed the under-cover agent to tempt Amman out to the streets. They'd flash a gun, push him into the van, and off they'd roll.

"You are looking well, my friend." The undercover said. He was none too happy that the last year he had spent working this Hezbollah contact, Amman—using him to infiltrate the political substructure of the area—was all going to go down the toilet with this capture. But the directive had come down some command chain that Amman needed hands-on interrogation back in Israel. That he might have information that could help America — and by America, they meant Jack and Suz and maybe the boys— was the icing on the cake, Jack was told.

Apparently, relations were frosty at the moment between Israeli and American leaders.

Jack didn't care about politics; his mission was to get Suz back and try to identify the children. If it was Ari and Caleb, that changed things considerably.

"You said there was an urgent transaction?"

There was a pause in the conversation and the jostling of glass against metal. Jack thought that the requisite tea was being poured and shared. It was part of the social dance performed by many Middle Easterners at meetings.

"Indeed. Monies from Slovakia need to be converted for use by our brothers. They need this funding with some urgency. There is an event that is time-sensitive."

"And in what form of currency—"

Another man's voice called out. "They have people watching the building."

The mark hissed, "Death to you," in Farsi.

That phrase instantly mobilized Jack. He strode across the street, skipping in front of a taxi that didn't want to slow, and moved across the crowded sidewalk toward the door.

In his ear, Jack heard their insider say, "He's running."

The van roared to life and battled its way through the morning traffic to circle the block. The Mossad undercover, looking every part the businessman, strutted out of the front door – he needed to keep his cover going in this part of the world, and that meant playing his bit no matter what. He folded his paper and looked at the sky before he walked down the sidewalk.

As Jack brushed past him, the guy turned his head to look the other way.

Jack pushed through the door, moving to the stairs, the only way to get to the back exit in this fire hazard of a building design.

Mossad Command was tense. "Alpha team, bring in the mark."

Jack pressed his index finger into the tag under his shirt. "Copy that." As he rounded the door frame, he pulled his Sig, wrapping the grip in his fists as he came to the first landing. Shoulder to the wall, he looked up for shadows, or body parts, or weapons focused down on him.

"They have eyes out front, he's on his phone, expect company," Command said.

"Alpha one, clear." Jack heard Ezra's voice.

"Alpha two. I'm almost to your floor," Jack replied.

"Roger." They were speaking in English for his sake. This team had been on enough missions with US special forces that they felt comfortable with American radio protocol. It was better that they weren't on the airwaves in Arabic or in Hebrew right now anyway.

Jack caught sight of the man, jumping and sliding down the back stairway. He was dressed in khaki pants and a blue dress shirt, trying to run in slick-bottomed loafers. Balding. Salt and pepper beard. Sixty-ish. When the man looked up the stairs, Jack caught a full view of his face — a hawk nose over a too broad mouth, fat purplish lips. His eyes bulged like someone with thyroid issues and were draped in heavy, sleepy-looking lids. The mark looked exactly like his intelligence photos.

This guy had been pictured on one of the packs of cards they hand out to soldiers. Play poker, memorize a terrorist's face. Effective. Efficient. Someone had been very smart. This guy's picture, on the seven of clubs, had cost Jack a bitter-cold all-nighter of watch duty when that seven busted him at blackjack, and he lost the wager. Jack wasn't going to forget that face easily.

Jack depressed his comms button. "Target confirmed. That's

Amman." How such a high-value terrorist found himself working in Paraguay was a very good question, and Jack was very interested in finding out the answers.

The last Amman had been seen was in Kabul.

That was a while ago.

U.S. forces had assumed he was dead.

"Be advised, X-rays are amassing at the back entrance." Command's satellite view was gold when it came to keeping an op safe. They could see the enemy's movements with a bird's eye view. "Get out of there now. And bring our mark in safely. That's an absolute—"

Command's directive was cut off by the strafe of machine gunfire. Jack dove behind a doorway, reached out a hand, grabbing Amman's back collar, as Amman crouched with his arms flung over his head. Jack jerked the man back up the stairs and pushed him into the hallway.

"Alpha Two. Mark acquired," Jack said into his comms.

"Let's bring him in," Command said.

"Alpha One. Threat neutralized."

"Copy that." Jack had Amman pressed against the wall, his shirt cloth wrapped in Jack's fist, and his forearm pressed across the man's back. Jack did a quick pat-down, removing a Glock from the guy's waistband.

"Alpha Three, what's your position?" Ezra called out as he rounded the corner and joined Jack.

"Alpha Three. Be prepared. Exfil ninety seconds." The roar of city life dappled Ruth's words as she responded.

Jack had Amman by the nape of the neck, using his clothing to keep him constrained, quiet, and on the tips of his toes. Jack maneuvered him toward the nearest staircase.

Ezra button hooked to take point.

"Ah shit, incoming," Jack yelled.

Ezra threw his body around the corner of the door as bullets pinged the exit way.

They took refuge in one of the empty rooms.

Jack peeked out the window. He saw the van almost to them.

Like roaches in sudden light, there was great scurrying as the street emptied. Screams echoed off the buildings.

"Shit, the mark took a gunshot." Ezra bent down and examined him. The thigh of the man's pants was wringing wet with blood. "Nah, damn it, artery. He's not going to make it."

The anger that rose in Jack seemed unmanageable, though he fought hard for control. He bent over, grabbing the man's jaw and forcing Amman to look him in the eye. The man was gray and fading. "You took an American woman and two little boys, where are they?" he asked in Arabic.

Amman lifted his chin, his eyes clouded as he bled out.

Jack squeezed the pressure points in the man's jaw. "The woman and boys. Where are they?"

Amman coughed and laughed. "You'll never know."

Ezra leaned in, so he was cheek to jowl with the man. "Very bad things happen to the families of villains who die. Hezbollah might just receive information proving that you are a traitor. You have one and only one opportunity to protect your family, Amman. Mossad never rests."

"I'm dying," he gasped out with more shock and confusion than pain in his voice.

"We have collected intelligence on you. You have been stealing money from Hezbollah. That will earn some vicious enemies for your wife and children. You are going to die now. Why not die knowing that you saved your family's lives?" Ezra raised his brow. "Tell me where the boys are. Where's the woman? Why do you have these hostages? Tell me, and I won't take your wife and children's lives in exchange." It was an empty threat, but it had a chance of working.

Amman seemed to pass out, but his lips moved. Jack leaned in.

He gasped. "Gregor Zoric needs . . . boys. Know nothing . . . woman." His eyes were mere slits.

Jack shook him. "A training cell let one of its jihadists go to America to get the boys. Do you know about this? Was he out of this area?"

Amman nodded. "Yes . . . a week . . .he went."

"Are the boys in the camp?" Ezra asked.

The wounded man's eyes rolled back, showing glassy whites

Jack smacked the man's cheeks until Amman roused.

"Where's the camp? Location?" Ezra demanded.

Amman's body trembled. "Tatí Yupí." On the front of his shirt, a small bloom of blood absorbed into the cotton. Amman cupped the hollow protectively. The much larger exit wound was streaming blood and intestinal fluids.

A puddle formed beneath the man.

Jack shuffled his foot away; blood made boots slippery and left trails that were easily followed. "Why did they take them?" Jack demanded, grabbing at Amman's shirt and lifting the dying man off the floor.

"The boys—"

"Three X-rays entered the building from the rear," Command said.

"Shit." Ezra stood and pivoted in front of Jack with his gun targeting down the hallway, guarding the interrogation. "Here, they come." Ezra pushed his shoulder against the wall and lowered his profile as boots hammered up the stairs. "We've got to move."

Jack bent to lift the mark.

"He's dead. Leave him." Ezra pressed his comms. "Target down. Repeat, target down."

"Shit," Command yelled.

Before they were trapped in the room, Jack followed Ezra into the corridor.

The back exit blazed bright as shots were fired by a gunman, trying to get the jump on them. Ezra took out their point man. "Move. Move. Move."

Bullets strafed the corridor.

Jack lunged down the stairs with Ezra at his heels.

They ran out of the building, down the street a half a block, and dove into the open side panel of the waiting van.

Jack's brace hit against the metal floor, and he sucked wind.

Ezra piled in behind him.

The van took off with their boots still sticking out of the door.

"Mission fail," Jack groaned as he rolled onto his back and pushed the heels of his palms into his eyes. "I failed you, Suz."

25

Jack

11:15 Hours Saturday, Feb. 19th

Mossad Base, Ciudad Del Este, Paraguay

Jack and Ruth sat quietly in metal chairs. Rivka was on the phone, obviously getting her ass chewed for failing to acquire Al Amman yesterday and deliver him to whoever up the food chain had called for his capture. Rivka Abelson was the head honcho running command and communications for the Mossad unit, situated in the center of what looked like an abandoned processing center behind high walls and metal gates. She was as hardcore as Jack had ever seen. Her body was athletic and battle-scarred, and there was a fierceness in her eyes that never left. He respected her from the moment they shook hands here at Mossad base this morning.

Rivka hung up the encrypted line and stared at the wall for a long moment. "Tatí Yupí is a problem," Rivka stated the obvious.

"This time of year, in particular. The heat. . .The rains make tracking all but impossible – unless you're so close that you can follow your mark before the next storm hits. It also makes survival tenuous."

Jack took that information in before shifting his attention to Ezra, who brought him a first aid kit and an icepack. "Your bleeding through," he said.

Jack looked down and saw red seeping through the pale gray of his pants. Jack pulled his knife and slit the cloth of the second-hand trousers he found in a box in the corner of Mac's place to expose the brace and reached to unfasten the straps. His knee was swollen and purple. The surgical site looked gruesome, where his stitches had torn through the skin during yesterday's shitstorm.

From the corner of his eye, he watched Ezra and Rivka catching each other's gaze. It was the silent communication that could happen after enough life or death situations had been experienced as team members. Words weren't really a requirement. Jack had it with Strike Force. But here, he was guessing at what they were telling each other – probably that Jack was a liability and should be benched for the game. That was unacceptable. With them – without them—Jack was going after Suz. He'd find her no matter what it took.

The day was passing, and Jack was antsy to get moving. The rains, though, beat down with such ferocity that visibility was a meter at best.

"We gathered a couple of nuggets from Al Amman before he was killed – so our efforts in securing him weren't a total loss," Rivka said. "We have Gregor Zoric's name. What do you know about that, Jack?"

Jack paused for a moment while he bit a piece of tape to finish dressing his wound. He repeated the intel that Lynx had passed him. "The Zoric family is Slovakian and has been running several operations in America to earn money to send home to finance terrorist activity, including Hezbollah. The East Coast US Zoric group was gathered up in an FBI sting last Friday, the 11th. When the special agents were searching through the leader's home, they came across intel that led them to intercept the attack on St. Basil's school, an elementary school outside of Washington D.C. This was a cover for a political tiger kidnapping of the two Levinski boys. From there, a member of the family, Simon Zoric, using the name Samuel Jones, traveled with Gillian Suzanne Molloy, Ari Levinski's teacher, to Brazil where you picked up the trail."

"The Americans think that Molloy is culpable in the kidnapping?"

Jack flinched. He hoped that wasn't what anyone thought. As far as he knew, Suz's movements were privy to him and Lynx. Right now, there was no connection between the boys and Suz. But once Lynx knew the connection between Zoric and Suz, she'd have to explain it to Finley and the FBI. What would that set in motion? "No, it is believed that Suz Molloy is acting other than her own will."

"Other than her own will?" Rivka let those words roll out of her mouth. "Do you care to define that?"

"We're trying to figure it out." Jack knew that sounded lame. These people didn't know Suz like he did. They had nothing to judge her by. An oatmeal chocolate chip cookie – Lynx's description pretty much did Suz justice – but certainly wasn't the whole story. She was a softy—a romantic.

But there was the other side of Suz — clever, smart, adaptable, and absolutely *tenaciously* protective of those she cared about. If she could do anything to help those children, he had no doubt that she would do it.

That's what Jack's gut said was at play here.

She was trying to help the boys.

"We are familiar with the Zoric family's connections and support systems," Rivka said. "Gregor Zoric has been an enemy to Israel for over a decade now. That his people have hold of these boys, not knowing the trajectory of such a mission, is concerning. That Al Amman indicated that a jihadist was sent to America to help remove the children ties this all together in a way that increases my concerns. It was brazen and extreme to attack the school." Rivka leaned her hips into the top of her desk and crossed her arms over her chest. "To explode St. Basil's like the Hungarians did to St Moglia's in World War II would have been a devastating loss of life. And while the number of students killed would not be comparable to the nine-eleven attacks in New York, it would be a historic attack. Unprecedented in the United States. Someone wanted to make a statement – to prove a point. And I believe that was Gregor – he is a megalomaniac and would like to be perceived as a world-class geopolitical manipulator. To make his name recognizable to everyone in the world like Osama Bin Laden did. So." She pushed off the desk and moved toward a screen with a satellite photo of South America. "We need to find the boys, return them to their family, take out a training cell, seize a couple of the militants for intel." She stopped to smile at her group. "Looks like we have our work cut out for us."

"And find Suz Molloy. Bring her back safe and sound." Jack's eyes were focused hard on the Mossad leader. Suz was not a big reward. She was an afterthought at best. Jack understood that. When a mission was coordinated, there was a hierarchy of wants, and that's how Rivka had delivered the information to her unit. Number one, the boys home safe and sound. That would cut off whatever political bargaining chip or strategical maneuvering that Gregor had put in play. Second, the training cell. That had been the Mossad objective before Jack had shown up on the scene. Three, if possible, keeping a couple of the jihadists alive might lead the special ops unit to their next source of danger. But Suz? She had no overt benefit to them. She didn't qualify as an important objective. Her name hadn't even come up on the list.

Rivka considered him. "How's your leg?"

"Fuck my leg, ma'am."

She nodded.

Jack knew that working with the Mossad unit was his best chance of getting to Suz, but once he got to her, he was going to be on his own to safeguard her. The Mossad had no skin in that game.

A clatter at the door and David, the guy from his first-contact meeting, pushed his way in with a box of food for lunch.

Jack took the opportunity to call Lynx.

"JACK, good, I was just going to try to get you. What were you doing?" Lynx asked over the phone. "Someone died?"

Jack paused and scanned the room for watching eyes or listening ears. "You must have had another *knowing*. Cause yeah, that last one 'I'll not give my fiddle to any man alive' was dead on."

"No pun intended. Can you give me an idea of what happened?"

"We were fishing for information, reeling a guy in. People tried to stop us. The guy with the information took a bullet to the back of his head and leaked what intel he had on to the floor. What's playing now on your psychic channel?" Jack scratched his fingers through the scruff of his beard.

"I'll tell you in a second. The pressure is pretty substantial that we find and rescue the boys. I haven't said anything yet, about you and Suz. And I won't until you identify the kids. I don't want to reroute resources in the wrong direction. And quite frankly, if you're already working with a team down there, more guys jumping in from different working groups, all playing capture the flag, is not in anyone's best interest. Have you heard anything more?"

"More rattle about boys – but I can't say what boys. Before the guy died, he said that a camp down here sent one of their jihadists to America. Take that for what you will. He was bleeding out when we interrogated him. So, nothing concrete." Jack put his hand on the wall and peeked over his shoulder to make sure their conversation was still a private one. "Speaking of nothing concrete, Spill. What did your *knowing* say this time?"

Lynx paused overly long, and Jack felt fear crawl up his neck. Jack wasn't a stranger to fear. He knew people didn't think guys like him felt afraid. It wasn't true. He felt fear *a lot* but had learned to push through it – to feel the fear and take a step anyway, and then another, and then another until the mission was complete. But this fear, Suz-fear, jeezus, this did things to his system that he needed to master. This kind of fear was debilitating. It felt like what Suz described to him after he had come to after being shot the last time. She said she lived in a cesspool of fear *all* the time. If this was what life was like for her. . . He closed his eyes. *Jeezuschrist.* He'd never ask someone he loved to walk through life feeling this way. It felt un-survivable.

"Jack and Jill went up the hill to fetch a pail of water," Lynx whispered.

Jack pulled his brow together while he played that through his mind.

Lynx sniffed on the other end of the phone. Her voice sounded wobbly as she said, "Did you hear me?" She cleared her throat and repeated, "Jack and Jill went up the hill—"

"I heard you, Lynx. Why do you sound upset? That's a good thing, right? It means that I find Suz, and we're working together."

"Probably, but. . ."

"But?"

"The whole rhyme is—"

"You didn't hear the whole rhyme, did you? Just the Jack and—"

"Yes, but—"

"I'm going to find Suz. And I'm going to see if I can locate the boys. And then we'll move forward. One step at a time – no reason to fight a battle that may never come about."

"Right." She cleared her throat, and her voice came back strong. "I want you to keep me informed. Let me know what you need, and I'll do my best to make it happen. Mossad is some of the finest special forces ops in the world, so I think you're in good hands." Lynx's voice lifted away from the receiver. "Hey, Finley, the report you requested came in. It's on the computer screen now. I was just looking it over."

"Great, thanks." Jack could hear Finley's voice.

"That's my cue to say goodbye. Before you go, any other pings from the SAT phone?"

"Nada. Let's check-in later. Good luck."

Jack held the phone in both his hands and leaned his head back onto the wall. *Jack fell down and broke his crown, and Jill came tumbling after.* Fuck.

JACK JOINED the others for something to eat. It seemed that lunch wasn't the only thing Adam—the first Mossad operator that Jack interfaced with—had for them to chew on.

After they ate, Rivka stood with her knuckles planted on the table. "Yesterday, our Alpha Team was in the city where they got a lukewarm verification from Al Amman that Hezbollah has a hidden cell in the forest. At the same time, Beta Team was turning over stones, following up on the last known location of Molloy. Adam?"

Adam wiped his mouth on a napkin, threw it onto his paper plate, and moved to the computer bank.

With a few taps, he pulled the satellite image of South America that was displayed on the screen into a tighter view.

Now the screen was filled with treetops, the entire area green. Toward the river, the trees seemed to make nice neat rows like soldiers on the parade grounds, then there was an open space and the tourism educational buildings.

Adam used a computer tool to circle the camping facilities and dorms. "After meeting with Jack on Thursday, we sent a pair of native speakers in to stay at the facility and check it out. The couple was asking folks who had been there for a few days if they had seen their American friend with red hair. No one had. As a matter of fact, in this weather, they are not allowing for campers. They have a few guests in the dorms. There are very few people on the site at all. Hiking in this heat is discouraged, and the rain makes the rock formations slippery and treacherous. The Center is asking people to stay with the educational guides and register their path if they decide to explore on their own."

"Did they check the paperwork for going to the dam?" Rivka asked.

"They did. The weather has been such that they haven't offered dam tours since Wednesday, the 16th, the day before we had eyes on the POI in this area. So that isn't a possible route for egress."

"So, nothing? She was let off by the taxi, and that was the end of the story?" Ezra asked.

"No, not the end. Our eyes found where Suz Molloy signed in for an educational walk. The number in her party was marked as two. It was the last one offered on Thursday." Adam typed and up came a photo of a registration sheet.

Jack looked at it and nodded. "That's her signature, all right. Did they talk to the guide? Did she get back to the Center?"

"The guide said that her friend was overcome by the heat, and they decided to go back on their own," Adam said. "It was a wide path, large enough for two horse carts to pass each other, and there was no concern that the two would have trouble returning to the bus and from there to the center. But the bus driver said that the two didn't show up for a ride back."

"Her friend?" Ezra asked.

"Male. Young. Dark. Non-English/non-Spanish speaking. No other description. The guide said the woman was wearing a heavy backpack, and the man had nothing with him. That's the last we have on Molloy. We have nothing on the boys," Adam said.

"Has the computer been able to weed through the satellite imagery?" Rivka asked.

Adam scratched at his cheek, then clicked the keyboard. "Okay, here's what we have. Clarity is compromised by cloud cover and precipitation. This preserve is the remnants of the Atlantic Forest left after the man-made lake was formed with the dam project. It's home to a variety of large constrictor snakes and wild cats, as well as other concerning animals – spiders, mosquitoes, wild boar, and so forth. From the images taken Thursday, the computer-generated five sites that our algorithms interpret as being deforested with a footprint large enough to allow for a training camp. We sent out a drone that night to try for heat signatures that might represent buildings and human activity." Adam tapped on the keyboard, and the images shifted.

"I think this one might be the cell's location." Using a laser pointer, Adam indicated what he was seeing. "Let me take you step by step through our thought process. First, the cell needs a way to get supplies in. It can't be that the jihadists are entering and exiting Yati Tupi through the front gates with those supplies. Here, just twenty kilometers to the north-west of the entrance, is a farm that has a landing strip. I've watched three small planes come in on radar just today. It's possible that this is what Hezbollah uses as an airstrip. There are other airstrips, but they are much farther away. Hours by car. Next." Adam pulled the view in even tighter.

"Wait," Jack said. "Help me work this through. If the boys who you saw were the American boys who are missing, in order to make the timeframe work, they'd have to have flown in. Since there's no border data on the boys, I'd say car to plane off a private airstrip *or* car to boat to plane from a foreign airstrip. If they were bringing the boys to the reserve, why didn't they land them in the farmer's field? Why'd they risk being spotted on the bridge?"

"Several things could have played into that choice," Ezra said. "What kind of plane were they on? It wasn't a legal flight — either commercial or supply plane. The boys would have needed proper documentation. They would have shown up on security cameras. The US intelligence would have that information as soon as it happened. No, they must have used a private airfield. Why not the Paraguayan landing strip? Could have been the time it touched down. There are no lights in the farmer's field. Could have had more to do with the amount of rain we've been getting. The wheels on a dirt runway might be a safety hazard that the pilot wasn't willing to risk. They may have needed a paved surface." Ezra flipped his pen into the air and caught it up again, then pointed it to Jack. "That's my guess."

Jack nodded. That all made perfect sense.

Rivka redirected the conversation. "Adam?"

"If you follow the road systems out away from the small airport, you see that this one runs along, indeed makes a boundary for this section of the forest. Early this morning, Ruth and I took scooters along that piece of real estate. Ruth?"

"Adam and I found two trails directly off the main road that are accessible by four-wheelers that would line up with the open space found with aerial intelligence. Adam, would you bring up the photos we took?"

"Roger that." There was a shift on the screen.

"The first one only went about fifty meters in and looked like it was used for dumping garbage. But the second — See? Here are the tire track ruts for ATVs and trailers on this one, like the first. Next photo, please. This is the path we followed back about four klicks. As you can see, the path seems well maintained, free of roots and debris, with no overhanging limbs to hit people in the faces as they move through on open motorized vehicles. Definitely human activity, not animal trails. That human activity is recent, too. Some areas appear freshly trimmed. This route could work for the cell's supply route. We didn't follow the path to the end," Ruth concluded.

Adam nodded. "And while we can't see it on satellite imaging because of tree cover, I can show you this." The image then changed to a dark photo with an L shape of squares lit up with varying shades of orange to yellow. "These images were taken by the drone we sent in for thermal images of the area."

"When was this?" Rivka asked.

"Around zero three hundred when we had a brief clearing from the rain. This time of night also worked because it allowed the forest to cool so we could see the demarcations. These images suggest buildings of some kind. Perhaps tents in that each give off a different heat signature," Ruth said.

Adam put his laser beam on the image. "In this scenario, if we believe this is the cell, then the tents of interest are this one, second from the northeast corner, and this one, the front of the short line of the L, in the southwest of the configuration. The heat signatures on these squares are much cooler than the others, suggesting that they are not housing as many bodies. From my experience, I would say the tents each have a centralized propane tent heater. I would guess that one distanced from the others might be that of the commander. And the POIs are sandwiched between two tents of soldiers." Adam pointed at the yellow square with no orange or red glow.

Jack had been looking at imagery like this for years, and he was coming to the same conclusions as Adam was.

"This all seems reasonable." Rivka paused. "I believe that when Al Amman was killed yesterday, that started a timer. I'm afraid if they think we have located them, they might dispose of the children as they flee. The boys will slow them down and make their movements more noticeable." Rivka lifted her brow and scanned the faces of her unit members. "The window on finding and destroying the cell is slamming shut as we sit here and discuss. We need to put a mission together, suit up, and head in. We'll reconnoiter and make a plan in the field. Time is of the essence. If this is the cell, we'll go in once they've settled for the night."

Rivka turned her gaze on Jack. "You may want to sit back and handle comms with Ruby," she said.

Jack had noted all the directional landmarks and coordinates. If Rivka thought he was going to sit back and let someone else go forward, especially knowing that Suz wasn't on their radar, she had lost her mind.

"With all due respect, ma'am, I'm taking point on this mission."

BUT THAT WASN'T how it had panned out. Not by a long shot. Saturday afternoon, the Mossad unit and Jack had turned out in their operational jungle camouflage raring to go, but Rivka ordered them to stand down. The skies opened, making the chance of friendly fire too great a risk. In fact, it would be all but impossible in this deluge to get their sights on a target or access their progress. She decided they'd use the extra time to gather more intelligence. She wanted verification that this was the cell they were looking for and not a bunch of drug squatters. She wasn't risking Mossad lives over an opioid raid.

Intellectually and professionally, Jack agreed with the move. Emotionally, he wasn't on board at all. Rivka knew that, and even though Jack had volunteered to go on the intelligence run, Rivka declined. She was right. If he saw Suz in there with the jihadists, Jack wasn't sure that his professionalism would win out over his desperation to get to her. Seeing her and walking away just wasn't part of his DNA.

So, it was Adam and his Beta Team who had been sitting under the torrents, counting heads, and making maps. Sunday night, they had come in from the field, muddy and exhausted, to share their intel. The camp was twenty-two klicks back in the forest. They hadn't seen any children. They had seen one person with a poncho that was unlike the others, moving freely during prayers. The group of thirty-seven men was all in Middle Eastern garb with beards, or attempts at beards. Some of them appeared to be barely out of pubescents. The camp was absolutely designed for cell training. At one point, Adam was able to run a wire into the eating tent. From this, they discovered that while the rains pelted down, the men were learning the various combinations that could be used to make successful suicide vests. The Beta Team recorded a lecture from the leader about the glory of being a martyr. The men in the camp each took a turn pledging their lives to the cause.

"The commander lives in the tent we believed he did from the aerial pictures, and the poncho is in the tent we believe houses the POIs. Again, though, the boys were not spotted."

"Did you position behind that tent?" Ezra asked.

"We did, but there was a distance. The four-wheeler path goes all the way to the end of the fence line, so another fifteen meters. With rain and distance, visual was difficult during the day. The last movements of the day that we saw from the poncho were during the last prayer. We were unable to run a wire that picked up voices from that tent. We did get an unusual heat signature when the poncho went into the latrines. If it's Molloy, she might have had the boys under the poncho with her. That or the children just aren't there."

"The poncho was only visible during prayers?" Rivka asked.

"Affirmative."

"Well, our first objective is to take out the cell. Which we will do. As planned, we will take the commander. *Alive,* this time." Rivka looked around the room, her eyes seeking out and making contact with each of them to make her point. "Perhaps he has more to tell us. I'm sure those up the chain of command will want to find out who is sponsoring the cell and what their objectives are. We need to demolish the camp so others can't move back in. And, of course, if we can free any hostages and bring them back to their homes, all the better. Let's get to work. We need a plan."

26

Suz

THIRD PRAYER OF THE DAY, MONDAY, FEBRUARY 21

Jihadist Training Camp, Refugio Tatí Yupí, Paraguay

THE CALL to prayer strummed a swath of reverberations across the air. Suz had been waiting just inside of the tent flap. There was a bustling about as the men hurried to the food tent. That is where they'd been gathering for the last few days instead of out in the open. The rain pelted down on the camp with a violence that exhausted Suz.

They had been offered little beyond hard-boiled eggs and sometimes some crackers or olives at each meal. Suz thought that resupplying was probably impossible in the weather. She wondered how meager their stores were and if rations would be cut any further.

With each prayer cycle, Suz had been making her way around the camp. Her feet would sink down into the soil like stepping on a sponge. Her footsteps instantly filled with water as she stepped forward, then their shape was abraded away by the vigor of the drops. Her movements were hidden from view by the curtain of gray. The drops pelted down so hard that she had taken to stuffing her shemagh balled up under the poncho hood to protect the top of her head with its cushioning. The visibility was so low that Suz was a little afraid of getting disoriented as she learned what there was to learn. There were twelve tents, for example.

When someone came in the main gate, if they looked to the left, they'd find the shower tent, then the latrine tent, and then the fence. If you turned right, there were seven tents. Each tent, except for the one that housed her and the boys, had cots. Each cot had a small trunk at the end. Each trunk held some basic supplies that the individual soldier owned. No weapons. The men always kept their weapons strapped to them. The tent she and the boys were staying in had no cots and no trunks, and the other tents looked overly crowded; this told Suz that men had been relocated to free their tent up.

Suz and the boys' tent was second from the last. This told her something too. What it was telling her was just on the outside of her thought process for a long time. For many hours, the boys sat in their tent with pieces of cord that Suz had cut for them. They had the survival book from her backpack open and were practicing knots. Suz was staring at the roof, willing her angels to come and whisper in her ear the thing that flitted ephemerally just out of clear view. But she got nowhere.

On her tour of the compound, Suz found that on the left side of the fence entrance, just in front of the shower tent, was the tent for feeding everyone, and in front of that was a tent that housed some 4-wheeler trailers but no ATVs. This is how the boys said they got in. Suz knew there must be a sizeable pathway, and that path had to take her to a road, and that road would have to take them to a house, and that house might provide them with safety. *Might*. That was her escape route right now.

She figured that they had brought her in through the forest so she would feel incapable of exiting successfully, so she wouldn't even try. Did they think that she wouldn't question the boys?

Well, the boys were here days before she was, so no one probably thought it all the way through.

If they were trying to intimidate her, take away all hope she could escape and survive to get to safety, they couldn't have done a better job. The walk with the refuge guide explaining that the waters were full of alligators and piranha, the trees full of killer snakes, that panthers and wild boar ran prolifically had kept everyone in a tight line behind their *Refugio* guide. Then there was the jihadist who marched her through the dense trees for hours on end. Completely daunting. Even knowing there was a path, it felt daunting.

Beside the garage tent was a tent that was the same size as the other sleeping tents; it housed the commander. It held a single cot but also had a desk and chair and boxes of supplies. Ammunition and the like. She couldn't find any extra weapons. And yes, she looked. And yes, she was now willing to use whatever she could lay her hands on. *Maybe*.

This wasn't civilization. These people weren't civilized. They weren't even animals. Suz had never experienced anything like this before. Couldn't categorize these beings. They weren't humankind in that she didn't experience any "kind" from them at all. Tolerance from their commander was as far as she could stretch. It didn't seem he was tolerant from goodness, though, but from practicality. Suz and the boys being here served someone's purpose. They were collateral, and that was it. Her world view had imploded.

The anger and sheer hatred that the soldiers exuded toward her and the children were palpable. Suz hid the children in the tent – wouldn't let them out of her sight. Though, being in her sight did zero to keep them safe. She had no authority here. She was hated even more than the children were. She was an American *and* a woman.

The children worried her. Suz couldn't get them dry. The feathers in the sleeping bag were sodden and ineffectual from the humidity, and while the days were still hot to the point where steam rose from the forest floor, the nights were cold by comparison. Wet and cold. Her meal replacement bars were growing fewer each day. The children would die here, she was sure if she didn't do something soon. She would die. . . Things were coming to a head. But she had a plan – sort of.

Finally! In the middle of the night, Saturday, her eyes had sprung open to the ubiquitous sound of falling rain. She knew why they weren't put in the corner tent. There were only twelve tents and no buildings. That meant that this camp had not been built to house prisoners. The commander had all but told her that when she was figuring out the latrine issue. "No animal. Fence," he'd said. The fence was there to protect the men from the animals. It was not constructed to keep people secured within. They needed to keep her away from the fence because it was vulnerable.

That morning when the chants called the men to their pre-dawn prayer, Suz had investigated the fence construction.

The shower was built where the ground sloped down, and the water from the showers ran away from the camp. There was no escape route through a ditch the way she had hoped.

The chain link fencing, though, that might work. The fencing was stretched tight, and she couldn't kick it to make it bend. That only served to hurt her foot even if heavily booted. She danced around, trying not to cuss.

At the corner post, hidden by the latrine, Suz found that the fence was held in place with fittings that bolted together. The bolts were rusted, but if she could get the bottom one loose, she could bend the fence out of the way, and they could slip out. Since no one ever checked on them, and she was only seen picking up their dinner and taking it back to their tent, she thought they could leave at the sunset prayer, after dinner. They'd still have a little light from the day. And they wouldn't be missed until breakfast, and maybe not even then. They'd have a good head start, and if the day progressed, and she and the boys were still in the forest, they could hide in the trees and wait until it was clear and hike some more.

It had to be soon, though. She was running out of food. The boiled eggs didn't have many calories.

Back at the tent, Suz had looked in the survival book for all the different ways to get a bolt free. It said, Coke, and banging, and cutting, WD40, and listed several other things to try. None of them would work in these circumstances. She had a small device that, ironically enough, was called a zombie card –it was the same size as a credit card and had little gadgets cut into the metal. One was for bolts. At the next call to prayer, Suz tried it out and got nowhere. She applied some Vaseline that had come out of her medicine cabinet and got nowhere. Back in her tent, she reviewed the list again, and this time she landed on heat.

She had a few hand warmer packets left. She thought they wouldn't get hot enough to help. And besides, the three of them were relying on that heat to help make it through the night. Thank God, the boys seemed to have pulled through their illnesses. Thank God, she seemed to have dodged the bullet and not become sick while snuggling the boys into her at night — for mutual emotional comfort as well as warmth. She examined the propane line on her tent heater and decided that that wasn't something she had the expertise to deal with – Jack would know. But she, for sure, was not Jack.

She took those thoughts into her dreams. *Jack, what would you do?* What? He'd be clever. He'd think outside the box. So Suz tried that. She thought. And thought.

Another day of rain. This was Monday. She knew because she had been marking the days in the back of the survival book. The jihadists had started chanting. The men had gathered. Suz went to use the latrine. Sitting there, examining the toilet paper, a spider jumped out at her. The sheer size of the thing made Suz drop the roll. The paper spiraled out across the latrine floor, stopping when it hit the lidded plastic barrel that held the lime bag. She remembered what the commander had told her about water and lime, her first day. That combination could burn skin. That was pretty hot. Boiling hot? Effectively hot? She wasn't sure. Hot for a brief time? Hot for a long time? She wasn't sure.

Suz thought about her go-to jar-opening technique when Jack wasn't handy – how she'd stick the spaghetti sauce bottle under running hot water at the sink. That and a good smack on the counter usually did the job. Suz ran back to her tent and found the folded piece of aluminum foil and tore off a length. She grabbed the zombie wrench and ran back to the latrine. She made a packet of lime and a drizzle of water and folded it shut. She wrapped it around the nut. It grew hot – really hot -untouchably hot. She waited as long as she dared. Carefully, she flicked the metal packet to the ground and tried the nut. It turned a quarter turn. That was it. She couldn't get it to budge any more. But Suz was elated. She swiped some Vaseline over the bolt, then tightened the nut back where it had been and ran back to her tent as she heard the last murmurings of prayer.

Each prayer cycle on Monday, Suz worked on that bolt. The first two prayer cycles of Tuesday, she did the same. After she climbed into the tent. She heard a call.

"Molloy. Here!"

Shit. Had they found her out? She quickly donned her poncho and went to the tent flap.

The guy outside held up three fingers. "You. Come."

The three of them?

She nodded and went back into the tent to help the boys to get their tennis shoes on. They'd be wet and muddy if they went out. Getting things dry was a little more possible now that the rain had become more sporadic, but still, was this necessary?

They emerged and went to the commander's tent. There he had the phone that Jones had given her.

"You." He pointed to Suz then to the corner.

"You." He pointed to the boys then his bed.

Suz moved to the corner. The boys sat on the bed. The man handed the boys an American newspaper from Sunday. Suz felt sure that a New York Times could be bought in a hotel, especially one that tried to attract US tourists, if not here in Paraguay, then just over the border in Brazil. The boys were made to hold it up.

The commander reached onto his desk and picked up a piece of paper and read, "Talk mama, say all good."

Suz's eye caught on an open Arabic-American dictionary sitting open on the desk.

The boys looked scared and sought her out.

"It's okay, guys. They're going to make a video, I guess, to let your parents know you're okay. He wants you to say something to your mom." She affected some semblance of a smile, hoping it would help them.

"Hi, mom, this is Ari. I'm okay. I haven't brushed my teeth

or anything. But I've tried to be good." Ari turned and looked at his brother.

Caleb was having a hard time. He sucked in his lip, and then it would stick back out in a pout. It took a few efforts before he pulled back his shoulders and said, "This is Caleb." He sniffed hard and wiped a tear from his eye with the back of his fist. "I want to come home now, okay?"

The commander turned off the video and looked at Suz. "Okay?" he asked. And she assumed that since he couldn't speak English, he was asking if the message that was going out was safe to deliver. For a moment, Suz thought of saying no and coaching the boys in how to get some information across to those who watched, but the thought was fleeting. She didn't know the distance this tape would travel, who would see it, and what the ramifications would be if they were caught trying a fast one.

"Okay," she said.

They walked back to their tent. Suz had a great unease settle across her shoulders. They were documenting the children's well-being. This wasn't good news. Strike Force had gone after their share of tiger kidnapping victims, and Suz knew the drill. Time was short – very short, sometimes only an hour. There was a very small window for the team to find the victims, and if they did, the next step was what they called a "snatch and grab" – the team just busted in and ran the heck out—no time for finesse.

Suz remembered this one story about a woman who had a bomb collar put around her neck and was seated on a chair. She had to hold a phone in her hand to Skype with the guys who were running the crime. They watched her from afar. If she moved, they said, they'd set off the bomb remotely. So, she sat very still. Meanwhile, the bank manager was being shown a Skype of his wife, who was sitting as still as she could, the bomb around her neck, tears streaming down her face, trembling and muttering over and over, "please."

The criminal explained the situation and that he needed money loaded into his car. The manager locked the front door, told everyone to go into the safety deposit box room, and locked them in. All the money in the bank was loaded into the van waiting at the back door. Off-site security saw what was going on and sent the cops. By the time SWAT arrived, the criminals were long gone. As soon as the criminals had what they wanted, they exploded the woman. There was never an instance that Jack knew of that the victims in a tiger kidnapping got to live. They were called tiger kidnappings because they were predatory and lethal. Once the tiger pounced, you were dead.

The camp commander was collecting verification that the children were alive. Someone somewhere was about to get a directive. And, just like the bank manager, this someone was going to do what they were told. Once they did it, the children would no longer be helpful. *She* would no longer be helpful. Suz wasn't willing to let her mind take that path any farther than it had already gone.

* * *

THE LATE AFTERNOON prayer had been called. The men were in the tent – the ground still too wet for kneeling outside – and Suz stood behind the latrine with her hand clapped over her mouth, trying not to scream. The nut had come free. It was free. They were free! Her feet did a happy dance. It took her a minute to tamp down the elation. She put the nut and bolt between her lips, for safety, then pushed the bottom of the fence. She wiggled out of the camp; she wiggled back into the camp. She put the bolt back in place, rubbing it with Vaseline, replaced the nut, then she made her way back to the tent.

Suz went through the backpack to find the things that she would need handy – light sticks, a compass, and the razor that she had fashioned into what she would call a shank, for lack of a better word. She made sure the camel bladder was full. She decided that she could leave the weight of the blow-up mattress and the sleeping bag, but they might need the tarp, especially if they got caught in another deluge.

As a second thought, Suz sliced the tarp in half. One half would be their ground cover and shelter if need be; with the other half, Suz made the boys ponchos of their own. The reflective side would help them stay warm as they walked. If they got overheated, they could just turn them inside out. She made a necklace for each of them with the chem-light sticks. If someone were coming after them on the trail, they could hide the lights underneath their arms. But they'd need something to keep them on track.

She picked up and thought through each piece in the backpack. She felt mildly more prepared for those decisions after reading through the survival guide. But not a hundred percent. She was over-thinking things. She needed to pare down the weight. She might end up having to carry the boys – one at a time to let them rest. But each thing might be *the* thing that could have kept them alive.

Jack, help me think. Please. Help me think. Guide my hands.

She decided she might need almost everything in there. The playing cards could stay. The Q-tips and Pepto-Bismol could stay. Yes, she might need the rest.

The boys watched her curiously, but she wasn't willing to

reveal the plan until they were standing in front of the fence. She made sure they were all clean, dry, and with moleskin preventively in place on their heels and the balls of their feet. For the first time since she had arrived, Suz opened two MREs. They were a lot of calories, and they'd need them. The boys shared a plate, and she ate the other.

Jack said they were fairly unpalatable, but right now, Suz thought they were a five-star meal.

The boys seemed uneasy, and Suz smiled to reassure them. She went to the food tent and brought back the hard-boiled eggs. If this was all the men were eating, they wouldn't have much stamina to chase after them. *They have the four-wheelers somewhere, and we don't.* Suz wasn't athletic by nature, and neither were the boys. . . All she could do was try.

They ate the eggs.

Suz staged their tent as if they were there tucked into their sleeping bag. She left the cards laying out. Suz wasn't completely sure that no one checked on them at night while she slept. In the dark, this charade might pass.

The sunset call to prayer sounded. She took the boys out the back of the tent, down the back of the row to the far corner of the camp. With shaking fingers, she undid the nut, pulled out the bolt, and put them in her lips. She pulled the fence in and pushed the backpack out of the hole. She signaled to the boys to be quiet. They scooted through the hole. She followed, searching the ground behind her for any telltale signs that they had been there. Seeing none, Suz put the fence back in place – bolt and all, pulled on the backpack, and with a little one's hand in each of hers. They fast-walked down the trail and out of sight.

27

Jack

18:00 Hours Tuesday, Feb. 22nd

Mossad Base, Ciudad Del Este, Paraguay

Ezra pulled up a satellite of the weather. It looked promising. According to computer trajectories for the next twenty-four hours, the heavy rains would be farther to the south and west, and they had a window of clear skies with intermittent drizzle.

Days had gone by, and Jack was chomping at the bit to get them operational.

Sunday. Monday. Now here it was Tuesday, and they were still sitting on their hands. There was nothing to be done, though it was making Jack nuts. The rain came down so hard for the last few days that visibility was measured in feet. Water ran down the streets like a riverbed. No one ventured out. It was a time to hunker down.

Jack had made his way back to Mac's during one of the rare

moments the rain let up a bit, to gather his MOLLE pack, and thank his friend for his help. Jack had been camped out in the corner of the Mossad operational base for the last few days on a cot that was a good six inches too short for his body size, using the time to nurse his knee.

When the time came, he needed to be in good condition.

Ezra had sewn him back together.

The antibiotics had kicked in. The ice packs had taken down the swelling. Resting seemed to be making the difference. The pain, though, man, it was whipping Jack's butt. He thought he'd probably prefer to take a bullet again rather than have another surgery on his knee.

Now, with the new weather maps green-lighting the mission, they were dressing in night gear. This was it. Jack could feel it in his bones. He was going to find Suz tonight or die trying.

28

Suz

SOMEWHERE BETWEEN MIDNIGHT AND DAWN, WEDNESDAY, February 23rd

The Forest, Refugio Tatí Yupí, Paraguay

THAT WAS IT. Suz had taken her last step. Each step of the way — from the time she had been at the hospital with Jack unconscious with post-surgical drugs, to the hide in the woods with the sixteen kids all giggling over Captain Jack stories, to coming home and Jones pushing through her door and her shouldering Jack's zombie pack — all she kept saying was this was it, she had pushed herself to the limit, she had nothing left. Each time, she had surprised herself and found courage hiding in her toes that she pulled up to her chin and powered on. This time was it, though, for sure.

The boys were walking in their sleep. With their fingers

curved into her pants loops and her arm wrapped around their shoulders, they had soldiered on, though their eyes had closed a long while ago. There was nothing to see, anyway, except for the orange glow from her chem-light stick. The night had descended quickly and completely after they left the view of the encampment.

She didn't know how long they had walked. The only reason she felt that they were headed out of and not farther into the forest was that this was the way the tire tracks had gone. There were none on the other side of the gate. She had no idea how far they had come or how far they had yet to go. But there was no going back. The decision had been made, and Suz felt it was the only one possible. It was the one that Jack would have made.

"Jack," Suz whispered. He was probably frantic or broken hearted. He was something. But the one thing he wasn't was here. Somewhere deep in her cells, she had believed that Jack would know she was in trouble, and nothing would stop him from finding her and helping her. But this was Tuesday. She'd been gone for a week. If he was coming, he'd be here, wouldn't he? He probably saw the start of her letter and the ring. Saw the plane tickets and the man's name. Thought that someone was supposed to care for her dogs and got hung up. . .decided she wasn't worth the effort.

Whew! That was a thought.

Jack might think that he was as equally done as she had been. They were done, and she wasn't worth coming after and confronting. She had been letting go of their relationship one finger at a time. She had known that no Jack in her life meant.. well, no Jack in her life. But somehow, that message didn't get to her cells, where she believed that no matter what, Jack would always be there for her in her time of need.

She cycled those thoughts again. And again.

Wow. I am such a hypocrite.

No one was coming. It was all on her. Everything that Suz knew and loved about Jack fought against the conclusions she just drew as she moved the children off the trail and behind a large rock that jutted up as big as a car. She sat the boys on a smaller stone.

Jack would come, no matter what. He would. *He just has no way to find me. That's the problem.*

"Sit here. I'm going to make a camp for us, and we're going to sleep." There was no response. The boys wrapped their arms around each other, holding their twin upright, their eyes still closed.

Suz ran some line from tree to tree in front of the rock as high up as she could reach. The tarp came down to the ground, and she used rocks along the edges to hold it outwards. Suz figured if the terrorists were out looking for them with night vision, the tarp and rock would help block their heat signatures. That's what the survival guide had said, anyway. She suspended the hammock. It was some kind of high-tech hanging tent system that she assumed would be considered hyper-cool by people who used this kind of thing. That it was a snap for her to get up and secure was the only thing that Suz really cared about. The guide had been adamant about staying off the ground. Suz couldn't agree more. The ground was a sponge, and it crawled with things that wriggled and squirmed as the foliage was consumed, digested, and biodegraded. She found the hot sack that Jack had included and put a hand warmer in the bottom.

She had the boys drink and pee, then helped them navigate into the bed. Suz couldn't figure out a way to fit in there with them without flipping the base over; she'd have to come up with something else for herself.

Suz sat on the smaller rock, poised to go through the backpack and make a plan to get some rest when she heard a mechanical noise from the path coming in from the direction they were headed out. She looked over at her handiwork; she thought the three of them were completely hidden from view. She pulled her pack behind the rock and checked the boys. They were sleeping with an intensity one wouldn't equate with rest. They were sleeping so hard, it looked like work, wrapped in each other's arms. Pulling the hood of her poncho up over her head, Suz picked up a stick and stood behind the boulder, watching.

Electric ATVs moved down the path. In the low lighting put out by their red headlamps, she couldn't see anything but black outlines. She counted heads; there were ten in all. That was all she could see. It didn't look like they were bringing in supplies – more food to bolster the hungry jihadists. She wondered who they were. Reinforcements for the terrorists? People who came to inspect their progress? People dispatched to do something to the children? Whoever they were, she was glad she wasn't in the camp anymore. Their automatic weapons poked into the air like something out of a dystopian battle scene.

Suz waited for a long time for more people to come in or to leave for an alarm to sound that they were missing from their tent, and a search was underway. The rain drizzled lightly down, and Suz was glad because eventually, it would obscure their footprints. Maybe. She hoped it worked that way. She wasn't sure what the terrorists would do to her if they found her. She knew it wouldn't be good – so she tried Jack's thought process – don't fight a battle you don't have to fight. Once again, she was smacked in the face with the fact that she was *not* Jack.

She moved around to sit with her back against the rock. Time passed, and Suz fell asleep, her head back, her mouth hung open. She startled awake and wiped the drool from her chin. That's when she heard the rata-tat-tat of machine-gun fire coming from the fort. Thoroughly confused, terrified beyond physical control, Suz crouched behind the outcropping and wept.

29

Jack

01:30 Hours, Wed., Feb. 23rd
The Forest, Refugio Tatí Yupí, Paraguay

The unit moved in a single, silent line at the edge of the pathway.

They each wore a communications system around their neck that allowed them to be heard by the movement of air over voice box. They didn't need to speak aloud.

The jungle could be tricky. Sometimes sound waves were muffled by the density of air and foliage. At times, noise carried for long distances, like it could over water.

The operators meant to limit the chances of arousing attention.

They intended to slip in and save the PCs –precious cargo— and grab their mark, get them out before they moved to the next step of their mission. Destroy the cell.

Their ATVs were hidden among the trees, two klicks out. They rounded the northern corner of the encampment, heading to the farthest side away from where the terrorists slept. They scanned for a night watch and found none. The jihadists probably felt complacent out here, hidden in the thick of the forest. The operators moved silently into the tree line as their breacher stepped forward, using the bolt cutters to open a pathway in. The sharp metallic snip echoed loud. As soon as the fencing was moved away, they held their position, watching for any movement coming from the tents through their night vision goggles. Nothing shifted or changed.

After ten minutes, Rivka pointed her open hand at Ezra and Adam and signaled them toward the commander's tent. She pointed to Jack and signaled him toward the tent they believed held Suz and possibly Suz and the boys. Low and slow the three edged through the opening. Keeping close to the fence line, they peeled off in their own directions.

Jack came up behind what they were calling "tent B" and used his KABAR to slice the tie downs to open the back flap. He stood for a moment taking in the scene. In the center of the tent a propane heater glowed red. That was the only heat source in the tent. His night vision didn't pick up the heat signatures of any human forms. He hauled himself over the edge of the platform and flipped up the blankets that covered humps, momentarily afraid that he'd find Suz's deceased body.

Rivka's voice played in his ear. "Alpha two, sitrep."

"Alpha two. Confirmation that Molloy was here. There is no one in this tent now."

"Alpha one, sitrep."

"Alpha one. We have mark secured. There are no other targets in this tent."

"Alpha one, hold tight. Alpha two, move to tent A and wait for the signal."

"Alpha two. Wilco."

The team moved quietly into place; each operator had one tent to disable except Adam; he'd take the whole south-western corner with the latrine, shower, and eating tent. All bullets were to point toward the western face to prevent accidental injuries.

"Males, not females or children," Rivka said. "Check-in."

"Alpha two. In position," Jack responded.

"Alpha three. In position." And so went the calls until everyone had done their check.

"On my count: three, two, one, move."

Jack burst through the tent opening, one step in, trained his gunfire on each of the jihadists. His bullets made popping sounds as they blew through his suppressor. He checked his work, did a headcount, and exited the tent.

"Alpha two. Complete."

As each unit member exited their tent, Rivka brought in a remote area lighting system. The terror commander was brought out and made to kneel in front of her. She spoke to him in Arabic. "We are looking for a woman and two boys."

The commander pointed at tent B.

Rivka looked at Jack, and Jack shook his head. She nodded at Ezra, who lifted the commander by the scruff of his neck and moved him to the tent.

"Here? Here is where you kept them?"

The commander nodded. "Yes, Molloy. Boys. Sleep." Everything about his face and body language screamed confusion.

"What were the names of the boys?"

He shook his head.

Adam showed up with the cell phone in his hand. He pushed

the camera file and showed the video of Ari and Caleb to Jack and Rivka.

“That’s them,” Jack said in English.

“And that’s the interior of the command tent,” Ezra said “The newspaper is from Sunday.”

“Ezra and Jack stay with me.” Over her comms, she called “Beta One, there was a thorough check of the latrine, the shower and dining tents? No sign of the hostages there?”

Adam responded, “Beta One. I have no one in my locations.”

“Copy. Let’s gather what intel we can. We’ll take it back to Base to examine.””

RIVKA CUPPED a hand around her mouth and hollered their names to see if Suz or the children would come out into the open. She shot a look at Jack, and he tried too, hoping Suz would know and trust his voice if somehow she were hiding somewhere within the camp.

Ruby came forward, “We checked the fencing. Ours is the only breach.”

While the rest of the unit finished up its task, Rivka worked on the commander, trying to gather where the precious cargo had gone. All he gave up was that he was supposed to send the video via satellite to the person who had requested it. Code name *The Bear*. The SAT phone had not worked in the weather. He was hoping to get it out today. It had to be out today.

Why?

He didn’t know. Or if he did know, he didn’t say.

“That’s it,” Rivka said into the comms in English. “Have we accounted for all thirty-seven in the cell?” Once that was affirmed, Rivka ordered the unit to exit. They would talk to the commander back on their own turf, where they could run his image through the computer system. Find out if he had any vulnerabilities they could exploit to gather more intelligence on the reason for their cell activity.

"Ma'am, I'm going to hang back," Jack said.

Rivka tipped her head to the side.

"Something happened to Molloy and the children. They didn't just vanish into thin air. The turd who was running this place seemed damned surprised that she wasn't in that tent. I need to stay here and see if I can't figure things out."

"I'm not going to leave support with you. You'll be parting ways with us."

"Understood."

"I can't leave you a vehicle, either. We need them to get everyone out."

"Understood."

"We'll be back during daylight if the weather holds. We need to pack the weapons and ammunition out of here—the bomb materials. We'll destroy the camp then. Depending on how things turn out, we can rally here."

"I appreciate that." To be sure, hiking that far to the road on his bum knee, and then finding a vehicle to requisition dressed the way he was and with an AK and MOLLE pack. . .Well, slipping onto the back of someone's ATV seemed the better route.

"Good luck to you. I'll leave the lighting and pick it up when we get back in." And with that, Rivka signaled the unit. The breacher clipped the heavy chain that laced through the front gate, and they trekked toward their ATVs, pushing their prisoner ahead of them.

Jack was in a camp with thirty-six newly dead bodies. The smell would quickly fill the forest and call the predators in. He shut the front gate without a lock. He wasn't sure how much good it would do. He'd seen it time and again when he was on maneuvers in Africa with the UN. That smell drove the beasts crazy. He needed to work fast.

HAVING ANGLED the lighting over to tent B, Jack did a thorough search. There was a small pile of wrappers from the meal replacement bars he had recently updated in Suz's zombie bag.

This was definitely her queen-sized sleeping bag and ground mat. She had definitely been here. Her bag had been, Jack corrected himself as Lynx came to mind. *Jack and Jill went up the hill to fetch a pail of water.* If Lynx's *knowing* was interpreted correctly, Suz should be here.

Even if it was just her body, he found.

Jack swallowed hard and dug into his conviction. He could feel Suz alive and thinking about him. That was what he was telling himself. It kept him sane.

He wondered if Lynx had any new intel. Any updates. That there had been a video made of the boys scared the hell out of him. Once the captors got what they wanted, there was no reason to keep the prisoners alive. The only flicker of hope he felt at that moment was Lynx's ominous *knowing.* He pulled out his phone and got nada. He hadn't expected to.

With his high-powered headlamp, Jack found Suz-sized boot prints where she jumped backward from the tent opening. Deeper than he would have expected, that meant she was carrying some weight. Perhaps her zombie bag.

It was interesting that she was allowed to keep it.

If she were the one staying in this tent, like the cell commander said, she definitely had the bag coming into camp. Perhaps she was allowed to keep it to supply herself and the boys.

He wasn't sure. That was odd.

But in the field, he'd seen plenty of odd things. Jack bent to examine the footprints. They twisted to the left, and two more sets of small footprints showed up in the muddy soil. Carefully, he followed along. The drizzle that had started as they stood in the tree line waiting to enter the compound had stopped. He could actually see a bit of the sky.

It was pre-dawn. Time for those of the Muslim faith to rise and pray.

He thought of all the devout Muslims he had met over his lifetime, and he was sad that the actions of the extremists, who used and manipulated the religion for their own goals, made life so difficult for so many really good people. He wasn't the least bit sad that this cell of would-be suicide bombers was history, he thought as he passed the silent tents.

The heaters were turned off now. There was no one to keep warm.

Where are you, Suz?

The tracks lead towards the latrine tent. He thought they would end there, and he was going to be out of luck.

Except they didn't.

At the far corner of the shower tent, Suz's feet had stopped, her prints side by side, weight on her toes. She had pushed off, leaving deep marks in the mud. The boys as well. At the front corner of the latrine tent, she had turned and leaned forward before turning back and walking on. She was checking to make sure she was alone with the boys.

He followed the tracks to the corner of the fencing where a wide puddle had formed. He checked to see if it was deep enough to show she had dug under, but it wasn't. As he rose, he found mud on the fence on either side of a fixing, where someone with short arms would have grabbed for balance. When he twisted the nut, it spun smoothly loose, despite the rust.

"Son of a gun," Jack whispered. "Suz dodged three dozen armed terrorists with two six-year-olds in tow."

He shined his light out of the fencing and could see scuffling at the edge of the puddle.

Jack backtracked, moving to the front entrance.

How long ago did she leave?

He pulled the opening wide and shut it again. If the Mossad unit was coming back in tomorrow, they'd appreciate it if they weren't fighting panthers and wild boar to gather up the munitions.

With a slow, steady pace, Jack followed the trail. *How far did you get, Suz?* You had to have left after they went to bed. We should have passed you on the trail.

A frisson of fear trickled like sweat down his spine.

Two kids in the forest?

He thought about how fast a predator could move and how little power even a trained soldier had against their attack. With his gun in hand, even he didn't have a huge chance against one of these beasts. On the way toward the camp, they hadn't seen any remains on the ground, but that didn't mean a thing. Jack forced his mind in a different direction. His head was on a swivel as he watched the forest and the tracks, slow and steady, he followed the trail. Until there was no more trail.

"Suz?" Jack stood on their last set of footprints that shifted into the tree line. "Suz?"

The sky was just starting to show color. The trees were still black. He faced his headlamp toward the tree line, then bent to examine their treads. Here, where the foliage was a thick carpet, the footsteps had to be found in the shift of flora instead of mud puddles. He took two steps in.

"Jack?" Suz's voice wobbled with incredulity. In a moment Suz had sprung into his arms and was sobbing hysterically against his chest. He leaned over and breathed in her scent — rain, dirt, and fear.

He wrapped her tight against him and let himself sob with her.

It was only now that he held her in his arms that he realized he had assumed she was dead. He had been mourning her. He hadn't believed he'd ever hold her again. Never believed he'd even get the closure of bringing her body home. She'd just be gone from his life, leaving an echoing void.

He kissed her hair. This was what a miracle felt like. This was the pinnacle of his life. This moment was every emotion that he had ever experienced balled tight and exploding outward.

He wrapped his palms around her cheeks and tilted her face up so he could inspect her. She tucked her chin and squinted her eyes against the bright LED in his headlamp.

"Sorry," he said. Flipping the light to dim. "Are you okay?"

Suz wasn't to the point she could speak yet.

Rescue was always a shock, and he had seen this particular look a few times. The brain stutters and tries to re-align itself with hope and relief when it had decided on consequences that looked very different.

"Just nod. Are the boys under the tarp?"

Suz nodded.

He bit at his middle finger of his tactical glove and pulled it off so he could touch her skin. He swept his thumb across her cheek, muddy from her tears, exposing a green and purple bruise beginning to fade.

"It's not safe out here. We need to go back to the camp."

Suz's eyelids stretched wide, and she took a step back. Not out of his arms – just enough that she could take in the information.

"I came in with a foreign unit working in the area. I jumped in on their mission because our intel pointed the search for you and the boys in this direction. The jihadists were eradicated, and the unit took the commander off to learn what he knows about life. The camp is clear."

"Of live people," Suz finally said.

"Yeah, you and the boys aren't going to want to visit the sleeping tents. We can go to the eating tent and wait. The unit plans to come back during the day. They'll have transport with them."

Suz snuggled back into Jack's arms, form-fitting her body to his as if she didn't want a molecule of air to come between them. "The boys are pooped out. I'm not sure they're going to make it back. We traveled far."

"You only made it a few miles, Suz. We're still a hell of a ways from civilization. Back is our best bet."

Suz nodded but didn't move.

"Come on, let's gather everything up. We'll help the boys. And you need some sleep." His voice was gruff. He bent over to kiss the top of her hair, she leaned her head up, and his lips caught on hers. It wasn't a passionate kiss. There was no tongue or desperately seeking lips. The kiss was soft and moved through his body. It was a kiss of exhaustion. And sadness. A kiss that tasted of a heartbreak that Jack didn't understand. A kiss that bruised his soul. And all Jack wanted at that moment was to get Suz safe and comfort her.

30

Suz

Breaking Dawn, Wednesday, February 23rd

The Forest, Refugio Tatí Yupí, Paraguay

"Walk through the fear." Jack had said with a chuckle as they heard snuffling along the trail.

SEALs feel fear. They just learned to walk through it.

She bet they didn't feel like she did. Their kind of fear surely felt different. They had skills, and she did not. Having a chance at coming out okay must feel different than feeling pretty darned sure that it was grace alone that kept her alive this far.

They were moving back to their prison, back to tents filled with dead bodies.

She put one foot in front of the other. That was all she tasked herself with. This was not the direction she had planned to head today.

Jack and his teams—all of them—planned, planned, planned, and practiced the plan until it was polished and seamless.

In. Out. Boom, done.

Except when it didn't work out that way. Every mission had a little bit of surprise.

She bet it surprised the heck out of him to find himself jumping off a building aiming for a car roof. She thought for a moment about how far off the ground three stories really was, how small a car roof would have measured from that distance, and how really lucky he had been to hit it dead center. Sure, he was trained to jump and hit a target. He had a better chance than most anyone else.

That was why he lived.

"Expect the unexpected," he said. Nothing was going the way Suz expected – or could even dream up in her wildest and hairiest dreams.

Jack was chatting with the boys. He had one sitting on each of his broad shoulders. Their hands held on to his backpack straps through their dangling legs. With his left hand, he held each of the kids' feet hanging in front of his chest – this allowed his right hand to hold his Sig. His head moved back and forth, scanning constantly.

Suz saw him favoring his right leg. But that was all she could see by way of fallout from his recent surgery.

Suz had missed the stream of Jack and the boys' conversation and tuned in when Ari said, "Maybe we could just make a raft and take it down to the river." They had just rounded the bend and were walking up to the gate.

"We walked all the way across the river when we go on the plane. It was really wide," Caleb said.

Ari kept speaking right over Caleb. "And when we get to the river, we can paddle to a town."

Jack set the boys down. His eyes moved over the area, taking everything in. He pushed open the front gate.

"We can't get near the water here, guys," Suz said as she maneuvered them into the encampment. "There are dangerous fish in the water called piranha. And there are alligators, too."

"Captain Jack can fight any old alligator. I'm not afraid of them. You?" Ari asked, searching out his brother's eyes over the top of Jack's head.

"Yeah, I'm afraid of them. I guess."

"You could fight an alligator, couldn't you, Captain Jack?" Ari asked as Suz reached up and took one boy then the other from Jack's shoulders.

"I never tried. I've eaten alligator, though. Have you ever done that? They cook them down in Louisiana. There are lots of alligators down there."

"*Ewww*." The boys sang out.

"What do they taste like?" Caleb asked.

Jack smiled. "Chicken." They walked into the eating tent, and Jack put his bag on the floor.

"Captain Jack has a best friend named Gator. Do you know how he got that name?" Suz asked.

"'Cause he swims like an alligator?" Ari guessed.

"'Cause he hunts alligators?"

Jack chuckled. "He wrestled an alligator, just one. But it was a big one. Bigger than Gator is for sure."

"Bigger than you even?" Caleb was wide-eyed at the idea.

"The alligator was bigger than me. It was about as big as if you stood on my shoulders and reached for the sky. It was a great big gator. What happened was, Gator was swimming in a swamp."

"You shouldn't do that. Swamps aren't good places to swim. He could swim in our pool with us, though."

"Shh Ari, I want to hear," Caleb scolded.

Jack moved to a bench and sat down. The boys had huddled in front of him. "Alligators are stealthy. They don't make any noise. This massive alligator snuck up behind Gator and grabbed him." Jack reached out and squeezed Caleb around the waist.

Caleb giggled.

"Gator knew he had to do something to get himself free, so he reached around the alligator and hugged him."

Both boys reached their scrawny arms around Jack and hugged.

"Tight. Tight. Tight. Tighter than that."

They scrunched their faces up and tried to squeeze Jack harder yet. Then Jack fell over onto the ground and closed his eyes. The boys looked at each other, astonished. Slowly they crawled up giant Jack. Ari reached out and lifted Jack's eyelid. Jack sat up with a roar and grabbed the boys to tickle them. They were laughing hysterically, and Suz's heart was warmed. She was so glad to see the boys looking like themselves, feeling happy and safe, even if they were in the middle of a tropical forest.

Suddenly, Jack froze.

"Redlight," he whispered. The boys instantly froze.

Something had caught Jack's attention. His eyes stared down at the ground, but Suz could almost feel the rings of his attention spreading wider and wider like a ripple of water after pitching in a stone. He flicked his wrist up and checked his watch at the same time as he pushed himself up.

"Come on, guys, we're going to take a little walk in the woods." He yanked the straps of his pack over his shoulders.

"But we just got here. I'm zonked. You?" Ari asked.

Caleb sat down on the bench. "I can't take another step."

Suz was on her feet, pulling the zombie pack in place. She

wasn't sure what was going on, but something had come to Jack's attention that wasn't right.

"Quick, quick, guys, we're going to need to run, okay?" He had pulled the boys up in his arms, not waiting for an okay. He was leaping over the single stair and dashing for the fence line just to their left. Now they were jogging along the perimeter. "We're headed to the far corner," Jack whisper-called back to Suz.

Suz wondered why they were taking this long route. Why didn't they just move across the open space? All too soon, she had her answer. The sound of ATV engines. As she ran, they came closer and closer. "Do you know who they are?"

"Don't think so – not willing to take the chance."

Suz had a stitch in her side that was a hot poker of pain, trying to double her over. She knew she was slowing Jack down, even though he had a full pack and both kids clinging to his sides. "Go, Jack, get the kids out of here. I'll catch up."

"Suz, I—"

"Just go!"

Jack's stride widened, and she watched his powerful muscles pumping hard. She did her best to stay up, but she was over a foot shorter than he was, and she didn't run ten miles a day with a heavy pack the way he did before breakfast. All she could do before breakfast was sit very still and wait for the coffee to take hold.

The ATV pulled up to the front gate. Jack had moved through what looked like an opening in the fencing and had the boys off in the tree line. She was out in plain view. She went down on all fours and started crawling. For the first time in her life, Suz was glad for her petite size. Dressed in jungle camo with a digital backpack, maybe if she was slow enough, she could get out of the hole before anyone saw her. She tucked her chin. How many times had she heard, "Slow is fast and fast is slow"? She knew from the Strike Force stories that sometimes these guys spent whole days moving into range. Creeping along at a snail's pace to get where they wanted, undetected.

It was an agonizing crawl. She heard the clang of chain at the gate and the call of confusion in a foreign language. She heard shouts and commands go up and the gate creaking wide. She refused to look at anything except for the open hole in front of her. She crawled forward. Slowly. Slowly. She had started to cry. Her arms shook with fear and fatigue. Suz tried to play a game. She thought of the Animal Kingdom reruns. Prey stalk their dinner slowly, so the gazelle never knew it was on the menu. She tried that on for size, *I am a panther, and that hole is my meal.* It felt silly and very unhelpful. Suz's hands sunk up to the wrists in mud, her knees went deeper. The wetness from the ground had seeped up her clothing, wicking up the cloth of her pants to her t-shirt, up her t-shirt, and into her bra. The light padding held the cold wetness against her breasts, sucking her core warmth from her body.

She heard the ATMs moving closer. Suz hoped they were just being brought into the encampment, and they weren't headed her way. Suz collapsed flat into the mud and held her breath. Now she heard shouts of anger and dismay coming from the tents. Jack said they were full of bodies.

How creepy was that?

She pulled her leg up and tried to push off, but it merely slipped back into place in the mud. She slowly rocked up to her knee and continued the crawl. She was up to the hole.

She heard Jack's low resonant voice. "Perfect. That was perfect. You're doing it right. Stay as low as you can, and keep moving."

While Suz didn't lift her head—she was hyper-aware that her

red curls stood out against the green like a neon sign—she lifted her gaze and scanned. She didn't see anyone.

"A little farther. Almost there."

He was right beside her, but Suz couldn't see him.

She pushed through the fence, and a green cloth flipped over her. She and Jack lay under his ghillie bush rag that made him look like a jungle Yeti.

"You okay?"

Suz shook her head.

"Let's get over to the boys."

Together they crawled into the tree line. Jack pulled back the camouflaging cloth and looked her over. He gave her a nod. He had taken in her tear-stained face, but this wasn't the time for cuddles. He rounded the massive tree and held his binoculars on the group. "Who are they, Jack?" she whispered in his ear.

"I don't know yet. But this might be a problem. They certainly aren't our friends who expected to give us a ride home. And they aren't Middle Eastern, not looking like Paraguayans either. They're too fair-skinned, and they're in civilian clothes. They've got AKs and sidearms."

"What are we going to do?" Suz scooted over a bit as Jack put his back to the tree.

"I'm going to move you and the boys to a safer distance, and then I'm going back to pick up what I can. We know that they made a video of the boys, but the commander couldn't get it out over the satellite. These guys might have come in to pick it up. Surprise. You and the kids are gone. The commander and recording are gone. The cell that was being funded by someone is dead. They're going to be pissed."

"The unit is coming back for us. If they're surprised…"

"Exactly."

"You have to warn them."

"I do." He nodded.

"How did you know that wasn't them to begin with?"

"We were using electric ATVs. Those ATVs we're hearing are gas-run and make more noise, which was to our favor. Also it's too soon to get back to the base, get cleaned up, fed, get some shut-eye, and rally."

The boys were sitting on roots wide-eyed and pale.

"You know, guys, how Captain Jack tells you all those great adventure stories?" Suz raised her brow and let them drop to show that she thought this was fun. "We are on one of the greatest adventures of your lives. You will tell this story to your grandchildren. We're going to take a walk to find a safe place to wait. I'm going to get some clean clothes on. And then Captain Jack is going to go and make sure our friends are safe and sound Good?"

The boys' coloring turned a healthy shade of excitement They were on an adventure. They were making stories to tell just like Captain Jack!

They moved silently through the forest. Jack tried to take Suz's pack, but it had become a safety blanket to her. Life-saving stuff was in that pack, and she wasn't about to part with any of it

She shoo-ed his hand away.

Besides, Suz could see his limp was getting worse. He was going to destroy his knee, then he'd be non-operational. Did she want that? Never. Nope, never. She wanted Jack's decisions to be made by Jack, not made for him by injury or anything else.

They came to a small outcropping of rocks. A spring bubbled up at the top, trickled over the stone and down into a shallow pool, then onward down the hill. On a large flat rock that was as tall as Jack's shoulder, he lifted the boys up. "Sit tight guys, Miss Molloy and I are going to walk over there and see if this is the best place to set up our day camp."

The boys nodded.

Jack took off his pack and slung it up with the boys and then did the same with hers. They walked toward the edge of the high area; a stretch of forested land was about twenty feet below. She stepped to the right, and Jack reached out his arm to stop her. "Careful, the rains have been heavy. You don't want to get too close to any ledges."

Just as she was about to agree, Jack slid down in front of her. It was the craziest thing. She was looking at his chest, then his neck, then his face, then the top of his hair. The ground around his feet seemed to disintegrate. And like an idiot, Suz leaned forward to visually follow his descent. The ground beneath her feet fell away. Gravity swept her downward. Without control, she was sucked down and spit out like one of those water slides at the amusement park, except with dirt and no splashdown. Jack was on a knee, his other foot braced below him as she slid past. He reached out and halted her descent.

She lay on her back, blinking. Earth rained down around and over her. Disoriented. Not understanding. She swiped at her eyes. Green filled her vision everywhere she looked. And then there was Jack's worried face over hers. "Suz, fuck, are you okay?"

"I think so." She said breathlessly.

"Lie still." His hands started at her head as he swiped and looked at his hands, swiped, and looked at his hands as he moved all over her body.

"What are you doing?"

"Looking for blood. Don't move."

Next, his hands started at her head and squeezed and palpated their way over her body. His eyes never left her face. "Does it hurt here? How about here?"

"How are you? Is your leg okay?" Suz asked in return.

Jack did a quick survey and found a tiny cut on his head swiping at the trickle of blood. He flopped on his back, his whole body shaking as he laughed silently.

Suz crawled over the top of him, her knee planted on either side of his hips, so she could look into his eyes. Was this a symptom of head trauma?

He hugged her to him and kissed her.

"Why are you laughing?" she asked into his neck.

"Jack and Gillian went up a hill to fetch a pail of water. Jack fell down and broke his crown. And Gillian came tumbling after."

"Cute." She pushed off his chest and stood up. Her eyes focused at the top of the ridge. "How the heck are we going to get back up there to the boys?"

31

Jack

07:20 Hours, Wed, Feb. 23rd

The Forest, Refugio Tatí Yupí, Paraguay

Suz and the boys were tucked safely in a hide. She had his Glock in her hand in case an animal got too curious. Jack was surprised that she had accepted it without protest, taken it without vomiting – not even a shake in her hands.

Jack had taken off at a jog to get eyes back on the camp. The day was advancing, and he was afraid for the Mossad unit. Through his binoculars, Jack saw a man with the bearing of leadership standing in the middle of the clearing with a SAT phone in his hand. The man hollered, “Yuri.” A man turned and jogged forward. The leader called out something, and Yuri about-faced and jogged to the commander’s tent, bringing back a notebook and pen.

The leader wrote something out, then checked his watch,

pointed toward the ATVs as he made his directive, and pulled th page from the notebook. Yuri saluted and folded the paper befor he put it in the side pocket of his pants. He pulled out his cel phone, nodded, and put it back in his pants. He moved towar the ATVs.

Jack took off running. Across the path from the camp, h made a sharp right and high powered his way through the trees crashing through the undergrowth. He had to intercept Yur before Yuri was able to get enough bars to call out.

Jack felt certain, that with a little luck, and his leg holdin out, he could transect the curve and get ahead of the guy. Hi knee burned, sending shock waves of pain through his whol body. Jack clenched his jaw and emitted a low-level growl.

He came to the tree line that was his only shot at getting thi guy without using a gun. Jack's nostrils flared as he sucked i oxygen and hissed it back between his teeth. He strained to hea the engine noise and got nothing. If he was too late, he'd need t jog out of here and try to warn the unit. Jack reached down an jerked his leg brace back into place. Twenty-two klicks woul feel like hell.

Jack flipped his pack onto the ground and pulled out a spoo of bank line. With a practiced hand, he drew the black cordag around the tree and ran across the path to affix it on the othe side. Coming around that curve, the guy would have no chanc of seeing the line in time to divert. It should hit the guy acros his shoulders.

Jack turned his ear toward a low rumbling. He pulled hi knife. Plan B was to throw himself onto the path behind the gu and get his blade between his ribs and into a lung. Shooting th guy was last on his list of intercepts. With the boys and Su hidden near the camp, and only his Glock in Suz's hands to sto the bad guys from recapturing them… It was like arming th enemy, he knew. Suz could never shoot anyone. But he had to leave her with something. And he wasn't willing to bring them to the men's attention by using a bullet to drop this guy off his ATV.

Jack stood in the shadow of a tree, his toes at the edge of the path, his knife in hand, perfectly still. As Yuri drove up, the cordage clothes-lined him. Yuri's body stayed in place as the ATV continued forward, dropping Yuri onto his back. The man was sucking wind, his eyes frantic.

Jack was on top of him in a second, pinning the man in place with his weight alone. The man couldn't breathe. His eyes stretched wide as he tried to flail. But Jack lifted his knife and planted it behind the man's clavicle, ending the fight. Jack patted the guy down, pulling out his wallet and ID, his phone, and, most importantly, the paper with the message. It was written in a language Jack didn't recognize, with lots of accent markings. He put it in a plastic bag in his pocket and zipped the pocket shut. Jack dragged the body back into the forest and moved to the ATV.

The forward momentum of the machine had slid the vehicle into the tree line and wedged it at an angle between two massive trunks. Jack's plans of riding the ATV to the road, making a call, and heading back into the hide were crushed.

Jack turned and jogged back to the camp to scope out the situation and devise his next moves.

Hidden behind a fallen log, Jack trained his binoculars on the x-rays. Using his thermal imaging, he had eight heat signatures.

Just on the off chance, Jack tapped his comms. "Zulu command this is Alpha two, radio check, over." Static greeted him. He wondered how close they'd have to be to get a radio signal. He checked his watch *Time flies when you're having fun.* The skies were still clear. He expected the unit in soon. He tried again, "Zulu command this is Alpha two, radio check, over." He'd keep trying.

Jack switched to his binoculars and trained them on the guy working behind Suz's tent. He bent and traced the outlines of four sets of footprints. He followed them to the corner of the fence line, and just as Jack had done, he bent and studied the puddle, twisted the nut, and stood with his gaze headed down the path. This man was a professional tracker. Jack needed to take these people out. As the guy jogged toward their leader, Jack put him in his crosshairs. His finger moved onto the trigger as he followed him with his sights. The guy stopped when the leader held up his hand. Through the rifle scope, Jack could see that the leader had made a connection with the SAT phone and was talking animatedly into the line. Jack held off. He didn't want the person on the other end to hear any gunfire and send more people in.

Minutes passed very slowly as the guy talked.

"Zulu command this is Alpha two, radio check, over."

"Zulu command, readable, what's your sitrep?"

"Stand by for a salute report. There are eight x-rays patrolling the camp. Caucasian. Civilian clothing. Arrival zero six forty hours. Heavily armed — AK-47s and sidearms. They sent a messenger out. He was neutralized. Intel gathered. I have eyes on the camp. They have a SAT link up and are in communication. All three POIs were located and shelved in a safe location to the north-west of camp."

"Solid copy. Alpha three picked up Serbian communications. A unit is headed in at the top of the pathway. We are three klicks from your location. Standby."

"Wilco." Jack switched his rifle sight for his field glasses and followed the activity. The tracker was out the front gate. He moved slowly down the trail, stopping every few steps to closely examine the pathway. He must have picked up the small boot prints from Suz and two sets of small tennis shoes, being tracked by his swim-fin-sized boot tracks. The tracks heading out of the forest looked differently than the dainty booted feet next to Jack's heading back without the little feet, two people instead of four. The militant stood and scratched his head. He looked back at the camp. He looked up the trail. He radioed in his findings.

Keep going. Keep going, Jack willed the militant on. This guy moved like a special forces operator. Trained. Confident. He knew exactly what he was doing. He'd easily follow the tracks at the camp to where Suz and the boys hid. Jack needed to take this guy out of the picture and keep Suz and the kids safe. The farther the operator got from the camp and backup, the better. Jack was on his feet, but his knee refused to hold his weight. Jack crashed into a tree. "Bite me," he hissed, reaching down and, through the stiff cloth of his BDUs, he snapped the lock on his brace so that his leg couldn't bend. He began his step-hop with as much dexterity and silence as he could muster through the heavy growth toward the tracker, now rounding out of sight.

"Alpha two, this is Zulu command. We're on foot, moving toward your location."

"Alpha two. moving, eyes on an X-ray tracker, heading up the path in your direction."

"Zulu command. Do not engage with firearms."

"Copy that." No, he'd have to take this guy out hand to hand. Jack took nothing for granted. This guy was big, but Jack would have the element of surprise. Jack kept pace with the militant, waiting for him to crouch and observe a print when his thoughts would be elsewhere. Jack knew the size and weight behind his boot print made for easy tracking in the wet loam. This guy didn't need to bend and think. The heat of the day rose with the sun, Jack perspired heavily under his battle fatigues and pack.

Sweat dribbled down from under his helmet, stinging his eye with salt.

The militant crouched in the shadow to make a low profile Stilled. His focus was down the path that was straight and down hill at this point, giving him a long view of what was ahead. He swung his rifle into position against his cheek and peered through the scope.

"Zulu command, this is Alpha two, you've got attention." Jack moved air over his tongue and lips, knowing that the tech-nology would fill in his words with sounds for the unit's ears.

"Copy. All units take cover."

Jack saw the militant reposition, dropping a knee to the ground, and moving his finger from the guard to the trigger.

He had a lock on someone.

Jack flung himself out from behind the tree and landed on the tracker, trapping the rifle under the tango so he couldn't fire. The man quickly twisted, yanking a knife from his leg holster.

He and Jack grappled, rolling and snorting over the ground into the trees.

Fists impacted muscles with dull thuds and grunts.

The guy was on top of Jack and had Jack's braced leg in a lock. The pain was excruciating. As the guy's knife swung toward his eye, Jack twisted the militant's wrist, snapping it.

The knife floated somewhere into the composting vegetation

As the man cried out, Jack reached up to grip the guy's neck and squeezed until the sound was silenced.

The militant was a machine. He kept coming after Jack. He had found a rock and was slamming it against Jack's helmet hitting into Jack with heavy thuds.

Jack's hands squeezed down on the man's neck.

The militant's last swing shoved the helmet off Jack's head the rock making contact with a stinging blow. The militant' weight fell onto Jack. Jack rolled the man's unconscious body off of him to the side. He lifted the guy's torso, and standing behind the unconscious man, twisted his chin and shoulders in opposition, cracking his cervical spine, and killing him instantly.

Jack gasped into his comms, "Alpha two, the threat has been neutralized."

"Zulu command, copy that. We're moving. The militant unit just passed us on ATVs. We counted fifteen heads, over."

. . .

"Alpha two, this is Zulu command. Do you copy?"

. . .

"Alpha two, this is . . ."

The ringing in Jack's head drowned out his ability to form words. He staggered forward a single step. He fell over a downed log. Rising onto his good knee, his bad leg stretched behind him, he moved his head in a slow circuit.

The greens of the forest kaleidoscoped before him.

Jack tried to lift himself to his feet and fell. He pulled off a glove and felt his head where the rock had crushed down on him.

The flesh was swelling.

Blood poured from his wound, down his collar, saturating his shirt.

His fingertips traced the opening, where Jack could feel bone.

Jack pulled his shemagh from his pack strap and wrapped it tight around the gash. At least he could keep the blood out of his eyes. He felt around blindly for his helmet and got it back on his head. Years of night operations allowed him to work without a visual field.

He leaned over and puked.

Wiping the last of the spittle from his lips with the back of his arm, he tried to formulate a plan. If he lay here, he'd be panther food. If he crawled to the path, the insurgents would find him. If he called in a unit member, they'd be one down for what came next. They were already outnumbered two to one. Jack was on his hands and a knee panting; his left leg stretched out at an angle.

If Zulu unit shot into the camp with AKs, the high-powered rounds would fly toward Suz and the boys. He had to get to Suz and the boys *now* and get them moved. He pushed to standing. He took a single, blinded step and was down again.

"Bite me."

Flat out on the carpet of leaves, Jack thought, *Jack fell down and broke his crown. . .*

Lynx had been crying when she told him that. She didn't say it out loud, but Suz would come tumbling after.

No fucking way he'd let that happen. No *fucking* way.

Jack pushed his palms into the ground, lifting his torso. The world spun to black.

32

Suz

MID-MORNING, WEDNESDAY, FEBRUARY 23RD

The Forest, Refugio Tatí Yupí, Paraguay

THE BOYS WERE LYING with their heads in her lap as the heat filtered through the loose weave of Jack's camouflage bush rag.

They were well hidden from sight.

After Jack left to help his unit, Suz had made the boys sit with their backs to the rock. She had stripped naked, her clothes right down to her bra and panties, were caked and heavy with mud. These clothes would never be wearable again. She washed herself clean in the cool spring water, then pulled out a different set of BDUs. Jack had packed her an array. This time she chose the digital print like Jack had on.

As they had hiked back to the camp, Suz asked him why he wasn't dressed in black, like she'd seen on TV. Jack had explained that black was all about fear – the shock and awe that would shut down a fight. They used black when they wanted to capture someone and take them into custody. People knew that when a unit, dressed in black with balaclavas hiding their identities, burst through their door, they had two choices – lie on the ground face down or die.

That had not been their purpose when they went to the camp. Their purpose was to sneak in and pull out Suz and the boys, then take care of the cell. Suz hadn't pushed him on what "take care of" meant. Though it looked like the boys were sleeping on Jack's shoulders as he carried them along, she couldn't be sure. She needed to keep the conversation mostly G rated.

"When you're out in nature, the trees and leaves don't lose their color at night," Jack explained. "There's just no light to see them with. So, it's not necessary to dress in black. As a matter of fact, if a light shined on you, and you were in black against green, you'd stick out like a sore thumb. On covert missions, the idea is to confuse the eye so you could stay operational."

Staying operational being a euphemism for not dead. He said their BDUs were chemically treated to help protect them from thermal-imaging and the digital pattern helped to keep them hidden from night vision. High-tech. He had grinned. "Yours too. You only have the newest highest tech equipment."

"Awesome," she had replied. It was a filler word – something to stick in the hole of sudden silence. She was thinking through their situation. "I messed up," she said after a while.

"How's that?"

"If we were in the tent, you would have pulled us out. Put us on an ATV and powered us out of here while your friends did what was necessary."

He was silent.

"Instead, I walked the kids into the forest and made this situation that much worse."

"You had no idea we were coming. You did exactly what I would have done. I'm very proud of you."

He was very proud of her. That thought didn't bring a smile to her lips. Her thoughts were whirring since this whole misadventure started way back when he was recovering in the hospital. The rock-solid ground she thought she stood on had a sudden fissure and shook with the aftershocks that kept her off balance. She wondered—as she stood beside the spring, pulling on her fresh panties—when she'd be able to draw some conclusions and understand her new normal. When she might feel confident about how she felt about the world around her. And Jack.

She pulled the straps of the bra onto her arms. Jack had packed these too. Funny how she had aggressively survivalist outerwear, but the underwear he chose was all lace with silky ribbons. She hooked the strap in place behind her back and pulled on the long sleeve digital print shirt, though it was hot as hades that day.

Dressed and ready for what came next, she had the boys eat and drink then had sung to them, trying to cajole them into a nap during the greatest heat. Now that they had drifted off, she fanned them as they slept, their cheeks bright pink. She was falling asleep, too.

Suddenly, rifle fire erupted from the camp. A piece of metal hit the rock beside her and ricocheted away. She flung herself over the boys as another followed.

Suz pulled the cloth from over their heads and pushed the boys onto the ground. She flipped over to her stomach. "Crawl," she whisper-commanded in her most authoritative teacher's voice. The boys crawled along beside her. She got them to the lip of land that had fallen away with Jack's and her weight. Down would be under the trajectory of the bullets, she reasoned. She had to get them down. She reached each of them over the lip and had them balanced on a tree limb that acted like a ledge. "Stay there."

Suz scooted back to their camp, crab crawling on her belly the way she'd seen it done in the movies. She wasn't nearly coordinated enough to make her body move that way. But the hell she was going to pick her stomach up off the ground. She grabbed their equipment, shoved it into the zombie bag. If she had to survive with the boys in the forest, she couldn't do it without their supplies.

The gunfire stopped. *Jack? What's happening?* Crouching behind one of the rocks, Suz picked up Jack's Glock from where she had tossed it on the ground. She wondered where she should put it, so it was safe.

A man chuckled. "There you are." His English was thickly accented.

Her eyes jumped up from the rock that came just below her shoulder and focused on a man dressed in black, not ten feet in front of her. Black was for fear. Black meant hostages. She wouldn't allow him to take her and the boys as hostages.

He raised his hand with his gun aimed at her head. "Now where are those boys?"

Suz moved without intending to. She did what Jack said. "Don't even aim, just put it in front of you at chest height, look at the target's stomach, and pull the trigger."

BAM! Her hand jerked up.

She was so surprised by the sound and the light. So confused by what she had just done. . .

The man fell backward onto the ground.

Agh! I shot him! Oh, no. Oh, no. I should help him. She started to round the rock when more bullets hit the trees.

The boys. Her priority was the boys. *Jack!* Where was Jack?

Was he all right? Why wasn't he here? She flung her pack onto her back and ran in a crouch to the falloff.

She grabbed Ari's wrist. "You're going to climb down the hill, okay?"

He nodded apprehensively but was doing fine skooching down on his bottom, crab walking with his hands and feet.

"Okay, Caleb, do it just like Ari is."

Caleb immediately started sliding. The earth loosened up as he pawed at the slope. He plowed into his brother, who had been making his way carefully down. They were flipping. Rolling. Stopping.

The boys' little arms and legs were splayed out on the ground, and horror-filled Suz like a balloon, pushing out against her until she thought she would pop. She couldn't move. She was too afraid. Ari pushed to his knees and shook debris from his hair like a dog. Caleb did the same.

"I'm okay. You?" Ari asked.

Caleb grinned. "That was pretty awesome."

Before a "Thank God" could form in her mind, more gunfire sounded. Suz turned her head in the direction of the camp, looking for another man in black with his gun pointed at her.

Something scalding hot pierced through her skin, and she reflexively clapped a shocked hand over the hole in her neck.

An explosion shook the ground. Shook her from her one-handed hold. She fell backward from the precipice.

In her mind, she screamed, *"Jack!"*

33

Jack

12:50 Hours, Wed, Feb. 23rd

The Forest, Refugio Tatí Yupí, Paraguay

"Jack!"

His name echoed and reverberated, not in his ears, but through his mind, along his nerve pathways, into his skin, pricking his hair follicles with apprehension.

Suz.

Suz was in trouble.

She seemed far away. Too far.

He fought against darkness and finally slit open his eyes. His sight was fuzzy. His head pounding. He reached up and touched the sticky pool of coagulating blood on his makeshift bandage. He pieced the scene back together.

Rifle fire.

The Mossad unit must be fighting the militants.

He needed to get to that fight.

Suz. Suz had called his name. Needed him. He had to get to her and the boys first. She was his priority.

He flipped over onto his stomach, pushing himself off the forest floor, and walked his hands back to his legs. The lines of the tree trunks danced, and he scrubbed a hand over his eyes to clear his vision. He sipped some water from the hose on his shoulder strap; it helped. He checked his compass and took a straight-legged step. That wouldn't do. He couldn't get to her like that. He bent and unlatched the brace. Took another step, his leg held.

A third step sent him flailing drunkenly sideways into a tree. He gripped the rough bark and panted. He thought about someone touching Suz. Hurting Suz. Someone putting Suz into their crosshairs and pulling a trigger. Something shifted in him and he became a wild beast with a ferocity that he had never experienced before; he could tear a man limb from limb with his bare hands. When he was operational, he was cold, calculating and professional. Now, his anger boiled through him like an inferno. He felt bigger, stronger, more deadly than he had ever been. He locked his jaw as a growl rumbled past his teeth. Any pain and confusion were hidden under the red-hot lava of his fury. He set off, racing through the brush.

Within minutes, he was near her coordinates, and he could circle around to get to where Suz and the boys were hiding. He dropped down as a bullet zipped past his ear. He crawled on his stomach like a lizard, keeping low as the bullets whizzed over head. The rounds sent resounding cracks through the forest as they pierced the bark and split the trunks.

Jack didn't know how many Mossad were headed down the path this morning and wasn't sure what caliber of training they would encounter. If the militants were all like the tracker, Zulu unit was in trouble. The Mossad was made up of some of the best trained special forces operators in the world. This unit had real-world experience and surprise on their side. Jack wondered how much ammo they had brought with them, how prepared they had been since they were coming in on a clean-up mission. He and Strike Force were always prepared, took nothing for granted.

Surely, this group was the same.

He hadn't seen misstep one since working with them – even if the Al Amman capture turned out to be a clusterfuck.

The Zulu Unit must have decided to engage, knowing full well what they were getting themselves into – otherwise, they would have slipped seamlessly into the forest and disappeared.

Jack's eye caught on the form of a man, lying on his back, dressed in black. Jack crawled over to make sure it wasn't a Mossad operator in need of rescue and quickly saw this was an x-ray that had been killed. The militant had gotten damned close to Suz and the kids when he took a bullet. As Jack crawled away, he wondered if it was friendly-fire that took him down or one of the Mossad. Jack worried that the x-ray had had a buddy as they tracked Suz and the kids to this spot, and the buddy had been successful at re-trapping them. Where were they?

Jack low-crawled toward the precipice now, where he and Suz had fallen earlier. He found the children's footprints, turning at the edge.

Good girl, Suz. That's exactly what you should have done.

He pulled his binoculars from the front pouch on his pack and searched the ground at the bottom of the hill. He saw nothing. No humans. No animals. No signs of movement. Just a thickly overgrown forest floor that could hide most anything.

He inched around to lower himself over the side, and that's when he saw blackened drops on the brown leaves. Jack pulled up his sleeve and touched a leaf to his skin. Someone or some thing was bleeding enough that they were dripping blood.

Jack slid down the side of the hill. At the bottom, he cam into a crouch. He cupped his hand and softly whistled the come here signal he used to call Dick and Jane from their woodlan adventures back in D.C.

In return, he heard Suz's sad attempt at a whistle.

He had tried to teach her, but her whistles always came out a almost all air and almost no tune. He gave himself a moment t exhale. Fear had replaced the oxygen molecules in his blood stream. He sucked in the fresh air. He moved forward to wher two little heads and two sets of eyes peeked over a rock.

"Hey guys," he whispered, moving toward them.

Over his comms, the Mossad unit was speaking in Hebrew.

The boys were wide-eyed as they looked at his head. "I cu myself. Heads tend to bleed a lot. Nothing to worry about." H used the calm, assuring voice that worked best when he neede to keep his precious cargo calm and functional.

"Miss Molloy is bleeding, too," Ari said.

"Okay, I'm here now. I'll help her." Jack skated down th second incline and came around the rock to find Suz with bloody t-shirt pressed against her neck.

"Hey, sweetheart." He moved slowly forward, knowin people who were wounded reacted with protective reflexes, an she had his Glock in her hand.

"Hey," she whispered.

He moved up beside her and took the gun, sticking it in hi waistband. "You need to work on that whistle. It's still prett pathetic."

She gave him a weak smile.

"What happened here?" The Velcro on his first aid ba rasped open.

"You know, just sitting in my comfy chair reading a good book, drinking a cup of coffee, when all of a sudden. . ."

"Okay, I'm going to take a look."

Blood was still flowing from her wound. Suz wasn't putting enough pressure on it to help seal the gash. The bullet had grazed her throat. Centimeters from...Shit. "This is a QuikClot bandage. I'm going to make the bleeding stop."

"Yes, please."

The shooting had ceased.

The forest filled with an eerie quiet as if the animals were holding their collective breaths.

Jack wondered what that could mean for them and for the Mossad unit. His gaze scanned their location, looking for any imminent dangers, potential threats, and a quick exit plan if one were needed. His mind ticked these off as he looked back at Suz.

She wasn't looking at him as he worked. "Hey Suz, do you know what day it is today?"

"No," she said.

An explosion thundered out in the distance.

He pressed the hemostatic bandage into the gash. "Do you know where you are?"

Her eyes traveled around. "Trees."

"Try, Suz, where do you think you are?" If she was going into shock, she'd need to be medevacked out to save her life, and that just wasn't going to happen. He applied pressure, knowing he needed to press hard directly over her artery.

"I'm in the forest. In Paraguay. It's about a week since I was kidnapped to help the boys."

"And what are the boys' names?"

Her eyes went wild, and she sprang upright.

He pressed on her shoulder with his free hand. "*Shh, Shh Shh*. They're right here. They're okay."

She sank back against her pack. Her eyelashes fluttered closed.

"Their names, Suz?" Jack's voice ticked up into a command to pull her back from her faint. "What are the boys' names?"

"Ari and Caleb."

"Good girl. Just rest."

They were quiet for a few minutes while Jack kept the pressure on. He processed through their predicament.

He pressed his throat comms with his free hand. "Zulu, Zulu this is Alpha two, over."

"Alpha two, this is Zulu actual. Welcome back to the land of the living. What's your sitrep."

"I have precious cargo times three. Injuries sustained, over."

"Copy that. Present coordinates, over."

Jack checked his GPS unit and got nothing. "Negative. GPS non-functional, we are northeast of the camp."

"Copy that. Over."

Over would be good.

34

Jack

16:05 Hours, Wed., Feb. 23rd

Mossad Base, Ciudad Del Este, Paraguay

The SAT phone rang.

"Hello?"

"Jack? We're getting pings. You must have found some sunshine to charge things up – everyone okay?"

Jack stood feet wide, with his fist resting on his hip. "Copy that."

"How's your head?"

"Painful, thanks. You must have gotten a new *knowing* if you know I broke my crown."

"Yep – this one was a good one, though." Jack could hear a smile in her voice. "Jack sprat could eat no fat."

He rubbed his stomach. "Yeah, I could eat some fat about now. I'm starving for a big juicy steak on the grill."

"Gotch yah. I'll put some in your fridge."

"Remind me of how that rhyme goes…"

"Jack sprat could eat no fat; his wife could eat no lean. But betwixt the two of them, they licked the platter clean. You each used your talents to get the mission accomplished. That's how I'm interpreting this – it's not showing up in red lights this time. It almost feels like a mellow *knowing*. I don't get many of those."

Jack focused on the ground in front of him. "I'm not married."

"You're engaged," Lynx said. "Close enough."

Jack watched Suz coming out of the shower. Ruth had come up with a dress and sandals for her. She looked like his Suz. Her beautiful red curls swirled down her back and framed her face in a soft halo. She looked like an angel. And his mind caught on Lynx's last sentence. Was she still his? Things felt different between them now. He couldn't label it – and that made him feel uneasy. "Maybe," Jack said.

Lynx let that one slide, and Jack was grateful.

She jumped the conversation forward. "Iniquus is arranging for a private jet out of Brazil. I talked to Rivka. That was a hell of a battle you all walked away from. The people in custody are some big hitters, Simon Zoric, for sure. Black and Finley are heading down to help interrogate them. We'll have to work out with the Israelis getting at least Simon back into the US so they can press charges."

"When are Black and Finley due in?" Jack didn't want the CIA or FBI talking to Suz and the kids. Not yet. They needed to get home and start to feel safe again.

"You'll pass each other in the air. Rivka said they'll escort you over to the airport and get you tucked into the cabin safe and sound. Just in case."

"Not trusting my skill set?" Jack affected his best wounded voice.

"Dotting 'I's. Crossing 'T's. You know the drill."

"Copy that."

"We'll hand the boys over to the Levinski family at Iniquus Headquarters, out of public view. How are Caleb and Ari holding up through all this?"

"They have Suz." His voice was gruff. Suz didn't turn to him when he said her name. She was staring out the window. A bright white bandage was taped to her neck. He wanted more than anything for her to walk into his arms for her to press her ear to his heart. She just seemed so far away.

"'Nuff said. She's magic with her kids. Speaking of her kids, Command had the ISO take Dick and Jane to your apartment, and they said you can take Suz there – you two can rest up without the world peeking in your curtains. The ISO will maintain security on her house."

"That's a stretch for command, letting Suz come to the barracks."

"Yeah? Well, you know, maybe they're thinking of hiring her on. That's how I got my job, taking down a bad guy on an Iniquus mission. Suz is the reason you found the boys. Other than her? They would have vanished for good. We'd never have seen them again." She paused, and it gave Jack a moment to absorb that thought.

Jack nodded but didn't say anything. Lynx didn't usually need words to be spoken out loud. He wondered if she was picking up on this whole conversation swirling around in his head.

"Of course, with Hound News creating the falderal about the president and the CIA, we can't let anyone else know her

specific role. We're going to come up with a story. Dumm
down her participation."

"Roger. We just got cleaned up and are headed to Brazil t
the hospital. Suz and I need some stitches. Let me know whe
you have logistics on our exfil."

"How's the knee?"

"We're not talking about the knee."

35

Jack

20:20 Hours, Wed., Feb. 23rd
Foz do Iguaçu, Brazil

After the doctors over on the Brazilian side of the river had sewn up Suz's neck, Jack's head, and given the boys a thumbs up and lollipops, they were transported under heavy guard to their plane. The boys eyed the AKs resting across the operators' knees in their van and huddled up against Suz. Suz kissed them and petted their hair. She held them closely, pointed out other things to look at – a bird flying past a tree and cloud shapes.

Once they were sitting on the plane and strapped in tight, Suz and the boys fell asleep before the wheels left the ground. The sleep of the dead. Jack had seen it enough times to recognize it for the physical and mental restorative that a body in a long-term trauma required to start the healing process. Once the body feels safe, it shuts down and tries to recuperate. They only woke up when Jack shook them gently and called their names, the ex door already open.

Iniquus had a limo in the hangar along with three Panthe Force operators. It was a quick and silent ride back to Headqua ters. There, the scene had turned awkward as the boys grippe Suz's skirt and hid behind her, not wanting to leave her side to g to their parents' outstretched arms. The parents were emba rassed, and therefore angry and accusatory. Jack got Suz out c there ASAP.

A car drove them to the garage under the Iniquus men' barracks, and the driver carried their packs. Jack was back o crutches. The doctor insisted. There was no infection – bu plenty of damage. Suz was still silent, and her face was a mask slack and emotionless.

Jack unlocked his apartment door.

Suz walked in, her gaze sweeping the room. It was built fc efficiency. A great room that had a galley kitchen and seatin area big enough for him to have his team members in for consult. Then a short hallway with doors that lead to a sma office, a bathroom on the right, and a bedroom on the left. Sh went to the kitchen and opened the fridge. It held some bee and some BBQ sauce. There was an unpacked paper bag th Jack knew would have the fixing for a steak dinner, thanks t Lynx.

"Are you hungry?" he asked.

Suz shook her head, walking over to the bookcase where sh scanned the titles. Her eye stopped on each of the framed photo of her. She was hugging her puppies. She was dangling a toe i the water at the lake. She was asleep with a smile on her face. . a dozen or so photos that he thought caught a glimmer of Suz' essence. Her brow drew into a scowl, or a thought, or …some thing. He couldn't read Suz at all.

This wasn't the same Suz he had left when he went away on his mission.

There was a dynamic shift.

Of course, there was.

Jack's uneasiness grew.

She moved to the bedroom and stood at the end of the king-sized bed.

"Suz, you don't have to stay here with me." He had to stop and clear his throat. "I can arrange something else for you if you don't want to be here."

She turned and looked at him and nodded.

What did that mean?

She moved over to the side of the bed he slept on – the right because Suz preferred to sleep on the left at the cottage in the woods. She picked up the picture of them. They had been dancing, in a moment of pure joy, they had both leaned their heads back to laugh, and her friend Emma had snapped the shot. It was perfect. It reflected how he felt every time he came home, and Suz was back in his arms.

She set it back down on the side table and then sat on the mattress. "I killed a man, Jack," she whispered.

So, it was Suz. The thought had crossed his mind out there near the hide. But it had been too hard for him to believe. He felt the blood drain from his face.

She looked up at him. "It didn't matter to me either. I didn't care a single thing about him when I pulled the trigger. I wasn't thinking about him as a person at all. I thought *he's wearing black. He's come for the boys*. If I hadn't had the gun, I couldn't have stopped that man." She bent down and slid her sandals off her feet, spun around, and put her back to the headboard, her knees were folded up, and she wrapped them with her arms.

Is she being protective or comfortable? What should I do to help her? Jack untied his boots and tugged them off, then moved to sit facing her.

"If you hadn't told me how to look and shoot, I couldn't have stopped that man." She squirmed down the bed until she was lying down and spun to her side, supporting herself on her elbow to look at him. "But at the time you were trying to teach me, hated the gun you put in my hand. It made me vomit. It was a symbol of violence."

"I remember."

"Do you?" Her voice faded off as she plucked at his comforter, a light shade of teal blue, her favorite color, the color of her eyes on a sunny day. "Do you remember how you walked me through it with nothing in my hands? We practiced three times, then you handed me the gun. I lifted it up, and you wrapped your arm around me and said, "It's not loaded. It's just to get the feel." I handed it back. Do you know why?"

Jack had laid down on the bed and mirrored her position, his head rested on his palm. He reached out and lifted one of her curls and rubbed it between his fingers.

"If I knew how to shoot it, and it came down to a bad situation, I'd be obligated to shoot it. Knowledge is power. I wanted to be innocent. And that's exactly what happened. I knew how to shoot a gun and kill a man, and I did it." She flipped onto her back and crossed her arms over her chest, squeezing herself like she was cold.

Jack reached for the throw at the end of the bed and spread it over her.

Suz didn't seem to notice.

She was staring at the ceiling. "After I shot him, I didn't go check if I could help him. Instead, I went to help the boys. Later as I sat on the rock, looking out over the forest, not knowing what to do next, I realized it wasn't my greatest fear that I would hurt or kill someone. It was my greatest fear that I would fail someone in their moment of need. If I didn't have the knowledge, then I couldn't really be held responsible, now could I? I had an excuse for failure." She swiped at a tear. "I have to get used to the new me. I am such a hypocrite." She covered her face with her hands.

"What?" Jack followed her reasoning all the way up to that last sentence.

She turned back over onto her elbow. "You. . . you know? You are such an incredible person. I loved every single thing about you, except that you went away from me and put yourself in danger, and I could do nothing to help you."

Jack caught the past tense of the word. She hadn't said love. She said loved—emphasis on the -ed.

"I was frantic every time you left me, and I think that's why I panicked about keeping my students safe after Sandy Hook. I was afraid that I wasn't as brave as those teachers who tried to save their kids. It would be my students' moment of greatest need, and I'd fail them. I was obsessed with it. I thought about it every single day. When I was out by the rock, bleeding, the boys by my side… I had just killed a man. And I couldn't have cared less about his life, about his family – his wife, his children. That astonished me. I thought that that would be the reason I couldn't save the kids. I'd be caught up on the fact that there was someone at home worrying for the bad guy the way I always worry about you. I would be hurting someone like me by hurting the person they loved. That thought loop probably makes no sense to you. You'd have to chew on those thoughts for a while like I did to make them make any kind of sense. But it doesn't matter anymore." She sighed and swiped away a tear. "I protected Ari and Caleb, and that was what mattered to me."

Jack tried to pick through the strands of information. They

didn't line up neatly. He needed to wait, though, before he aske questions. Sometimes Suz needed a second for the next idea t pop up – the one that she really wanted to get across to him. H wanted to know where she was headed with this.

"But I had this other thought while I sat there on the rock. thought that I failed you our whole relationship."

"No." Jack shook his head emphatically.

"I have, Jack. You know, moments of urgency and crisi they aren't part of my everyday life. They're part of yo everyday life. People in this world *need* people like you. N everyone can do what you do. There are, in fact, very few wh have your combination of mental and physical attributes an moral conviction. So few. Too few. You have to do what you d I had no idea how important it was until I felt it myself. Oh, de God, it was, *whew*. . . and add the responsibility of childre in..." She shook her head, making her curls jiggle.

"Sweetheart, please." He laced his fingers through hers.

She curled her lips in and shook her head again. "Hypocris My dad would be so disappointed in me. I wanted to keep you t myself, so I could feel safe and happy. But when I was in dange and I thought you were in the hospital, I wanted someone lik you to rush in and save the day. I wanted a hero to pull us out o our mess even though I knew someone else, someone like m would be wishing their guy was home mowing the lawn o something. Don't you see?"

Suz was revved up. That he could see. Her words were a over the place, the way she got when her thoughts and emotion collided when she was overwhelmed with what she needed t say, especially when she knew that what she was going to sa would hurt someone. Jack felt his heart squeeze.

Was she going to tell him that they couldn't be togethe anymore?

Was this her breaking up with him?

"I told myself my greatest fear was that I would fail someone in their moment of need. And yet I failed you. For four years, I failed you."

"What? No. I—"

"It's true, Jack. When you were home, I should have relished you. I should have brought you peace instead of all the crap I gave you about your job."

"Suz, you have to stop talking in the past tense. *Please*." His muscles bunched like he was taking blows.

"I'm not going to live like that anymore. Forgive me. I'm so so sorry."

Tears distorted his vision. His breath caught in his lungs.

Suz lifted herself up, and Jack tightened his fingers in hers.

He couldn't let her go.

She turned and swung a leg over his hips, and he rolled onto his back, so she was straddling him. She leaned over and kissed him lightly on the lips, anguish in her eyes.

Jack didn't kiss her back; his lips had pulled tight as he clamped his jaw down.

"I love you, Jack," she whispered. Tears ran freely down her face. "Tell me you'll forgive me someday."

Forgive her. He'd forgive her, but his heart was breaking into bits. He felt it coming apart in chunks in his chest. The shards stabbed him. It was so painful it took his breath away.

"Tell me you'll forgive me for all of my anger, for not being there for you, for not supporting you. Tell me you'll let me make it up to you. Please?" She was gripping both of his hands and holding them over her heart, staring down into his eyes. "Give me a chance to show you that I can support you the way you support me. I can be a better person than I've been. Please don't stop loving me."

Jack sat up and wrapped his arms tightly around her. He tucked his head into her shoulder and sobbed. For the second time in his life, since he was three years old, and his mother picked him up off the ground after a fall and said, "Boys don't cry," he sobbed. Once because he thought he had lost Suz, and now because he had found her again.

He cupped her face in his hands. "Gillian Suzanne, you scared the life right out of me."

She wrinkled her brow, confused.

Jack kissed the tip of her nose, her eyelids, her lips. He laid her down and found his place of serenity nestled between her thighs. He kissed down her neck, his thumb lightly petting the bandage of a wound that very easily could have ended things so much differently. He groaned at the thought, laying his forehead against hers.

He moved backward and pushed his weight into his elbow as his fingers fumbled to undo the delicate buttons of her dress. He celebrated each success with a kiss. She moaned as he reached her belly. Arching into his hands as his tongue traced along the top of her panties. His hands skated down her hip and under her leg as he pulled her tightly to him, grinding his hips so she'd make that little mewling gasp and sigh.

It was the sound of everything good in this life. The sweetest sound he knew.

"Jack," Suz whispered.

All right, the second sweetest. His name on her lips definitely came first. He slid back on the bed to rest his head on her stomach, stroking a hand along her beautiful legs, kissing along the inside of her thigh, to make her giggle and swat at him.

"Stop, you're tickling!" She kicked to get away from him.

He held her ankle tight and reached up for her panties, sliding them free.

. . .

JACK HAD HAD a lot of firsts over the last week; when he made love to Suz, it felt like a first, too. They had a wonderful sex life, for sure. But this time, it was different. This was a baring of souls instead of just bodies. And when they were done, they had collapsed in a tangle of utter exhaustion.

Suz had obviously done some soul searching while she was captive. Jack tucked a lock of auburn hair back over her shoulder and kissed the delicate bone under her neck.

He'd made his own discoveries. How vulnerable he felt when she was in danger. That was one hell of an eye-opening experience. How he had felt terror instead of fear. You can walk through fear. There isn't much you can do about moving through terror. He had walked in her shoes and was humbled by her strength. They'd have to come up with a way to deal with that. He wouldn't ask her to live her life that way. But he felt absolutely certain that together they could figure it out.

Suz was still asleep when Jack climbed from the bed and brought back the engagement ring. He sat with his back against the headboard, looking at it. It was his grandmother's stone in a Suz setting. His grandmother had raised him after alcohol took over his mother's life. Grandma was his idea of what a woman should be — smart, caring, strong, and gentle at the same time. He thought Suz embraced some of the best of his grandma's qualities and added some that were distinctly Suz. The whole oatmeal chocolate chip cookie-ness of Suz – warm, sweet, and healthy but never obnoxiously so. That image brought a lopsided smile to his face.

Suz opened an eye. "What are you doing?"

Jack palmed the ring. "Thinking about how wonderful you are and how much I love you."

"Funny, that's pretty much all that's been on my mind for the last week or so – how wonderful you are." She leaned over and kissed his hip. The only thing in kissing range. She pulled herself up to sit facing him. "How much I love you. How much I am *in* love with you."

She was watching him closely and tilted her head. He closed his eyes and took a deep breath, then focused on her with earnestness as he held up the ring. "Gillian Suzanne, will you promise to say those very words to me for the rest of our lives?"

"Oh." She sighed. "I absolutely will."

She held out her left hand this time, and he slipped the ring into place. She slid into his lap, lay her head on his shoulder.

"*This* is where I've always belonged."

The end

I hope you enjoyed Jack and Suz's story.

Please follow along with the rest of the Iniquus world characters as they live, love, and fight for the greater good in the tight-knit Iniquus family.

Would you like a sneak peek at the next book in the Iniquus chronology?

Keep reading for Chapter one of Deadlock

Readers, I hope you enjoyed getting to know Jack and Suz. If you had fun reading Jack Be Quick, I'd appreciate it if you'd help others enjoy it too.

Recommend it: Just a few words to your friends, your book groups, and your social networks would be wonderful.

Review it: Please tell your fellow readers what you liked about my book by reviewing Jack Be Quick on your favorite retailer. If you do write a review, please send me a note at hello@fionaquinnbooks.com. I'd like to thank you with a personal e-mail. Or stop by my website, FionaQuinnBooks.com, to keep up with my news and chat through my contact form.

Turn the page for chapter one from DEADLOCK!

DEADLOCK

He'll get her home safe…or he'll die trying…

Honey Honig is used to infiltrating the most dangerous places on Earth and thwarting kidnappers. But he never expected to end up in Tanzania, at the wrong end of a hostage situation with the most intriguing doctor he's ever met. Now, he'll do *anything* to get them out of the deadly web they've landed in—and keep the woman of his dreams safe. Should be easy for an ex-Delta Force operator, right? He wishes…

No one kidnaps animal migration specialists. Or so Meg Finley thought—until she found herself in the clutches of terrorists, that is. She needs to keep her wits about her now more than ever. She can't let herself be distracted by an untimely attraction to her ridiculously appealing protector. But…she is…

. . .

It will take all of Meg and Honey's combined strength, knowl edge, and skill to survive. But when all is said and done, will i be enough to get them to happily ever after?

Deadlock is an intense, action adventure military romanc suspense thriller filled with spies, conspiracies, and internationa terror.

1

ROOSTER

JIBOUTI, DJIBOUTI

BEFORE WE BEGIN, I need proof of life."

The radio crackled with static in return.

Rooster scraped his teeth over his top lip, waiting.

"Mr. Honey." The buzzing and mechanical channel whines ere replaced with the cheerful sound of lighthearted banter. You know, every time I say your name, I laugh at the irony."

"How's that?" Rooster stretched his long legs out in front of im and crossed them at the ankle, settling into the conversation.

"Oh, if you knew, you would kick yourself." The man's ccent sometimes rang with Arabic notes, sometimes with rench, but his English was quite good. He had obviously spent me in America. "As for your proof of life, you must realize by ow that I am an educated man. I'm not a Somali pirate raised ith minimal thinking tools. I've done my research. I know your ctics. The Bowens are worth three million dollars. I will hold irm to that number. That number is *not* negotiable. The only

things we are to negotiate are how the payment is to be made an
how you are to retrieve your people."

Rooster was pleased. "Brilliant" had never strung so man words together at one time. Up until now, his responses had bee monosyllabic, sometimes just grunts, since their communication had begun over a month ago. Rooster had made a career c hostage negotiations. It took him to some of the bleakest, mo: godforsaken parts of the Earth. Now, here he was in Djibouti o the Horn of Africa, sitting behind his radio set with a wet tow draped over his neck in a poorly air-conditioned rental house o the outskirts of the capital city. Djibouti was a country of dr scrublands, volcanic formations, the amazing Gulf of Tadjour beaches, and temperatures that ran over a hundred degrees, da and night. *It's a dry heat*, Rooster reminded himself.

Though he drank water constantly, he hadn't peed in day: His clothes were covered in white scum from where his body' sweat had left its residue.

In hostage situations, when Rooster introduced himself as th negotiator, he used the radio call sign he'd been given way bac in boot camp some twenty-odd years before, Honey. Well, h made sure to say *Mr*. Honey, so things didn't get weird. Not t say that most of the people he negotiated with were fluer enough in English to understand that the noun was often used a a term of endearment.

Most of the men who negotiated from the bad-guy side chos to be called names like "Glock" or "Chief," sometimes "Boss. Rooster knew these were words they thought, in their limite grasp of English, gave them power. This was the first time a English speaker had wanted to be called "Brilliant." A narcissis Someone who's ego swelled to cover up his lack of convictio and probably the fact that he had a micro-dick. Rooster ha steered his psychological tack accordingly.

Right now, though, Rooster needed to push things along. Time was the enemy. There was a statistical trajectory for good outcomes, and that section of the graph had come and gone. Hostage negotiation was a slow game. But they were now in the orange zone, the time when people without training, who were psychologically and physically unprepared for the challenges of captivity, folded under the weight. If the captors recognized their victims' decline, a deal was often possible. If they didn't, then Rooster's team would be trying to get the corpses back, so the victims' families would have closure.

Bad things could happen—did happen—to hostages held under kidnappers' thumbs. But so far, Rooster was batting a thousand, bringing his clients home at least alive, if not always safe and sound. He reached out to knock on wood. He tended toward the superstitious when his ego bubbled up some wise-ass thought like good batting averages.

His teammate Randy sent him a chuckle when he did it, then refocused on his task at the computer.

Rooster pressed the comms button. "It's been a while since I heard from the Bowens. Before our conversation continues, I need proof of life," Rooster said, not a trace of emotion in his words. The captors wanted him to be passionate and work from the heart. Rooster knew the only way he could save these people was to keep an emotional distance. He had to think of these negotiations like a businessman buying office supplies—necessary supplies, but objects all the same. Compartmentalization was a honed skillset. Boxes were a handy tool. His emotions belonged to a different part of his life and not his career. Emotions equaled mistakes.

Brilliant laughed. "I am not stupid enough to be in the same area as my hostages. If you have some new communications tracking device, it will not work. I am a moving target."

Rooster rubbed at his chin, his focus sharp. "Okay, let's se up a time. I need to hear their voices. I need to verify that the are still the right people, and they're still safe and sound."

"Bowen is holding up under the strains of his conditions. Hi wife, on the other hand, is not. We believe she needs immediat medical attention. I am very worried for her."

"She has a heart condition. You know that," Rooster saic "Does she have her medication? Is there a drop point where I ca provide supplies?"

"With a tracker attached? No."

"Can you tell me her symptoms?" The longer Rooster coul keep this asshole talking, the better shot they'd have of pickin up ambient noise—clues to his whereabouts.

"I believe the heat and stress, along with her particular loca tion, are all problematic."

"She doesn't work for Hesston Corporation. Why don't yo let her go? Call it a good-faith gesture."

"I would like nothing better. As soon as the payment is made I will take her immediately to the hospital."

"Is the hospital a far distance? Should I arrange for helicopter?"

"Ah, you think you can trick me into giving you informatio about where the Bowens are held. Listen to me. Anjie Bowe needs immediate attention. I want to get her that attention. It i you who prevents me from doing this." He let his words seep ir Waited for Rooster to panic.

Rooster knew all the tricks and traps. He sat silently listening to the static.

"I realize how this works. It will not be Bowen's corporatio that pays the ransom monies. It will be the insurance company You don't work for this man, Mr. Honey. You are paid by th insurers. But if this man or his pretty little wife dies, your reputa tion will be tarnished. The insurance contracts will go away, as will your paycheck." He paused. "Really, it's self-preservation that should make you wish to come to a happy conclusion."

Rooster leaned forward, his forearms on his thighs, staring down at the mic. He took a breath, making sure Brilliant had finished his communication before depressing the button to talk. "This is a business transaction. Your opening bid was three-million dollars, and you aren't coming down. I can tell you straight up, the insurers won't pay that. Not even close. And while Derek Bowen works for Hesston, Anjie Bowen does not. I'm sure you understand, from a businessman's point of view, why letting Mrs. Bowen go still gives you all the leverage you need." He paused to slick his tongue over his teeth. "And it shows everyone on this side of the table that you're acting in good faith. I need proof of life, and I need a more reasonable number."

Another man's voice could be heard in the distance—the sound of a car's horn. Then the crackle of radio static.

Rooster waited. Brilliant gave no reply.

ROOSTER SNIFFED HARD, setting the handset back in its indentation on the radio. He focused on the shadowy corner of the room. As he let his thoughts percolate, he reached for the jug sitting beside his chair. He upended it and chugged big gulps of the warm water. Swiping the back of his hand over his mouth to catch the drips, he turned to Randy.

"Almost ten minutes. That's an improvement," Randy said, sending the audio file back to Iniquus's Headquarters in Washington D.C. "Still full of himself. He's convinced he holds a winning hand."

While Randy sounded like the name of a man raised on football and apple pie, he was actually from El Salvador. Randy wa his call sign. He'd come to America over a decade before to pu his considerable athleticism to the test, hoping to gain citizenshi from his US military service. He'd served two rotations in th sandbox as a Ranger, tough as nails, with the brain and stomac for the hairiest of missions.

Now, Randy and he got their paychecks from the for-hir security complex, Iniquus, that worked civilian contracts as wel as running black ops for the government. While Randy was Strike Force member, commanded by Striker Rheas, and Rooste was on Panther Force, commanded by Titus Kane, those designa tions were often fluid. Operators went where they were told t go, based on capability and availability.

Randy had just finished up a close protection detail for a American businessman and put the guy on a flight from Keny back to New York. The boarding call had sounded over the P.A system, calling for Randy's flight to Tahiti where he planned t take his R & R. But Randy answered his phone and thus pulle the short stick. Now Randy was sitting in this rat hole wit Rooster.

"Brilliant gave up some stuff this time," Rooster said. "Pla that bit at the end again before the horn honk."

Randy tapped the computer, cocking his head as he straine to weed out what hid under the ambient noise.

"Do you hear that guy in the background? Can you isolat that voice?"

Randy fussed with his software, hit enter, and they listened t the man's voice, free of distractions.

"I don't recognize that language. Any guesses?"

"Nada," Randy answered. "Let's see what I can find."

Africa was a continent rich in languages and cultures. Tradi tion. Segregation. And turbulence. If Randy's software coul ranslate the sentence and give them a dialect, they might have omething useful to work with.

Rooster pulled his headphones into place to listen to the ecording. He believed what Brilliant had said about Anjie 3owen. She was in dire straits. With her medical history, xtremes were perilous. Why she'd followed her husband on his oat trip along the coast of Africa at this time of year was a nystery to him. But it wasn't Rooster's job to second guess eople's decision making. It was his job to save their lives. And ˄njie felt fragile to him.

Rooster knew that Brilliant had already figured out Anjie vas disposable. It might even work in the kidnapper's favor to et her die. Rooster had hoped that Brilliant wouldn't realize that act. But Brilliant's tone and word choices told Rooster Brilliant ad already drawn that conclusion. He would use her as a argaining chip as long as he could but didn't care one way or nother whether Anjie made it home to her three young kids r not.

Word choices were everything. In people who negotiated in nglish as a second language, those word choices came from ow deep their vocabulary well ran. This guy was fluent. That vas a win for the good guys. It meant he had a wide range of hrases to use, and therefore specific meanings could be weeded ut. Rooster moved the recording back to the beginning of their onversation when Brilliant had laughed.

"Mr. Honey. You know every time I say your name, I laugh t the irony."

The irony of my name. The irony *of my name.* He pressed lay. "Oh, if you knew, you would kick yourself."

My name is part of the puzzle. Not Mr. Just Honey. Honey *is ronic.* Rooster stretched his arms above his head, laced his ingers together, and cradled the back of his head in the hammock they made, flicking his thumbs against one another a he let his mind wander. He worked to put a pin in the irony c "Honey."

"Got it." Randy's voice held a grin. It pulled Rooster's atter tion to him. "The man's speaking Afar."

"Translation?"

"He said, 'They bring the salt.' And that belching sound yo hear isn't a man dying of indigestion. It's a camel's grunt."

Rooster tapped at his computer. His eyes scanned over th screen, then he leaned back in his chair and laughed with hi hands covering his face. He scrubbed his palms up and dow over his cheeks, around the back of his neck. "Oh, the irony," h said as he focused back on Randy. "The Afar tribe harvest sa spheres from Lac Assal. They bring them to the harbor on th backs of camels."

Randy waited patiently for the piece that made Rooster react

"The Arabic name for that lake is *Buḥayrah ʿAsal,* whic literally translates to Honey Lake. I do believe that Brilliant ha failed to live up to his name."

Ready to find out what happens next?

Get Deadlock, Book three of Uncommon Enemies, part of the World of Iniquus.

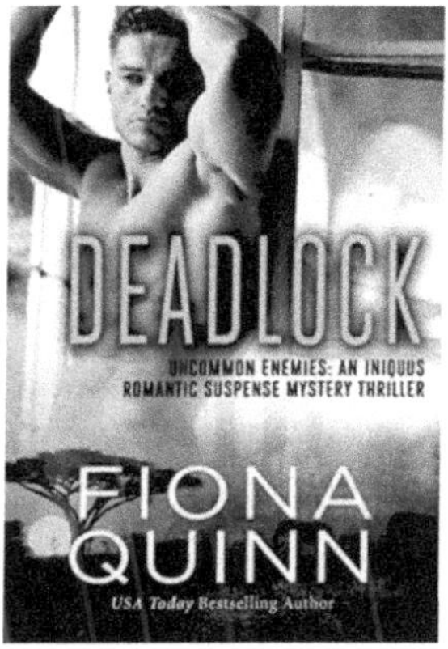

Would you like a list of Iniquus World books in chronological order? Turn the page.

THE WORLD of INIQUUS

Chronological Order

Ubicumque, Quoties. Quidquid

Weakest Lynx (Lynx Series)

Missing Lynx (Lynx Series)

Chain Lynx (Lynx Series)

Cuff Lynx (Lynx Series)

WASP (Uncommon Enemies)

In Too DEEP (Strike Force)

Relic (Uncommon Enemies)

Mine (Kate Hamilton Mystery)

Jack Be Quick (Strike Force

Deadlock (Uncommon Enemies)

Instigator (Strike Force)

Yours (Kate Hamilton Mystery)

Gulf Lynx (Lynx Series)

Open Secret (FBI Joint Task Force)

Thorn (Uncommon Enemies)
Ours (Kate Hamilton Mysteries
Cold Red (FBI Joint Task Force)
Even Odds (FBI Joint Task Force)
Survival Instinct - Cerberus Tactical K9
Protective Instinct - Cerberus Tactical K9
Defender's Instinct - Cerberus Tactical K9
Danger Signs - Delta Force Echo
Hyper Lynx - Lynx Series
Danger Zone - Delta Force Echo
Danger Close - Delta Force Echo
Cerberus Tactical K9 Team Bravo
Marriage Lynx - Lynx Series

FOR MORE INFORMATION VISIT
WWW.FIONAQUINNBOOKS.COM

ACKNOWLEDGMENTS

ly great appreciation ~

To my editor, Kathleen Payne

To my publicist, Margaret Daly

To my cover artist, Melody Simmons

To my Beta Force, who are always honest and kind at the ame time, especially M. Carlon and E. Hordon

To my Street Force, who support me and my writing with uch enthusiasm. If you're interested in joining this group, please end me an email. **Hello@FionaQuinnBooks.com**

Thank you to the real-world military and CIA who serve to rotect us.

To all the wonderful professionals whom I called on to get e details right. Please note: This is a work of fiction, and while always try my best to get all the details correct, there are times hen it serves the story to go slightly to the left or right of erfection. Please understand that any mistakes or discrepancies re my authorial decision making alone and sit squarely on my houlders.

Thank you to my family.

I send my love to my husband, and my great appreciation. ˜ you are my happily ever after. You are my encouragement an my adventure. Thank you.

And of course, thank *YOU* for reading my stories. I'ı smiling joyfully as I type this. I so appreciate you!

ABOUT THE AUTHOR

Fiona Quinn is a six-time USA Today bestselling author, a Kindle Scout winner, and an Amazon All-Star.

Quinn writes action-adventure in her Iniquus World of books, including Lynx, Strike Force, Uncommon Enemies, Kate Hamilton Mysteries, FBI Joint Task Force, Cerberus Tactical K9, and Delta Force Echo series.

She writes urban fantasy as Fiona Angelica Quinn for her Elemental Witches Series.

And, just for fun, she writes the Badge Bunny Booze Mystery Collection with her dear friend, Tina Glasneck.

Quinn is rooted in the Old Dominion, where she lives with her husband. There, she pops chocolates, devours books, and taps continuously on her laptop.

Visit www.FionaQuinnBooks.com

COPYRIGHT

Jack Be Quick is a work of fiction. Names, characters, places, and incidents either are the product of the author's imagination or are used fictitiously, and any resemblance to actual persons, living or dead, business establishments, events, or locales is entirely coincidental.

ISBN: 978-1-946661-32-6
Chesterfield, VA
Library of Congress Control Number: 2021910731
Cover Design by Melody Simmons from eBookindlecovers
Fonts with permission from Microsoft

CPSIA information can be obtained
at www.ICGtesting.com
Printed in the USA
LVHW091532240821
695995LV00014B/78

9 781946 661326